PRAISE FOR *MAN, UNDERGROUND*

"With *Man, Underground*, Mark Hummel has crafted a novel of rare insight. It is sincere but never sentimental, life-affirming yet clear-eyed, and timely while possessing a timeless wisdom. Oh, and it tells a great story, too, equal parts rollicking caper and dark night of the soul. A worthy addition to the canon of misfit lit!"

— Luke Geddes, author of *Heart of Junk*

"A lovely and moving novel about loss and recovery that's thoughtful about these topics, alongside art and violence and how we use one to narrate the other."

— Fiona Maazel, author of *A Little More Human* and *Woke Up Lonely*

"In *Man, Underground* Mark Hummel takes us on a wild journey of American gentrification; the narrator, voluntarily trapped in his basement, a sort of transplanted Dostoevsky's *Underground Man*, dreads encroachments by real estate schemers, the state, commercial Americana, and finds rescue from his paranoia in an unlikely friendship with a young counter-cultural activist, with whom he has amazingly witty conversations. The dialogue sounds like a Raymond Chandler movie script, so sharp and clever, and the descriptions and narrative comments are all interesting and original, and many could be quoted as aphorisms. This cultural and psychological critique and satire will entertain you for sure."

— Josip Novakovich, author of *Rubble of Rubles* and *April Fool's Day*, shortlisted for the Man Booker International Prize

"Funny, tender, and shimmering with optimism, *Man, Underground* asks: 'What if we were all just a little kinder? A little more understanding?' It's a delightful, heartwarming story of an unexpected friendship that leaves the reader with hope. I look forward to what Hummel does next."

— Meagan Lucas, award-winning author of *Songbirds and Stray Dogs* and *Here in the Dark*

"Mark Hummel has certainly written a novel for our time. From the very first pages, I was drawn into the story through its sparkling, muscular dialogue, and then lured on by a series of plot moves both arresting and entirely plausible. This truly wonderful novel reminded me that grief met with patience and the willingness to listen can be grief gently and incrementally eased."

— Liza Wieland, author of *Paris, 7 A.M.* and *Land of Enchantment*

"*Man, Underground* is witty, endearing, and full of surprises. I loved watching the transformation of our "underground man" into something resembling a blossoming flower."

— David Abrams, author of *Brave Deeds* and *Fobbit*

"Mark Hummel's animated descriptions, knockout dialogue, laugh-out-loud wit, and narrative momentum create a story relevant to everyone. In his canny and compassionate prose, Mr. Hummel lets us know that we are all bewildered and vulnerable, that fate comes for every one of us, and it is only by relating to each another that we can heal our communities and maybe the world. Delicious wit and tender observations combine to tell the story of a lonely man and his quest for reason. This is Mark Hummel at the top of his game."

— Jean Ryan, author of *Survival Skills* and *Lost Sister*

"Hummel is a master at dialog, and as each chapter unfolds through the unexpected—city bureaucracy, gnome relocation, under-bridge karaoke—the real story emerges brilliantly through the asides, the quips, the sudden truths. *Man, Underground* is a story about discovering hope. Every page is a joy."

—W. Scott Olsen, author of *Neverland: Adventures, Wonder, and One World Record in a very Small Plane* and former editor of *Ascent*

"*Man, Underground* presents an astute, equally comical and terrifying portrait of modern society, described by a narrator who has removed himself from most human interaction. Hidden In his surprisingly well-equipped subterranean fortress, the narrator has become an 'other' in a city that values conformity. When his peculiar lifestyle triggers a property review, a talented, quirky teenager named Monika launches a funny, ill-advised diversionary campaign. Author Mark Hummel brilliantly draws the reader deeper and deeper into the narrator's life, peeling each layer to challenge our assumptions about 'others.' Hummel's descriptive, deeply engaging prose is surgically precise and insightful, revealing the beauty and heartbreak of our shared human experience, and the redemptive power of unlikely friendships."

— Ginger Pinholster, author of *Snakes of St. Augustine* and *City in a Fores*

"Using sharp dialog and exquisite prose, *Man, Underground* takes the reader on a comedy/tragic journey through a learned man's existential crisis and a precocious adolescent's coming of age. Think Lolita, but with Humbert Humbert as an erudite, reclusive, curmudgeonly gentleman, and Lolita as a wisecracking, teenage Mensa. Every Hollywood screenwriter should study Mark Hummel's dialog. He's a genuine master."

— James A. Ross, author of *Hunting Teddy Roosevelt*

MAN, UNDERGROUND

Mark Hummel

Regal House Publishing

Published by
Regal House Publishing, LLC
Raleigh, NC 27605
All rights reserved

ISBN -13 (paperback): 9781646033881
ISBN -13 (epub): 9781646033898
Library of Congress Control Number: 2022949415

Regal House Publishing, LLC
https://regalhousepublishing.com

Printed in the United States of America

for Jennifer, Abbey, and Sydney

I am convinced that fellows like me who live in dark cellars must be kept under restraint. They may be able to live in their dark cellars for forty years and never open their mouths, but the moment they get into the light of day and break out they may talk and talk and talk...

Fyodor Dostoevsky, *Notes from the Underground*

1

I don't have a doorbell. Actually, because accuracy matters, the more factual statement is that I only recently installed a doorbell after a long history without one. The events I describe largely pre-date that installation and perhaps help explain it. When I built this house, I didn't exactly picture people stopping in for a visit. It's not as if anyone in his right mind wants to encourage solicitors, be they salesmen or missionaries preceded to the door by their cologne or the sheen of their bible. I have lived that life before. Building an underground house struck me as a sound way to keep strangers away. And a doorbell felt like putting out a welcome mat.

If I tried to describe my home and its one visible portal to the world, I likely would fail. I suspect people would imagine a two-dimensional world with a door isolated in space like a magician's show. When I see my front door as I approach it after an exhausting Thursday of running errands, I like to think of the entrance as inspired by a root cellar. I picture a place meant to preserve vegetables within the consistent cool womb of the earth, only this one preserves the sanity of a man. Maybe it would be easier for strangers to accept its presence if they considered it as belonging to another age or another function. Perhaps I would be easier to accept if considered in the same way.

As I said, this story starts before the installation of the doorbell. It came as something of a surprise then when I was startled from reading by persistent knocking. It took a while for the sound to register. Eventually it dawned on me that someone was banging on my front door, for not only am I unaccustomed to visitors, mostly I am unaccustomed to outside sounds, insulated as I am. And I mean banging, because not only is my door isolated from the rest of the house way up there above my head, I've got a second door—a heavy metal fire door—at the bottom of the stairwell that creates a kind of airlock. Moreover, I'm not exactly the sort from whom neighbors come seeking a cupful of sugar, and the neighbors I do have apparently want to see me gone, and that very fact is related to this one, related that is to the insistent banging that continued so long it snuck into my consciousness and finally forced me to put down my book to investigate its source.

The door at the top of my stairwell, my thin barrier of protection from the noise and the nonsense, has a good deal of glass in it, and when I reached the stairs, I could see just enough of the motion of a leg through the glass that it was evident the persistent knocking was the collision of a foot against the door. A rhythmic thumping. Climbing the stairs, I could see the leg attached to the sound, which was a bare, feminine leg, if one that seemed preternaturally thin, like the leg of a famine victim, a leg that disappeared from my view within a skirt that seemed, from this distance on my upward-looking angle, fashioned from armor or black electrical tape. I couldn't be sure.

When I reached the landing, I stood level with the young woman. One square-toed engineer boot abused my door at an absent, regular interval, while the girl had her head turned away as if watching something on the road that crossed some hundred yards distant and where a rusted and dented Honda Civic that dated to the past century sagged on underinflated tires. Graced as I was by the appearance of the back of her turned head, I examined, with some curiosity, her hair, which was cut short and unevenly like it was meant to form a jagged silhouette. If forced to describe its color, say in a police report, one would have to respond "brunette," for that was the predominant color, though it was terrain frequently interrupted by clumps of black and blond and something the color of a navel orange allowed to over-ripen. She wore a jacket that looked the texture of leather but which was silver. It hung from her thin frame as if from a wire hanger unfit for the task. The sleeves were too short and I saw the fine down of hair at her forearm before the skin disappeared at her wrist in a tangle of leather, hemp, and silver bracelets. Beneath the jacket she wore a dull gray T-shirt. I couldn't quite see its logo but guessed by the remainder of her attire that she advertised for a band, no doubt a band that exuded a certain amount of rage captured in a logo fit for emblazoning on drum skins and young women's chests. I was intent on deciphering that logo, for just two letters were visible, F and U, and it was rather like trying to read mail through an envelope when you can make out letters but not entire words and your head starts to map out the possibilities as if solving a word scramble.

Now that F and that U chided my inability to reach beyond the most obvious and profane assumptions. They nagged at me. I really wanted to know if indeed it was a band name. The evasiveness challenged my music critic brain and I thought through the fog of past articles I'd written and the troves of research materials I'd consulted. Thinking backward only causes me embarrassment, for I have given up on the world of such publications where I once routinely published. Magazines only add to the din. As if there isn't already enough noise. My specialty was contemporary rock, and contemporary rock at my heyday placed me in the '80s and I was equally guilty then of sincerely believing that the counterculture of art and music offered a bold and needed counterpoint to the dominant culture and the myopic worldview of Reaganomics and Cold War posturing. I was no stranger to dishing out bullshit, and eventually I came to doubt my own posturing, my pieces in those days all written from the safe confines of a two-story, three-bedroom, three-bath Tudor in the Boston suburbs. Suburbia is nowhere from which one can write meaningfully about economic policy, international politics, or for that matter, counter-culture. Not when surrounded by bubblegum pop and talk of lawn fertilization products, even if I fooled myself by saying that I believed in the world-changing potency of art—just before I got back to waxing the family sedan.

Since I do still write about music, or at least I try, I've kept my one contact with the external world via my mailbox, and when I followed the turn of this visitor's head, I saw my lonely mailbox at the road edge near her car. The mailbox held my attention, for I was caught thinking that it and my front door were my two lasting connections with another world, at least the world beyond memory, something I find lonelier than an empty mailbox.

I purposefully shrugged off the past and returned to deciphering the logo on her shirt. When I at last opened the door to put a stop to her infernal banging, I had not realized she'd turned her head toward me, for her first words were, "Getting a good look, Daddy-O?"

"I was trying to read your shirt," I confessed, startled.

"They always are," she said.

"No, seriously," I said. "Is it a band logo?"

"Looky, no touchy," she said, unzipping her coat and holding it open.

The letters ranged up and down the fabric like an EKG chart. "Frankfurter Alley. We Do Dead Dogs," I read aloud. The letter "D" in the word "dog" was crafted to look like something resembling a dog, or perhaps a frankfurter with skinny legs. The two "Ls" in "alley" formed the walls of buildings. All in all, it wasn't the work of an artist who had passed beyond the third grade.

"Isn't it great?" she asked.

"It isn't a band?" I questioned. "It's a restaurant?"

She shrugged. "Orange tag special—half off at the ARC—forty-nine cents. Sweet, right?"

The shirt ended about an inch short of her skirt, and while she was generally built like an adolescent boy, I couldn't help noticing that the intentionally erratic spacing of the shirt's lettering was exaggerated by the curves of her breasts, and the thin, oft-washed material had no success in camouflaging the presence of a bright purple bra.

"Show's over," she said, closing her jacket.

I expected piercings to interrupt the lines of her face but

none were present. It was a face incongruous with her hair and attire and directness, a face of unblemished, very white skin and thin, angular features, slightly elflike and youthful though her eyes looked older. I guessed her age between sixteen and twenty. She did not hold my eye, instead turning her head aside when I asked her why she had kicked my door so energetically.

"No bell," she said. "How are you supposed to know when people are at your door? How do you know when you have packages?"

"Packages?"

"You know. The FedEx guy in his dorky shorts."

"I don't get packages."

"Everybody gets packages."

"Well, I don't."

"That's impossible."

"Why is that impossible?"

"Because everybody needs stuff."

"You've heard of stores."

"Duh, everyone shops online. My uncle bought his second wife's wedding ring on eBay. Did you know that even in years of rising gas prices, UPS remains a high-growth company?"

"I didn't," I admitted. "I'm afraid I get a little out of touch."

"It's beside the point anyway," she said.

"What *is* the point?"

"I'm here to offer my services."

She spoke in a fashion as odd as anyone I had ever met, for though her voice offered confidence, a presence you could say, her body language made her appear she was about to take flight. One limb or another was in constant minor motion, a quiver here, a repetitive twitch there, a tapping foot. I wondered briefly if she suffered from Tourette Syndrome and then dismissed the notion. She looked away as she spoke, then abruptly turned back to me and held my gaze. She had chocolate brown eyes so dark they approached black.

"Just what sort of services?" I asked.

"I, well, you see, I thought you should know there's someone who's got your back, man, you know, with what's going on and all. With what they're trying to do to you and everything. Someone who could help you fight them."

"I have absolutely no idea what you are talking about."

"The city," she said, looking again over her shoulder.

I looked that direction too, as if the entire population of the city might be hiding near a sparse line of weedy trees that edged my property. "City?"

"This city. You know."

I did know, or I thought I knew, although I had no idea where she fit in. When I moved here seven years ago, the acreage opened onto an abandoned gravel operation, hence the south-facing cut-bank I'd been able to build into. I was attracted to the place primarily because there was no one else here, no development, and given the former gravel operation, one would have thought, not much capacity for development in a place still within walking distance of a grocery store. I moved for the privacy. It is something of an uninteresting city, tedious even in its ordinariness. Classically midwestern. But then that's precisely why I had chosen it.

I had, stupidly so, underestimated the American will to sprawl, and over the brief years the city had grown and a neighborhood had sprung up around me. Houses and streets and sewers and a convenience store all appeared alongside the other fruits of modernity. Now I had neighbors on either side of me, although my acreage gave me some breathing room. No one could build behind me because of the zoning restrictions to preserve open space at the former gravel pit, and I had no windows besides those cut into the south-facing slope, so I was able to live my chosen life with minimal impact from these insurgents. Only it seemed of late many of my neighbors petitioned the city to investigate my home, believing its presence—even though all they could ever see of it beyond a grassy landscape was my garden and my lone door—offended them. Apparently, they were convinced that the existence of my home would drive down the prices of theirs. I assume, if pressed, they would argue that the nature of my underground habitation was dangerous, based on how opposite it was from their own.

All of this properly translated suggests that my neighbors likely think *I* am dangerous. And the city, in its eminent wisdom, had begun an official investigation into their complaints. City officials had taped notices to my front door indicating my residence was "under review" to insure adherence with city codes and zoning ordinances.

I burned the notices in my woodstove, and when they planted a wooden stake at the road edge to which they'd attached a larger version of the notice declaring the "under review" status of my property, I burned that too. I poured a trickle of fuel on the sign and lit it with some small satisfaction. I'd not ever talked with any city officials "officially," but I felt I'd made my thoughts regarding the review status clear by my little act of pyromania.

"The city," I repeated in response to the girl fidgeting before my door. "And who are you again?"

"Oh, I didn't say. I'm Monika. Hold on, I've got cards and everything." She fumbled in a jacket pocket before retrieving a colorful business card that read simply "by Monika." I nearly commented on the *k* in her name, remembering '80s era bands that displayed their politics by spelling *Amerika* with a *k*, thinking, I guess, that the letter *k* inherently holds communistic tendencies. I'd argue that such choices show alphabetical prejudice.

"I'm sort of an artist," she said. "I do murals. Well, I've really only done one full-on mural so far. Maybe you've seen it. It's on the side of the Wharton building on Sixteenth. There's a hair salon in there now, and a Christian Science reading room, and a coffee shop. Maybe a palm reader too, but I think she may be dead. My stuff is on the wall of the coffee shop."

"I haven't seen it."

"You should. It's really something."

"I imagine."

"I do other things too. All kinds of other things, I mean, but other art too. I like to work with textiles. And found art. Regular stuff too. But I think I like murals the best. I like the scale, you know? I think art should be out in public. Art should be fun, not for profit."

"Then why the business card?"

She shrugged. I wasn't sure how I was intended to interpret the gesture.

"It's been very nice meeting you, Monika." I started to shut the door.

"I wanted to see if you needed help."

"No wall space for a mural," I said, waving my hand toward the empty air on each side of my door.

"Not art help."

"What sort of help then?"

"To fight the city."

"I am in no fight with the city."

"Maybe you don't see it as a fight, but it will be. I've seen their notices before. I volunteer for an organization that preserves historic buildings. Whenever we have a building get tagged with a notice, the fight is on. The city will say that gentrification is healthy, but not at the loss of preservation or diversity. The notice is like the city's little declaration of war. You just don't know it yet."

"I don't think my place exactly qualifies for historic preservation. I think you've picked the wrong battle," I said.

She either didn't hear me or chose to ignore me. "I heard my parents talking about you the other night," she said. "They said they thought eventually the city would declare eminent domain and take your place. Isn't that terrible?"

"I would find it quite terrible, you know, given that I live here."

"They did it to a sheep farmer last year. There was a new neighborhood near him and a park and everything. Soccer fields. People said the sheep smelled. They were worried about asthmatic soccer players or something. He wouldn't budge so they ousted him."

"No sheep."

"I'm just telling you what my parents said, that the city would probably do to you what they did to him. They use law to enforce their will."

"Who are your parents?"

"Just parents. Just people in the neighborhood."

"The neighborhood," I repeated. "And who are you?"

"I'm Monika."

"I got that."

"I'm your neighbor."

"Neighbor?"

"I live up the road in Cedar Ridge Farms. That's the next development over."

"You know there never was a farm there, don't you?"

"I know," she said, although I still thought she looked disappointed.

"And no cedars either. They wouldn't be indigenous if there had been."

What might a therapist remind me? That I redirect emotion with sarcasm? That isolation makes one quick to paranoia? I'm certain I could provide a therapist more than enough billable hours to create a jump in tax brackets.

Miss Fidgety, who could do with a little therapy time herself, confessed to not knowing about the native range of cedars.

"See, your visit has been fruitful," I said. "Thanks for stopping by." This time she stopped the door with an engineer boot.

"Don't you want my help?"

"Not particularly."

"I know you've been targeted before. You can't think that last summer, when your garden was trashed, was random."

Now she had my full attention. The previous summer, just as my plants had really started producing, that time as a gardener when you see hope returned to the universe as flowers begin turning into stubs of peppers and cucumbers, someone had destroyed my garden by driving through it. Not just driving across my land and into the garden, they must have spun donuts there because they'd effectively ruined almost every bed. As infrequently as sound reaches me, it had taken me some time to realize the revving engines came not from four-wheelers racing through the old gravel pit but from my rooftop. I reached the top of the stairs only in time to see their receding taillights. Three over-powered contraptions like Frankenstein hybrids of a golf cart and a motocross bike. "What kind of game are you playing?" I demanded. "Have you come back to gloat?"

"What?" she stammered. Then she looked offended. "I didn't have anything to do with it. Besides, that's not how I would have done it."

"The destruction of my property was not thorough enough for your tastes?"

"That's not what I meant," she said, throwing her arms out in apparent exasperation. "If they wanted to send you a message, they could have shown some creativity. They're bullies. They targeted you because they don't like you. Well, it's not exactly that they don't like you. They don't actually know you. You're more like an easy mark." She puffed out her cheeks as if she'd just run a sprint. "They wanted you to notice them."

"By destroying my property? That's a neighborly way of saying 'hello'? What the hell is a matter with you?"

"That's not what I meant." She shook her head in odd little jerks. "They're just stupid kids who don't know any better. They're like terrorists. They destroy what you care about to get your attention. They make you focus on them by taking away what matters to you." She released an audible sigh. "I felt really bad about the owl."

"So, you were involved," I shouted. "Talk about terrorism. And now what? You want to rub it in? Or you think you can extract some kind of protection money now?" I wanted to wring her scrawny neck. "Go away," I said, pleadingly, when I'd wanted to sound defiant.

Remembering the owl had struck a chord. It was something my wife had given me ages ago, in an altogether different time. It was a piece of sculpture, even though she had presented it to me as a means of scaring birds away from our berries and fruit trees. It had never worked for that purpose, but I had always liked the whimsical look of it, constructed as it was, from rusty washers and gears and nuts and bolts. Apparently, the rust had taken its toll, and in the violence of the garden attack, when it was toppled from a post, it had shattered. It was one of the few sentimental items I'd moved with me when I arrived here. That, and my music collection. Everything else had gone pennies on the dollar at auction. Amid the deep ruts left by the vandals' tires and the broken boards from the raised vegetable beds and all the violence dispensed on the poor plants, it was seeing that owl that made me feel violated and helpless and angry.

"No, no," Monika said in a rush. "I came by the next day. I saw what they'd done, and I felt terrible. I wanted to help you clean things up, but I didn't. I've regretted that."

"Why do you care?" I said harshly.

"I should have helped you," she stuttered again. "Because I should have seen it coming and stopped them. It was my brother and some of his friends who did it. I heard them talking later. Bragging." She seemed to be contemplating her boots. "It's really sad. Just a few years ago they were kids who'd play in the open space as an excuse to get a glimpse of you. Little kids. Curious. Now they sneak around your property and smoke dope and talk about what a crazed loser you must be." She looked at me. "People have no right to condemn you just because you choose to live differently. The whole purpose behind the founding of this country was to protect the right to individual freedoms."

"Your government teacher would be proud of you."

"My government teacher is an asshole. He was probably the first one to sign the petition against your property. He's just another of the self-righteous hypocrites that run our schools."

I had to admit that I liked her spunk. "I bet that position makes you popular with him."

"You said it, Jack. That's all high school is—a popularity contest. The popular kids all do just fine in his class just so long as they keep their hair straight and their noses brown. For everybody else he treats his desk like it is an altar. Bring on the virgins and the knives. Although, good luck finding a virgin."

"So what do you do if he's already decided your fate?" I regretted the question as soon as I asked it, prolonging, as I was, a conversation I didn't want to have. I wished I had turned the garden hose on her or, once I saw those skinny legs through the glass, never answered the door.

"Mostly I stay at lunch," she said. "Some days I go to the art room. Other days I go to his class and just sit and fume and make myself miserable because I don't speak up."

"But you're going to defend me."

"Yeah, sure."

"Why?"

"Because it's right."

"That's righteous of you, sister," I said, suddenly aware that, embarrassingly, I had spoken in a manner that sounded just like her. "Just why is it you think I need your charitable defense?"

"Just because you've decided to hide doesn't mean your choices have less value than other people's."

"Who says I'm hiding?"

She gestured to the empty air outside my door. "The rabbit hole theme you've got going says that you're totally well-adjusted and living in the mainstream. Just what awful thing happened that made you run away and hide?"

The question gave me pause. Perhaps I'd taken a page from her approach to her government teacher, for I found myself empty of pithy comebacks. At last, the best I could manage was the lame barb: "I guess it's time to invest in the No Soliciting sign."

"Don't get me wrong," she said, ignoring me. "I respect that you choose to live differently. People deserve to live as they choose. I'm down with that. We all get along the best that we can. That's why I want to help you."

"That's sweet," I said, re-gathering myself, "but I don't need defending. Some horrific crisis will divert the city's attention. There will be a sudden presence of rabid squirrels or a lack of adherence to recycling bin labels, and the city will have to step in and restore public order."

"That's a great idea."

"What is?" I asked, confused.

"A diversion."

"You watched a lot of TV as a child."

"You can't fight the system so you sabotage it," she said.

"Right. You get on that. That'd be terrific." She shifted her posture in one of her continuous nervous movements and I seized the opportunity to sneak the door past her boot. "Bye now," I said as I swung the door closed.

"I'll be back," she said, waving like she was featured on a homecoming float.

2

Mostly I had lied to fidgety, anorexic Monika. I'd begun to worry a good deal about how far the neighbors and the city might push. Recurrent nightmares I'd suffered years before returned. I'd awaken in a lather of sweat. I thought I was long done with them and the memories to which they were inextricably linked.

At first, I'd dismissed the city's notices. Maybe I was being avoidant. Honestly, though, what possible stance could they presume? I'd had no confrontations with my neighbors. I'd never met any of them. When I built the place, I'd waited through the lines, filed all the proper permits. What could I possibly have to worry about?

Yet more and more while working in the garden my gaze shifted to the small rise of buildings on a distant hill, home to the city offices. Several such hills sprout from the landscape, the closest occupied by an upscale neighborhood built over the last two years that looks down upon my garden plot and my lonely door. Their lights interfere with stargazing and I'm certain all that fake stone and stamped concrete leaches carcinogens.

None of those homes existed when I moved here. If they had, I most certainly wouldn't have bought the land. While I could never have imagined the circumstances that had instigated such a move, once I'd made up my mind, the relocation was carefully planned. I wanted to go somewhere I could be a stranger. My needs were few. The land was cheap. A place of laughing cows and amber waves.

What right would the city have to push me out of my home? Could they? Had I broken laws of which I was unaware? If it came to it and they pursued legal action, I couldn't begin to imagine facing a protracted engagement with the judicial system. I'd been an unwanted participant in one major proceeding in my life. I wanted no more.

Let the city go battle the old junkyard on Ninety-Fifth Street and its graying hippy or the dairy operation near the river swaddled in cow shit. How about that dead zone that once pretended to be a downtown? What did they want with me? Is it too much to ask to be left alone?

I realize my tone sounds a bit hysterical. Let me clear the record. First, I don't really live in a hole in the ground. There was intelligence behind my home's design, a simple understanding of why temperatures below ground remain within a small fluctuation zone, an elementary knowledge of the sun's path. My home may be unconventional but it's not primitive. Quite the opposite: complete with two large freezers and a well-stocked pantry, not to mention an energy-efficient washer and dryer. In a designer color no less—candy apple red. I have wants same as the next guy, and I need any help I can get when it's time to face laundry day. Sometimes, however, I like to dry my laundry on a line, and I make it a point to fly my boxers with particular flair. (Is it possible that our culture will be remembered one day for the colorfulness of the images we are willing to print on boxer shorts?) I take advantage of what the good earth provides— wind to dry my underwear, soil to provide natural insulation during cold winters and hot summers.

Few people have crossed my threshold, not even to complain about the patterns on my boxers. I imagine they take one look at my front door and assume that I'm a few bricks short of a load. I suppose I shouldn't blame them. I'm not so thick-headed I can't realize how odd my door looks. Maybe it's natural that people assume I live in the dark. If they'd only consider the perspective of my home they don't have from the road, they'd see it is purposely built into the side of a tall cut-bank, that the south wall of my home is visible from above ground and is full of windows and that in the winter, when the sun is low on the horizon, I get long hours of good light and fine solar heat. They don't see the overhung roof that blocks the angle of mid-day sun in summer or the tile near the windows that absorbs and retains heat. Of course, people don't ask such questions, like why I built my front door in the manner I did or why I sought this underground life. Instead I assume people see my lone doorway and know I must be stone crazy.

Not that I go out of my way to correct them. Not that I didn't build that door for the opportunity to offer the world my middle finger. If the presence of my door turns people away, that's fine with me. People bring complications.

Of course, I'm not privy to other's conversations. I can't really know what they say about me. I stick to myself. If, when I am out and about in the above ground world, I speak to others; I like talking to kids best because they aren't afraid to say what's on their mind. If children approach me when I'm on my way to the library or the grocery store, I make it a point to answer their questions. I'll admit that sometimes I tease them. When they ask if I live with snakes, I'll tell them I do, that the place is rampant with poisonous diamondbacks and that I cook them for my supper and decorate my Christmas tree with their rattles. I like watching as their eyes grow wide and then the moment when that wrinkle of healthy skepticism furrows their brows. Mostly though, I answer their questions honestly—the way I like my questions answered—and mostly kids know when they are being teased.

Through talking with kids, I know there are stories about how I bury people down here or that I've filled the walls with sacks of money, but in my experience most folks wouldn't know the truth if it bit them on their backside. Such stories are a way of categorizing something outside a range of experience. It's like people who collect insects and keep them neatly labeled, the wings all shiny and rigid with shellac and safe inside their glass cases. They just seem to forget the pins stuck through the thorax that allow for this bit of otherness to seem permanently knowable and contained. We live in an age when people don't build houses with basements anymore. It used to be that we re-treated to basements for cool in the summer, just as we planted wind breaks and maintained root cellars.

There is ample evidence we no longer live in such times. I'm easier to accept with my label—the crazy man who lives in a hole. It's no great mystery that people talk about anyone who is different from them. We fill our lives talking about others. People who live atop hills must know they are the topic of conversations, for the house on the hill is a concept nearly as old as time. I know if I lived down in the street-level sewage and plagues of the Middle Ages, I'd focus conversation on the guy up there with his clean hair and silk stockings. It is human nature to label him feeble-minded or assume he's got warts in places better not talked about in mixed company. As if the king on the hill doesn't talk about the peasants below, living among their hogs and their excrementally transmitted diseases. The poor talk badly about the rich and the rich about the poor and the powerful about the powerless and on and on.

I know people talk about me. I'd be a fool not to know. The recluse with his spiders and snakes. Mr. Underground Man. Funny how people who don't have anything to say to you always have a lot to say about you. I say let them talk.

I suppose it's not fair to compare my life to others. I've got time on my hands. Time to think or time to *ruminate*, as a therapist might wish me to say. Others have jobs to which they must attend, families to feed, mortgages to pay. I have none of those. I have my distractions, the scratch of vinyl on the turntable or the scrape of graphite on paper. Otherwise there's not much that reaches me down here. Not much distraction to get in the way of thinking. So I do my share of ruminating.

Ruminations. Like this one:

The world of men, like the world of trees, is a vertical one, such that when isolated in a horizontal landscape—when we emerge from our cover like prey within the hunter's field of vision—we are always seen. I wonder if this is where evolution has landed the species. We gave up our trees and prehensile tails for what, to be bipedal and vulnerable?

We gave up our trees but traded them for vertical dwellings in which to hide, like skyscrapers and houses. Anyone who challenges such a convention is immediately ostracized. Think of the horizontal human. How does the average person react to someone sleeping in public? Our species sleeps a third of our lives, but we've matured beyond slumber parties. Encountering someone sleeping in public disobeys the expectations of our upright world. We find their presence incongruous, just as we find something awry, maybe even sad, in the tree that is no longer upright, knowing as we do, that life has gone out of it.

Or at least that's the smell of the shit I'm dishing today. I'm not one to be trusted. It's not like I haven't taken a chainsaw to a tree before.

Trees have been on my mind lately. I'm preoccupied by them. Is there any manmade object as graceful as a tree? There's a crabapple nearby I admire. And I respect the way evergreens shed snow in such a practical fashion. Don't even get me started when it comes to hoarfrost on bare winter limbs. But then I tend to obsess over things. I like to think I am able to see what others don't. Maybe that's another brand of shit.

Yet I have been handed a life—not one of my choosing—that has made me look where others do not. To see the weeds in the cracks. Here is an example: people are so accustomed to trees, just as they are to made objects that occupy the vertical world, like walls and doors, that they look right past them. When do we notice the stranger? Only when he is sleeping on our front sidewalk.

I realize I sound cynical. I am. Life has taught me so. I've lost things. But I shouldn't compare my experience to others. The truth is, I don't know about other people any more than they know about me. Since I no longer understand our culture, I've withdrawn from it. I have a history, like all do, and my particular history helped me see that the world was a dangerous and painful place. So I retired underground.

My decision to "unplug," as it were, offered no agenda or statement. I'm not Ralph Ellison's invisible man. I pay for the electricity I use same as the next guy. I can't claim that I was used for a greater cause or that I became a spokesman for those who are alienated and dehumanized or that I came close to a power that I saw as corrupting. No, I am an ordinary man. Each year a bit less hair where I want it and a bit more where I don't. I think of Timothy Leary's phrase: "Tune in. Turn on. Drop out." I dropped out. Maybe I still wore cowboy pajamas when he said it and it took me another forty years to heed his advice, but I opted out, as the insurance folks like to say. If I were trying to settle an insurance claim, I'd argue that there were mitigating circumstances. Those circumstances changed me. I'm not sure I would recognize the man I was before I decided to settle here.

I came along a good while after Leary. A Cold War kid. Tuck your head and kiss your ass goodbye. By the time I cast my first ballot, we had already forgotten most of the lessons of Vietnam and, along with a few missing brain cells, we had pretty much forgotten Leary too. We'd hired an actor to pretend to be president. We'd watched John Lennon killed. We'd long since stopped selling planes to Iran and started selling them to Iraq and had watched a Sea Stallion helicopter fly into its refueling plane. Yeah, those blissful, turn-your-head-and-cough days of "peace."

I shouldn't complain. I've got no room. I chose the path of inaction. I have become Melville's Bartleby responding to the world around me with a continuous "I would prefer not to." I only encountered Bartleby within the past year. I wasn't much of a reader, even if my degree suggests otherwise, but I'll admit I've taken solace in the world of books in the last years, and when I met a character like Bartleby I had no difficulty understanding his actions, or his inactions as the case may be.

Bartleby makes perfect sense to me. Just as I get Ellison's invisible man much more clearly in his below-ground squat than I do when he was the one behind the podium, I understand his blind rage more than I do his youthful hope. I get his learned silence. I crave silence. There's so much noise in the world. Everyone is vying for attention, so they try and shout louder than the next guy. When was the last time quiet existed? My little place, snug down here inside the earth helps. It can't block out the world, but with enough insulation between all the noise, it helps.

3

Monika reappeared as threatened. I was above ground working in the garden. Hearing her Honda squeak to the curb, I'd begun to wish I had installed an escape hatch and a fire pole. All I had was the meager camouflage of plants, and though it had been a productive year in the reconstructed garden and my compost had done its job, a grown man can't hide forever among tomato plants. Monika walked directly to the garden despite my having dropped to my knees in the pretense of weeding. I waited, not daring to look up.

"I've been thinking about your problem," she said without preface.

"The only problem I've got is with unwanted solicitors," I grumbled. I'd been polite the day before—even accommodating, the way you treat the mentally incapacitated with respectful forbearance. A new tactic was in order.

"Mostly I've been thinking about your suggestion."

"I had a suggestion?"

"Diversionary tactics," she said. "Refocus the energy, so to speak. Give the neighbors a different cause to fight. All they really crave is something to break the monotony of their lives. Something to change their own mendacity, this selfish dishonesty they focus on in the belief that their lives actually mean something. They want to feel important."

"Did you just use *mendacity*? That's like a bonus word in vocabulary, right? You must be the darling of your English teacher."

"Actually, she's whacked. Can't stay focused for more than thirty seconds. Last week she forgot to give us our vocab test. Meds, I think. Probably bi-polar. I've seen her type before. I also happen to think she's a Wiccan. But you're right, I get a word like mendacity into something I've written and I'm gold-en. That's not the point. Well, it is actually, because that's the reality of the 'burbs, man; they're all wallowing in the self-deceit that there is meaning in their big plastic houses. Their Tup-perware. Their mandatory, conservative color palette. Do you know what color my house is? Autumn Blush."

"That sounds pretty."

"It's one of three colors the homeowner's association lets you pick from. Autumn Blush, Emerald Forest, and Sahara Sands. They send you a letter telling you when it needs painted."

"Well, then I'm on a bona fide double bonus plan," I said. "No homeowner's association and no walls to paint."

"See, that's exactly what I'm talking about. We need a world where people can go their own way. People get so locked into their puny generic lives, they can't figure out why they're all so sad. They lead these lives of, of, how do you put it, lives of…"

I waited her out.

"…of…lives of quiet desperation, like what's his name said." She appeared more agitated than she had the day before. She turned a little circle and threw her hands up, looking more than a little desperate herself. "Oh, why can't I remember shit?" she said. "You know. The dude. What's his name? There's probably something I ingest everyday against my will, some additive in my food that's eating my memory cells."

"Could be drugs," I suggested.

"What's his damn name?" she said, ignoring me. "Ugly dude. The writer. Hung out in the woods. He wrote that book about it."

"Thoreau," I offered.

"Bingo. That's him. 'The majority of men live lives of quiet desperation,'" she recited now, beaming. She had a pretty smile. "I just loved that the first time I read it, you know. Like it just clicked," she mused.

"The first time. You've read *Walden* more than once?"

"Of course. Didn't you?" She looked at me, incredulous. "Doesn't matter. What was I saying?"

"You were describing the psychic atmosphere of the suburbs. Why, I have no idea."

"Oh yeah. It's because they hate you."

"Pardon?" I stopped my weeding and stared at her.

"Not you. They don't even know you. They hate that they aren't you. No, that's not right. That they don't understand you. That's not quite right either. You're different from them and they don't get it. Maybe they hate that you're not them." She fingered the leaf of a tomato plant.

"I had no idea I was at the heart of such consternation."

"You're not. I mean, it's not really you, it's the idea of you."

"And what about you?" I asked

"Oh, they don't like me at all. I mean, how could they? I dye my hair."

"Why don't they like you? Besides the hair."

"Mostly because I'm young, but also because they think I'm a rebel."

I had been hoping for something more from her. I stood with my little handheld hoe. The day remained warm despite being late in the season. The green peppers needed more mulch. I prayed the insects stayed away and frost held off.

"I'm not really much of a rebel," she said. "I mean not in the real world of rebels. It's not like I've taken really significant stands or anything. It's not like I believe in something I'd lay down my life for or that I would take on the establishment in so vivid a way that I'd be seen by everyone for the commitments of my beliefs. I'd like to aspire to that but I doubt I have it in me. I'm just enough of a rebel in their eyes to remind them that they're not rebels themselves. Or heroes either, for that matter. That's what they really hate. To be reminded of how they all conform to the status quo without a second thought."

She had my attention again. But I thought it wouldn't go well for me if I paid too much interest in the ability of her mind to turn corners as she'd just done. I had better take evasive action quickly. "You should take up gum chewing," I said.

"What? Why?"

"To give yourself some other way to exercise your jaw." I saw the barb arc on a trajectory targeted for flesh, but then it veered away as if her clothes really were made of armor. Today she repeated the silver jacket but wore baggy brown corduroys and had added a stocking cap despite the heat. I liked it better when you could see more of her hair.

"Give a cow a cud," she said, "and maybe they'll all shut up."

"That's a messy metaphor."

"I realized that as soon as I said it." She blushed. "I wish I could think faster on my feet. It always gets me in trouble, you know. It's like I need a good day to find quiet and think up the perfect comeback. It should be declared a syndrome. Delayed comeback syndrome. Because once you miss the cue or if you come back with something lame, the moment just passes you by."

"You're right," I said. "You should probably be medicated or find a good therapist."

"Yeah, I should join the zombies. My mother has tried that."

"What? Kill the undead?"

"Sending me to a shrink. She thinks I have issues."

"I can't imagine how she could think such a thing."

"The first time was all over vegetables. I was like eleven or twelve."

"Vegetables?"

"I wouldn't eat them. I refused."

"All vegetables?"

"Yep."

"Why?"

"Because she wanted me to."

"You are a rebel," I said, retrieving my pocket knife in order to harvest some broccoli.

"No, the funny thing is that now I'm a vegetarian."

"Of course you are."

"Which, ironically, really pisses her off."

"I'm sensing there is a great deal of vegetable tension in your house."

"You shouldn't joke about such things. I have a brother who is a vegetable."

"Root vegetable or flower vegetable?" I asked, trying to be cute. A frequent mistake.

"As in brain dead. Feeding tube, shit in a bag vegetable."

"Oh," I stammered. "I'm sorry. I thought you were joking."

"You should pay more attention."

I felt terrible. Such was the risk of being above ground. "I didn't mean to be insensitive. I didn't know you were being literal."

"How could you know? Besides, my therapist says it's healthy to talk about it."

"Do you mind if I ask what happened?"

"Botched suicide attempt. He tried to hang himself from the ceiling fan in his bedroom after downing a bunch of pills, only he didn't succeed in breaking his neck, just in cutting off his air supply. He probably still would have gotten the job done except the ceiling fan broke. It was the sound of him hitting the floor that finally got our attention."

"I really am very sorry."

"Yeah, aren't we all? My mom goes and visits him every day. There's loads of guilt there as you can imagine. The whole family makes this grand production of a trip on Friday nights, all of us tromping into his room at the care facility. We dress up like it's Friday business casual, and we'd look the model family, straight off the Family Channel movie of the week if it weren't for the vegetable. Or maybe that's what gets you on the Family Channel, that and anorexia and murderous affairs. Or is that Lifetime? Or Oxygen? I don't know. Anyway, it's quite the production. A lot of the time Dad stretches the little fraud out and takes us out to dinner after, says it's quality family time and then it all turns into an Applebee's commercial."

"Please accept my apology and my sympathy."

"Stop apologizing," she said. "I thought you'd be the sort of person you don't have to pussyfoot around."

"Why would you think that?"

"Because I figured you don't care what people think. I figured you had cajones."

"Ca-whatits?"

"Cajones. Balls, man."

"People probably make that mistaken assumption."

"Apparently."

"Look, I really don't know why you're here," I said. "I don't know what it is you're looking for."

"Like I said yesterday, I just thought you might like a little help."

I looked at her carefully. She seemed to stand without fidgeting for the first time since I'd laid eyes on her. "You really think there's something to this. You think the city is going to take some action."

"People will force them to whether they want to or not," she said. "The people around here are totally crazy. I mean off-their-rockers nuts. Mostly they're bored. But they're also a little scared. Deep down they realize that there is very little they control. It makes them feel good when they believe they are doing something to stand up for middle class values."

"I don't get how I'm opposed to middle class values," I admitted.

"You don't have to be. Like I said before, they don't know you, so they're free to believe whatever they want to believe. It's all about the image you project."

"What image do I project?"

"You live in a hole in the ground, dude."

"Good point."

"They can't see anything they have in common with you."

"I bet if they knew me, they'd find out I'm not so different than them."

"Oh, right, you keep thinking that," she said, then paused. "Besides, it doesn't really matter who you are or what you think if you don't project the image they are comfortable with. With you, there's no lining up with the things they value. You go head-to-head, you lose."

"There's weeds," I said.

"What?"

"Weeds. Why don't you put in some work while you explain why I'm so outside of convention?" I nodded to a hoe atop one of the raised garden bed rails.

She picked up the hoe and set to work but didn't miss a beat. "Consider the things they talk about. Like they all work. All the time. Even if some of them couldn't really tell you what they actually do; I mean, even if mainly their days consist of going to meetings and answering emails, they still like to think that work matters. They like to think of themselves as productive, maybe even invaluable. That way they feel better when they see someone else roofing a house or pouring asphalt in July. Work matters to them. They wear shirts with their company names on them. Do you work?"

"No, not in the conventional sense."

"See. Strike one. That's something they expect, like where you work defines you. Your work is something they value. Just like they value their cars. They drive everywhere. They'll drive to their neighbors two blocks away to drop off little Cindy-Lou Who. They have really nice cars. Expensive cars. Do you even have a car?"

"No."

"Strike two. They can't imagine walking. Don't ask them to take a bus."

She was really going now. I felt it might be dangerous if I attempted to stop her. The upside was that her pace of hoeing matched her speed of talking.

"And they love their families. Oh, they are quick to tell you just how much they love their families. Only a whole lot of them are so busy working all the time they really don't see much of their families. Still, they talk, you know, especially if their kids are in sports. They just have a harder time talking about them when they're living with their boyfriend the tattoo artist and they're pregnant or asking to live in their basement again until the restraining order takes effect. Do you have a family?"

This one hit home. "No," I said.

"Strike three, boss. You're out. See, they don't have anything in common with you. Are you starting to see all the incongruities here?"

"Yes," I said flatly. I felt embarrassed and I wasn't sure why.

"Don't forget religion. It's very important that you're seen as religious. Nothing that's not Christian of course. Do you attend church regularly?"

"No."

"Electronics?"

"Pardon?"

"They love electronics. You have to have the newest of everything to keep up. Is that your secret pastime? You've got a high-res flat screen and a home theater digital surround system that you blast the groundhogs with?"

"Not exactly."

"Oh, and they love their yards. Don't laugh, this matters a lot. See, it's the appearance thing again. Oh, wait, you don't have a yard, you have a field."

"I have a garden," I said.

"Exactly. That's quite nineteenth century of you."

"So I'm screwed," I said.

"Hopelessly."

"That sucks."

"That it does."

"It appears I am destined to be forever unliked. No neighbors borrowing garden tools and no invitations to pool parties. I can live with that," I said.

"You won't have neighbors at all."

"Even better."

"I don't see how homelessness or a forced move could possibly be better," she said.

"You're being paranoid," I said, beginning to feel a little paranoid myself.

"Have you been asleep your whole life?" she asked. "You've

seen how people treat anyone who is different from them. Difference creates fear. They circle the wagons."

"No one sees me."

"That's an even bigger problem. What's invisible scares them way more than what's real. It just takes one vocal egomaniac to incite their hatred. Then it's game on."

"You mix a lot of metaphors."

"You're worried about my metaphors when your neighbors are going to find a way to have you evicted."

I couldn't help but wonder if Monika was right. Did I really have to worry that I could lose my home? Could nosey neighbors strip away the only thing I had? I shook my head. I was letting an addle-brained teenager fuel paranoia.

"The good news is that they're like racoons. Easily distracted. We need to refocus their attention. Get them thinking about something else instead. That's how they do it in Washington."

"What exactly do you have in mind?" I asked, suddenly drawn right back in.

"I was thinking after we talked the other day. About your garden. About what my brother and his friends did to you. I don't imagine the neighbors came around with words of consolation or baked goods. If somebody else had been targeted, the neighborhood would be up in arms. They need to think they could be targets. So, I kind of already started on a bit of a campaign last night."

"Campaign?"

"Let's just call it a diversionary action."

"What did you do?"

"Kid stuff. I figured if they thought there was a problem even more in their backyards than you, so to speak, something that got at their sensitivities regarding their vision of home and family and pristine lawns, it would get their attention."

"Kid stuff," I repeated.

"Yeah. You know, harmless, silly pranks, stuff that doesn't hurt anything but pisses them off."

"Just what exactly did you do?"

"It's all innocent really. A couple of houses now sport toilet paper in their trees, maybe three houses, five tops. Toilet paper is more expensive than I thought. Next time I think I'll raid all the bathrooms at school first. Now shaving cream is cheap."

"Shaving cream."

"A little on some car windows, nothing much. Don't worry. I only did the houses of the kids who vandalized your place. I made up my own gang sign. Want to see?" She scrounged in the frayed army backpack she had flung at her feet upon picking up the hoe and then removed a small piece of paper inscribed in black ink with something that looked like a cattle brand.

"Very artsy," I said.

"It's hard to render in shaving cream."

"I imagine."

She looked momentarily embarrassed. "I might have driven over a couple of mailboxes," she said sheepishly.

"Mailboxes."

"They belonged to people who were really mean to me when I was in middle school. Cruel really. Still, I didn't mean to hit them."

"You didn't mean to."

"Not with my car. You know how you hear of boys driving by and knocking off mailboxes with baseball bats? That's what I had in mind. I borrowed my brother's bat, but I hadn't quite factored in how hard it is to drive and swing a bat at the same time. I've never been exactly what you'd call an athlete. I felt terrible after."

"You're certifiable."

"And there might be a lawn ornament living in my trunk. A gnome. That's what I was really going for. That's when I knew I was on the right track."

"Pardon?"

"A gnome."

"I got that."

"I don't understand why people find them cute. They give me the heebie-jeebies."

"Why do you have a gnome in your trunk?"

"I liberated him, so to speak. They're really heavy. You probably didn't know that."

"No, I didn't."

"I had a bitch of a time getting him in my trunk. I named him Frodo. I thought naming him might lessen the creep factor. I can't say that really worked. He's thumping around back there like I've got a body to dispose of or something."

"You don't, do you?"

"What?"

"Have a body to get rid of?"

"Very funny," she said. "No, just the gnome."

"Why is it you're doing this?"

"To help you save your home," she said, and she put down the hoe and picked up a bushel basket that I'd placed vegetables in. She smiled at me.

"And how is it you're helping me?"

"By diverting attention off you. Hey, you've got a lot of good stuff here," she said, indicating the basket. "You don't think I could park Frodo here for a while?"

"Frodo?"

"The gnome. You need to pay more attention."

"But I thought you were trying to keep the heat off me."

"Right. Good point. Maybe I'll have to rent a storage shed. It's not like I want to be accused of stealing him."

"Of course not. You're just helping me."

"That's right." Holding the basket under one arm, she slung her backpack over the opposite shoulder and then pointed with her chin at another basket I'd filled at the end of the row. "Twice the people means half the work," she said and started walking to the front door. Stupidly, I picked up the other basket and followed.

I do have a second door. French doors, in fact. Few people know of their existence, although they are plainly visible, as is the entire south-facing glass wall of my house. Of course, to see those windows would ask people to put on some comfortable shoes and move their feet without the aid of a personal trainer, so the open space beyond my house is largely unvisited with the exception of a few children. I'm sure it would be a place highly attractive to motocross riders and recreationists on ATVs (if you can really call another mode of driving recreation), but the neighbors convinced the city to place a ban on such activities—preserving the abandoned gravel pit as protected space—and are quick to employ their phones if they see someone in violation. They probably have the number set to speed dial. It is not without irony how sometimes it is industry and progress, those great destroyers of the natural world, which conspire to save small slices of it. The old gravel pit forms something of a boundary for the city to limit its growth and preserves my privacy.

It is not a place without its beauty. A lesson in the recuperative strength of nature resides here, for slowly she reclaims this scarred land, repopulates it with frogs and a few rebellious trees. Knee-high grasses can fill spring with clouds of redwing blackbirds. On morning walks here, I often encounter deer and always I see rabbits and muskrats, and on mornings of especially good fortune I glimpse a red fox. It is a place that is reserved in the way women used to be when a glimpse of a bare thigh came as a kind of thrill. Perhaps it is a beauty you must look harder to see, but it can arrive on a butterfly's wing or in rain drying on a spider's web. Often, looking into this small preserve beyond the framed opening of my french doors, I feel like I am in a savannah, safe within cover but able to see into the distance.

In this instance I can side with the neighbors for trying to preserve the simple pleasure and beauty by employing their phones whenever they spy the unwanted ATV. Or the undesirable neighbor for that matter. Monika just might be onto a tactic that holds some logic.

At any rate, such are the circumstances that allow so few people to know of my second door. It was not there that Monika carried my vegetables, of course, but to my front door. I thanked her for the assistance, and when she offered to help get them to the bottom of the stairs, I politely said that I could manage. Though visitors to my front door are few, she is not the first to have shown curiosity in gaining entry. She, to my surprise, offered no protest and promised again to return with an update on her actions battling those at the helm of a misguided municipal system. I asked no questions. I could only imagine what was next in her campaign against her—correct that, our—neighbors: absentee doorbell ringing, egg throwing, dog feces in paper sacks. My hope was that when she was caught, as she inevitably would be, she would not suggest that she was doing so in some illogical attempt to assist me. But I do wonder about the neighbors. Even the smallest of the homes that have sprung up around me are exponentially larger than mine. Some I would label virtual mansions. I suspect they harbor a fair number of lawyers. Perhaps the fear Monika had incited in me was not without merit.

I watched Monika walk to her car. I heard the car start and watched as she completed a swift U-turn. Just as she completed the turn, she waved at me, and I surprised myself when I realized I had returned the gesture without so much as a thought.

4

More rumination: examining my habits I suspect that, among the many labels surely used in reference to me, the most common is likely "hermit." I suppose it is fitting. Listening to myself it sounds as if I have a psychological disorder that traps me in my home. Untrue. I remain a great believer that in most elements of life people are granted choices. I believe this despite past circumstances that offer contrary evidence.

I did, however, choose the lifestyle I now lead. A calculated retreat seems an apt phrase. I have not removed myself from the company of humans entirely. However, I have become a creature of habits. Does that make me so different? Who does not live by routines? Among mine is my Thursday schedule of errands. While I find most aspects of culture curious, if not objectionable, I will admit that I offer my Thursday errands as a kind of treat to myself. I suppose a useful metaphor is to think about the human relationship with zoos. We may find a certain cruelty in locking animals behind bars, yet we still go and amuse ourselves by watching them and justify their presence in the name of preservation. Sort of like going to see the monkeys is how I view my trips to town. I suspect most would want to turn my metaphor on its head, but I think I've got it about right.

It is on Thursdays that I go to the library. Not only do I gather books—fiction and poetry entirely, I have no more need for what is real—I take the time to read the Sunday *New York Times*. Now I understand that it is the oddest sort of juxtaposition to remove oneself from a culture and then still spy upon it by reading one version of its comings and goings. Still, I draw a distinction between distancing oneself from a culture and being ignorant. Call it an indulgence. I long ago divorced myself from television and from radio, phones, computers, and social media.

Several of the librarians address me by my surname and I like the respect such a means of greeting offers, even if they are simply reading my name off their computer system. I converse with them, briefly, chitchat mostly but sometimes we talk about books. Such conversations can buoy hopes that not all is lost for humanity. But lately, since the appearance of the city's notices on my door, I have begun to skim the local paper before leaving the library, and my hopes for humanity are questioned once more. It is a paper that seems exclusively filled with stories of crime and tragedy, violation and corruption. I am convinced that their photo editor held previous employment with a forensics department.

After Monika's introduction into my life, I've also taken to doing some research while I'm at the library. I've learned a good deal about municipal powers and the use of eminent domain, and from the regularity of abuses I have learned about it's enough to make me lose sleep. Apparently, it is no longer uncommon for cities to declare the purchase of properties useful for "the public good" to sustain the appearance of a neighborhood and then turn around and sell acquired properties to private developers and benefit from higher tax income. I'd begun to wonder if Monika knew more than she was letting on. More and more my mind focused on what I'd learned about the abuse of municipal powers upon my departure from that quiet, civilized respite of books.

From the library it is my habit to walk to a used music store, a place at the fringes of what used to be downtown that is now terrain featuring empty storefronts and enterprise dependent on low lease rates—pawn shops and used clothing stores ('vintage' their signs declare), a nearly extinct furniture store, and a number of businesses that boast signs in languages other than English. Like the others, one can see the neglect of the record store in the brick exterior that seems to be shedding layers like so much snakeskin and by the dirty windows with their fading window paint and dead flies.

The perpetually scowling proprietor does not speak beyond

the requirements of a transaction. I can respect his apparent desire not to speak and require no acknowledgement. I am there for the music, and he does have an enviable collection of vinyl records and within it there are occasional treasures. Music, an ally all my life, though sometimes an enemy too, mostly still offers me pleasure and comfort.

Each Thursday I treat myself to one other indulgence, lunch out. I have three places I frequent and rotate through each once a month and each month I have a bit of a mental battle over which one I will visit a second time. At each restaurant I am guilty of having a menu favorite. I start the month with lemon chicken at The Forbidden City Café. Week two is reserved for Los Dos Hermanos enjoying the #6—a chili relleno and cheese enchilada in a blue corn tortilla smothered in green chili. That's followed by Marv's Burger Heaven for a double decker bacon burger, a sure ticket to heart procedures and a prescription for Lipitor.

Despite my chosen desire for isolation, it is not without pleasure that I sit at a restaurant once a week and listen to the clatter of dishes and the chatter of a kitchen at full service. That it is an environment I can exit when I choose heightens my pleasure.

After lunch I complete the necessary errands that simple life transactions necessitate, irregular visits to the bank and post office, a trip to the grocery store for fruit and other perishables. I also frequent a musty book store (what is it with used book stores anyway, the particular funk that attacks the nostrils—the dead skin of previous owners, a gathering of geriatric cats?), where I occasionally augment my library reading with the purchase of a book that withstands rereading and for the regular purchase of puzzle books—word games and number puzzles and crosswords. I fear I will one day exhaust such a market. They occupy my time and I like to believe they help keep my mind sharp.

Time is a commodity of which I have reserves. Perhaps I have come to value its presence too late, for in my former life, it always seemed in short supply. Each Thursday I remain surprised at how quickly time passes.

I go out into the world other days too. I walk miles and miles, but these walks take me along ravine bottoms and among river trees and into small woods. Such walks are peaceful whereas on Thursdays I am reminded of the constant movement of the modern human, the noise of cars moving fast, the heat that rises off so much asphalt, the fumes that are expelled into the air. There is simply so much commotion that it infiltrates and pollutes my mind. I can't think straight. Walking in traffic makes me recall what it was like to face the barrage of television or the internet. I can only imagine how both these forms of electronic anesthetic have evolved. There are regular articles about both in the *Times*, but I skip those. They hold no relevance for me. Nor does most of the news. I am largely immune to it. For example, apparently we have recently plunged into an economic crisis, what they have labeled "The Great Recession," although given the nature of my own economics and the comfort of home ownership without a mortgage, I believe I have been safely vaccinated against economic woes.

The few periodical publications I briefly indulge are mostly filled with advertisements, a fact that is no surprise given the predominant nature of our culture. I must say it is the omnipresence of advertisements screaming for my attention that presses my pace home on Thursday afternoons every bit as much as the pollution and the general din. Indeed, it often seems to me that the source of the din is advertising. Car radios, bus stop benches, store windows, flyers taped to light posts, billboards—even as removed as I am, I remain surrounded. Perhaps I need blinders like a horse bedazzled by distraction. That and a pair of earplugs.

Such was my state when a car horn sounded repeatedly. I paid it no mind. The horn sounded again and seemed so near I wondered for a moment if a car were careening down the sidewalk behind me. Then I saw Monika's Honda Civic pulled to the opposite side of the road. She waved from the open window. I believe she shouted something, but I could not hear over the traffic so I waved and resumed walking. I watched as she rejoined traffic, nearly cutting off a pickup, which prompted another horn blast and a raised middle finger from the driver. Her rusty little car receded in the distance before abruptly changing lanes and making a fast U-turn at an intersection. Within seconds she pulled alongside.

Her passenger window was down. She leaned across into the passenger seat. "Need a ride?"

"No thanks."

"You have all this stuff."

"It's not far really."

"I'm headed home anyway."

"I like to walk." A large truck rumbled by and I felt buffeted by its passage. "Go on," I said. "You'll get yourself killed parked here."

"And you won't? You could die from what it's doing to your lungs alone."

"You're not contributing to the speed of my death in this rattletrap?"

Monika looked embarrassed. Another truck passed so closely that the wind from its passage visibly shook her car.

"I have an update for you," she said. "Get in."

I shrugged.

"Come on, bucko," she said. A car honked a high-pitched squawk and disappeared fast. We nearly shouted in order to be heard over the traffic. I felt absurd. Reluctantly, I got in her car, an action that felt immediately absurd as well. The door closed with a metallic shudder.

"I felt safer on the sidewalk," I said as she pulled into traffic.

"Well, if you wanted to be safe, you should have booked a flight. Statistically speaking, of course. I'm not implying that I can fly." She jerked through the gears like a NASCAR driver on amphetamines, the car lurching at each transaction. The knob of the gearshift had been replaced with an eight ball. The dials on the radio featured beer bottle caps. A miniature Buddha was glued to the center of her dashboard. The car made a high-pitched whine as if it were taxed beyond its abilities. I looked around as if I could identify the source and saw that the back-seat was filled with textbooks and art supplies—canvas and poster board, quart paint containers, along with messy tubes of acrylics. Among the mess there was a rifle painted entirely in white.

"You're on the drill team?" I asked regarding the rifle. "Or are you an arctic assassin?"

"Freshman year."

"I wouldn't have guessed that."

"It was a phase. First marching band, then drill team, then academic decathlon. The full geek quotient. I didn't last a month in any of them."

"Yet you kept the rifle."

"They never asked for it back. I keep meaning to paint peace signs and flowers on it and then return it anonymously. Maybe I could use it in an installation. It could make a dramatic state-ment, don't you think?"

"I'm sure the Pentagon would close up shop the moment the Joint Chiefs saw it."

"Are you always so sarcastic?"

"Only on Thursdays."

"It gets annoying."

"A character flaw. I'm sure I'm compensating for some-thing."

"For what?"

"What?"

"What are you compensating for?"

"Oh, nothing. I was only being sarcastic."

My joke was met with a dramatic frown.

"Sorry," I said. "I'm not around people much. A therapist would probably say that it's a kind of defense mechanism."

"Why is that?"

"That I'm defensive?"

"No, that you're alone."

"Do you always ask so many questions?"

"How else do you get to know someone? If people don't ask each other questions, how will they ever understand each other? Besides, any of us could SPLAT!" she said, making a loud, wet sound. "Drop dead any second and the opportunity would be gone forever."

She had a point. I looked out the window. I hadn't been in a car for a long time. In the past, I liked to drive and sometimes I used driving as an excuse to think. "What if you don't want to know people?" I asked.

"There's not much doubt that most people probably suck," she said. "I mean, let's face it, like two thirds of the population is of below average intelligence, so it's easy to think you might want to avoid them. But what if you passed over the person who might change your life just because you refused to talk to people?"

"There's something wrong with your math," I said.

"How do you mean?"

"You said two thirds of people were of below average intelligence. If there's an average, then couldn't only half of them be below average?"

"When's the last time you took a math class?"

"Longer than I can remember. Before you were born. It's quite possible much of the world was covered in ice."

"I'm in AP calc. So you probably don't want to have the whole mean, medium, average discussion with me. I'd kick your ass."

"I concede."

"That was entirely beside the point anyhow," she said, turning onto my street.

"What was the point?"

"You know exactly what the point was."

I did.

Two minutes later she pulled to the curb in front of my property. I had rarely considered my door from this vantage point. I wondered if I shouldn't plant a tree on each side of it to soften its line. What surprised me most was to recognize that I had worn a discernable path from the road to the door. With rare exception, I departed from the front door on Thursdays. Otherwise, for gardening or recreational walks I use the french doors on the south side of the house. Imagine that my steps could impress such a wound in the earth in just seven years. How right Monika's Thoreau had been.

Monika interrupted my thoughts. "You haven't asked for an update."

"Was I supposed to?"

"It's your ass on the line, not mine."

"True."

"Rumor has it the city is going to hold a public meeting about your property review, one that will invite public comment."

"What review? They haven't done anything more than plant a sign in my yard. No one's spoken to me."

"Supposedly they've tried. They believe you are being uncooperative."

"How do you know this?"

"I took acting my freshmen year. The teacher was seriously demented. Can you believe he thought a group of pimple-faced high school kids could understand *Kiss of the Spider Woman?* I think he took a little trip back in the day and never returned."

"Acting?"

"I'm not saying I was particularly good at it. But to make a phone call posing as one of your concerned neighbors wasn't exactly Oscar material. I said I was afraid you were making meth."

"Thanks, Monika. Having them believe I run a meth house is really going to help my situation. Now I'll probably be assaulted in the middle of the night by storm troopers wearing gas masks and carrying grenade launchers."

"Who knew you were so dramatic," she said. "The clerk I reached was very talkative. Everybody likes gossip."

"Apparently."

"By law they have to post a notice for a hearing at least thirty days in advance. That's when they share the findings of their review. I imagine you'll be receiving unwanted visitors any time now."

"It seems to be a trend. Thanks for the ride," I said, opening the car door.

"Need help carrying anything?"

"Do I look infirm?"

"I was just trying to be nice."

"Oh."

"Believe it or not, there are nice people in the world. Plus, there's the whole social convention thing, even if you're lying."

"Sorry."

"Obviously you don't need help. I always thought homeless people were kind of sickly, you know—from meds or booze or malnourishment or whatever. They always either look kind of wiry, like they're made of springs or else like they're on their last legs."

"I'm not homeless," I nearly shouted. "For Christ's sake, you approached me because you said you wanted to help defend my house."

"I know that," she said. "I didn't mean that you were homeless. It's just that you act like you're homeless, walking to the grocery store and all."

"I look homeless because I walk?"

"Not homeless. That was the wrong word. Vagabond-ish. Or is that the same thing? Give me a break. I just meant eccentric people. Most eccentric people are older, that or crazy, and you act older, kind of crotchety. And you talk like a professor."

"Oh, so now I'm eccentric *and* crotchety."

"If the shoe fits."

Clearly, she had an argument I couldn't effectively rebut. "You really know how to hurt a guy."

"Hey, are you like some sort of ultra-marathoner or something?"

"Yeah, you caught me. That's exactly what I am."

"So you don't need help with the groceries," she said, smiling. She had a pretty smile.

I closed the car door and walked away.

"Forty-eight," she shouted from the car.

"What?" I asked, turning.

"You are wondering how old I think you are. I'm guessing forty-eight."

"You really know how to hurt a guy," I said. "I'm forty-six."

"You're the same age as my mom."

"Lucky me," I said, turning and once again resuming the path I had eroded into the soft skin of the earth.

5

On Friday I suffered no invasions from Monika or from city building inspectors. Monika had told me about the weekly family trips to visit her brother that consumed her Fridays, although I wondered if I had perhaps seen the last of her. After all, clearly she was impulsive and unpredictable and would likely depart from my life as suddenly as she had entered it. Good riddance.

However, anticipating the arrival of city officials left me feeling I was becoming my own jailer. Typically, I spend a large portion of days listening to music, but I feared I would miss the knock at the door in a drum beat. I vacillated between my "prefer not to" desire to avoid officialdom and a nagging worry that if I did not accommodate their inspection, I was endangering my defense. On any other day I could listen to music as loud as I pleased, one of the benefits of my home's construction and my isolation. Music is meant to have some muscle behind it. Music accompanied my days—smoky, languid jazz while I wrote or read, old rock while I worked out, fusion or blues when I drew.

I had been knocked from the balance beam of my routines. I couldn't concentrate. I walked to the turntable repeatedly and then resisted the impulse. More than once my imagination manufactured the sound of knuckles rapping above. All of this was silliness, for after seven years of living here alone, I know every sound the place can muster, from the hum of the refrigerator fan to the flush of water through pipes.

When I retrieved the mail on Friday afternoon, a small royalty check awaited me, which was pleasant enough even though my needs are few, but accompanying the check was a notice that the publisher wanted to begin making payments electronically, along with directions for completing the necessary paperwork required for such transactions. I felt a slosh of queasiness in my stomach. Instantly I envisioned writing a check at the grocery store only to find my account had been emptied.

The sums from my humble percentage were not grand. Yet I remained shocked at the odd, lingering interest in a kind of soft exposé on '80s hair bands, a book I remain mildly embarrassed for having written, laden as it is with episodes of binge drinking, sex with groupies, and other predictable behavior from dropouts turned rock stars. Indeed, the royalty checks had grown significantly larger in recent years, for evidently there is some renewed interest in such bands. Would that they followed Neil Young's advice and burned out. Perhaps, I thought, I should have heeded his counsel too.

I must admit there are days when I awaken and wonder why I am still here. By here I do not mean this simple, comfortable rabbit hole I have fashioned. I mean here in the metaphysical application of the word that is as slippery as the just-caught fish. I seldom participate openly in the civilized transactions expected by my fellow humans, but I sometimes wonder why I persist in participating in the larger transaction of exchanging oxygen for carbon dioxide. Why indeed?

Such ruminations are, I suppose, an accompanying product of spending one's time alone. Too much presence within my own head. And yet, incredulously, here I am. More than that, I contemplated how I would preserve my home, and by simple logical extension, the lifestyle I have chosen. What does it mean to want to fight for a thing I never would have asked for in the first place?

Of course, even the most visionary have difficulty seeing the future. When I allow departure from anything but concentration on whatever simple task occupies my fingertips, my focus is almost entirely on the past, and the past is visible with a clarity that arrives whether bidden or not.

Moving here and choosing a lifestyle that tried to keep the clutter down was part of what I now see as an illogical attempt to forget. On my best days, I am capable of admitting my shortcomings: I am a hypocrite and a fool. The past haunts us no

matter how far we run from it. And clutter, well our lives, like
our minds, constantly accumulate it like leaves adding to forest
detritus. Why just yesterday I purchased two albums. My life
has been accompanied by a kind of soundtrack, each memory
back-grounded by music, although that is another kind of clutter, I realize. These albums will join the multitude of bins filled
with their cousins, so much vinyl that if I lived above ground,
I fear the structure could not hold the weight. A hypocrite and
a fool. What is it I seek as the needle rides the grooves like a
junkie searching a vein?

What sort of clown fails to recognize that alone one finds
loneliness?

If I were a drinking man, my Saturday morning would have
found me hungover. I felt restless and tired. I had reserved one
of the newly acquired albums, John Lee Hooker's *How Long Blues*
for Friday night, a kind of gift to myself the way a child might
squirrel away his favorite candy from the Halloween bucket. The
music failed to offer escape. It is an accomplished album, one
that should have fit my mood perfectly. I slept poorly. The only
cure I knew for my perceived ailment was routine, so to routine
I returned with weight lifting and a cardio workout. There are
days when exercise is mindless, days even where one might label
the exertion euphoric, and there are days when each step seems
taken underwater. Such was Saturday's regimen.

From the workout I moved to the garden. The morning
held a cool fall chill that can feel exhilarating, though this day
it offered only the reminder that the garden neared its annu-
al death. That knowledge, the image of drooping stalks and
curled leaves, made the work laborious, as filled with effort as
the workout had been.

The day proceeded in the same pattern, each act a struggle, the day's writing more like a clubbing of the head with a
blunt object, the sentences adolescent and acne-pocked. The
day's drawing proved a fumbling of pen lines wishing for the
abrasive rub of the eraser. If only I could erase whole days and

leave no smudge.

By dinnertime cooking simply seemed more effort than I had energy for, so I ate cold cereal and toast. Twilight found me outside. I had fashioned a pocket garden beyond the french doors, using rock from my home's excavation to form a tiny stone patio into which I'd dug a fire pit. It was a pleasant place to write or read or simply to remain still on summer mornings when the pond edges were full with birdsong and the fluctuating patterns of flight and on summer evenings when the frogs took over.

I started a fire and sat close to its warmth. I watched the occasional fleeing ember stray into the night sky. I contemplated the stars.

Sunday passed identically. I had slept fitfully. I worried that I was coming down with a cold. I fell asleep in the middle of the afternoon, awakened in fact, only by the thump of a book slipping from my lap onto the floor. I feared I was regressing into childhood behavior—afternoon naps and cold cereal for dinner. How long before I would awaken to a urine-soaked bed?

At one point I was so convinced I heard the backup warning beeps of a piece of construction equipment that I raced up the stairs and out the front door to stand blinking in the sunshine. That evening I gathered every scrap of paper regarding the house and its construction and placed them into a folder. I secured the whole thing with a rubber band. There were pages with numbers and drawings, pages with the tiny print of legalese, more pages with bloated words of insurance coverage and easements and soil samples. So much paper for so little a house.

I found, during my search, another file for another house, the papers that demonstrate the buying and selling of property, the commodity of walls and floors and ceilings—so much bulk for paper that proves so incapable of containing the heft of memories. I tried not to read its yellowing label as if it bore the spores of contagion.

6

On Monday I dispersed with routine and took the bus to the library where I knew they had copy machines available to the public. I suffered a momentary panic that I would not be able to operate something so simple as a copier. The panic worsened as I encountered an LCD screen crowded with graphics that included arrows and hatch marks and numbers that did not coincide with a need I could imagine necessary. I contemplated abandoning the project when I saw that some kind-hearted librarian had typed a simple placard and taped it to the top of the machine: "Place original face up here and press start." I felt a wash of relief. Then a new wave of panic curled. Like most legal documents, many were oversized and some of the pages were as flimsy as tissue paper. A few were yellow and one was pink and many were dense with print on both front and back, and instinctively I knew that simply inserting them in the feeding slot would prove insufficient, worse, would clog the machine and set off some sort of warning alarm. I had visions of documents emerging from a shredder.

The panic must have been visible on my face or worse, perhaps I'd muttered my frustrations audibly, for as I stood contemplating retreat, a kind-eyed woman asked me if she could offer assistance. She was blond and attractive in the sort of way you would want a mother of toddlers to be attractive. She wore a nametag that declared her as Jessica. I had never seen her before, but then, I thought, I'd never been to the library on a Monday and I'd never entered the little glass-walled copy room. "These things can be persnickety," she said, smiling. "I'd be glad to lend a hand."

Jessica, upon learning that I wished to copy all of the folder's contents, efficiently separated the single-sided pages from the double-sided, and then she had the whole lot copied and arranged in a neat packet within minutes. I thanked her profusely, all the while wanting to explain that I wasn't incapable, that I possessed a college degree, that I had once worked professionally and had successfully operated computers and fax machines, copy machines too (even if I'd always struggled with the precise workings of corporate phone systems), yet she smiled at me again in a way that suggested no such explanation would be necessary, mollifying my embarrassment by the simple statement: "Don't tell my boss, but it took me a year to figure out double-sided." The readiness of her smile provided a momentary renewed hope for humanity and I made a twenty-five-dollar donation after I paid for the copies.

Returning home, my confidence deflated when I saw the plain brown sedan with city plates parked at the curb. Two men sat within, their windows down in the pleasant weather. My first thought was to continue walking.

What would an ordinary person do? I wondered. Walk to his house and not assume every car parked along the road had the potential to change his life, I imagined, for starters. As I drew close, I saw the words "Code Enforcement" stenciled on the car door. The two men wore identical polo shirts, indiscriminate beige in color, and the one in the passenger seat wore a baseball cap. The dashboard was a litter box of papers and fast-food wrappers.

I turned at the little path I had worn across the property, trying to make certain I appeared nonchalant. I was halfway to my door when I heard: "Excuse me, sir. Can we have a word with you?"

It struck me as an archaic expression: "a word." I thought a word was all I should offer them: "No." How would that be for "a word"? Would they know how to react? Instead I said nothing at all but simply stopped.

Baseball Cap arrived first. He wore sunglasses and walked as if he spent his days on horseback rather than pasted to the vinyl seat of a city sedan. The driver lagged fifteen feet behind and breathed as if extricating himself from the car had been undue exertion. He was pear-shaped and possessed little folds of man boobs that I couldn't stop staring at. A stencil in the shape of a city logo bounced with his left breast. As he neared I saw he had milky blue eyes that seemed gigantic behind thick lenses.

"We're with the city," Baseball Cap said redundantly, as if the insignia on his hat suggested that together the two men had visited a "gently used" clothing store and purchased matching outfits.

Big Scary Eyes spoke. "We're here to complete a preliminary property review in accordance with the official notices you have received." I suspected he had memorized the line and had no idea what he'd just said. He stood blinking, apparently awaiting a response.

"I made copies," I said, thrusting the thick sheaf of papers at them. "Everything you might need is there."

"We just need to make a brief external visual inspection and ask you a couple of questions," Glasses said, ignoring the paperwork.

"We just have to walk the survey lines," Baseball Cap said.

"Survey lines?"

"The property lines," he said, beginning to unroll a large plat map.

"Are you the lawful owner of record for this property?" Glasses asked, reading from a clipboard.

"Yes."

"And you can confirm that this is Lot 53 of South Lake Terrace Estates?" He went on to name the county and the state.

"It's 1974 Nixon Road."

"Same diff," Glasses said. "It's just the legal description, the one bankers and tax collectors like."

I began shuffling through the sheaf of papers in a panic, looking for the legal description. "It's all right," Glasses said. Baseball Cap had returned to the car and was carrying a large reel tape measure and some kind of instrument toward the tree-line at my property's edge.

Glasses chewed gum I saw now, or rather I heard its annoying popping while I continued to scan the papers in my file until I realized that the legal property description appeared at the top of nearly every page. "They match," I nearly shouted as if I were a game show contestant. I indicated the description with my finger for him to see.

Ignoring my triumph, his eyes moved from my property sales disclosure form to his clipboard. His voice was monotone. "Do you harbor any livestock on the property?"

"Pardon?"

"Livestock. Chickens, goats, cows, that sort of thing."

"Not the last time I looked."

"Do you conduct business enterprise from these premises, either the manufacture of goods or their retail sale?" he asked, and then he looked around as if trying to locate the factory floor. His eyes settled on my front door.

"No."

"Have you sold any part of your property or otherwise subdivided your holdings?"

"No."

"Are you aware of any current legal proceedings regarding this property?"

"No, aside from this review."

"It's not really a legal proceeding."

"Oh."

"Okay, well, we'll be out of your hair in twenty minutes or so. We'll just locate the property corners."

"That's it?"

"Yep. That's all we've got to do at least. They'll verify your well and septic permits downtown at Records. They'll double check your tax payments. That should about do it."

"That's the review?"

"It's not like you're running a puppy mill. You're not, are you?"

"Huh?"

"Just joking."

I had been shocked into silence. There must have been something he wasn't telling me.

"Okay, have a good day." He turned, then stopped, turned back and said, "By the way, I couldn't help admiring your garden. I wish I had more space for my garden," Glasses said. "The wife and I grow a handful of things out against the fence, some more in containers on the patio, but most of my place is concrete."

"That's too bad."

"I envy the space you've got. We practically live on top of the neighbors," he mused. "Well, I better get to it."

"Thanks," I mumbled, although I didn't know what I was thanking him for. He walked to where Baseball Cap stood near the road. I went to my front door. A hundred questions I should have asked flashed through my mind. I didn't know whether I should be relieved or suspicious.

I went inside and found myself pacing an indistinct geometry from kitchen to bedroom to woodstove. I imagined what they might really be doing up above, no doubt something altogether different than they had told me. I often thought that of the broader world too, that, up there, away in the light, things transpired I could not imagine, patterns of behavior entirely expected from which I was removed.

I gave them an hour. I imagined investing in a periscope so that I could reconnoiter my surroundings before emerging into the open air. A vision of such a thing appeared in my head, mildly cartoonish, informed by childhood memories of watching *Hogan's Heroes* and peering around corners with the aid of my G.I. Joe Green Beret kit. Surely such a thing could be had, for they retired submarines just as regularly as every other once-demanded piece of the military-industrial complex. Even periscopes must join the detritus. After an hour I stood outside my front door and saw the city vehicle was gone. Indeed, there was no evidence they had ever been there.

I tried to persuade myself that was the end of it, that I'd

gotten worked up over nothing, but an unfamiliar pain had taken up residency in my left side just under my bottom rib. I decided fresh air might do me good and I exited through the french doors and went for a long walk along the ravine bottom. The movement helped, and although not dressed for it, I broke into a jog and soon the deeper regularity of my breathing became my companion and the sweat began to flow and I focused on the movement of running and eventually reached the end of the ravine where it sloped toward the river. There, after navigating the curving roads of a new subdivision, I took the paved jogging paths the city had recently built. A number of joggers and bicyclists eyed me as the curiosity I was, running in street clothes at a pace that could have made Olympic hopefuls envious. I ran for miles before eventually turning around and retracing my steps, still on the run.

7

I promised myself I would return to routine, as if habits would allow me to accept that the city review was as benign as my odd couple's visit. A routine is not necessarily built upon a plan that is predetermined. My schedule was more in the realm of evolution of incident.

On Tuesday, I started by writing such drivel that I was rapidly reducing my winter dependence on firewood. I contemplated igniting the pages one at a time while I was still in the act of writing them and thereby excising the middle step between pen and woodstove.

My drawing project fared no better, and given that my daily rituals shared the common medium of paper products, for a time I pondered making their destruction identical.

My usual forty-five minutes on the treadmill proved particularly uncomfortable due to a certain chafing that was the result of having run in street clothes.

And so the day progressed. I tried to start the book recommended by the kind librarian the day before, a vacuous piece of "adventure fiction." I quickly wished the protagonist would succumb to his adventure. I retreated to Rilke to save myself.

Typically, as the weather cooled, it made sense to work in the garden at midday, opposite the pattern of summer when the heat drove one to labor in the opposing ends of a day. I used our continued pattern of dry fall heat as an excuse to procrastinate and waited go above after three p.m. A poor decision. I heard Monika's car before I saw her, for it offered a distinct high-pitched knocking, the sort of sound that if its equivalent were found by a physician during an exam, the patient would be awarded an ambulance ride to the hospital.

I watched her walk from the road to the garden. She appeared to be dancing, for lack of a better word, and as she neared, I heard her mutter an occasional vague lyric. Only allowing voice to every eleventh or thirteenth word, the song was impossible to identify. The words came in a register she really couldn't reach, and I counted myself lucky that I didn't have a dog.

She stopped singing, although her head still bobbed and her eyes appeared half closed. She offered no greeting. White cords dangled from her ears and disappeared into some invisible place on her person, and momentarily I feared that in my absence the world was experimenting with cyborg technologies and I was faced with a flawed prototype.

At last her head stopped bobbing and Monika made a sweeping wave motion. "Hey, Skipper," she said. She removed the left earphone.

"What are you listening to?" I asked, pointing absurdly at my ears as if she might think some of our species were able to listen through another appendage.

She looked embarrassed and shrugged before answering. "Retro," she said.

"Retro," I repeated. "Which retro?"

"Come again."

"Isn't everything that's passed fair game for the retro moniker?"

She looked embarrassed again. "Sometimes I like to listen to old stuff. People give me a hard time about it."

"Like what?"

"All kinds of stuff. I'm not a music snob. But a lot of times I listen to stuff I download from my dad's CD collection, you know, stuff from the eighties."

"Ah," I said. "Ancient history, like practically before the invention of the electric guitar, almost before metallurgy. What is it you just had on?"

"Queen. 'Death on Two Legs' to be precise."

"Eighties? That's 1975."

"Whatever."

I nearly laughed out loud but stifled it. I must have made a facial expression.

"I happen to think Freddie Mercury was way ahead of his time," she said. "A genius."

"A lot of critics think there was no good music produced in the second half of the seventies and virtually all of the eighties," I said. "They think there was a good ten- or fifteen-year gap void of anything worth carrying forward, a dark time best forgotten. Apparently, you have pricked a hole in that theory."

Stabbing the toe of her big boot in the earth, she said, "You know their lyrics. What do you think?"

"I remember 'Bohemian Rhapsody' as the craziest thing I'd ever heard. I remember thinking Brian May's guitar made the most unusual, most identifiable sound of the age. Mostly I remember loving the poster that came with *Jazz*. All those 'fat-bottomed girls' in their nude bicycle race. Very exciting stuff for a frustrated adolescent. Mercury was laughing all the way to the bank on that one, getting soft porn into every teenager's hands. A few suburban moms probably had heart attacks. If only they knew then that Mercury would have preferred it to be a poster full of skinny-bottomed boys."

"There was a poster?"

"Yeah, a poster full of nude girls on bikes. All the less overt implications were lost on most. Because they'd made it as a mainstream band, they could have impact that the punks and others couldn't, even if the punks had great fun ridiculing them even when they were stealing from them. I find it tremendously ironic that Freddie Mercury got filthy rich on a song like 'We Are the Champions' because it gets played at every sporting event in the world when he wasn't exactly your stereotypical sports guy, though he did love his soccer."

"You know a lot about music."

"It's not like I live in a hole in the ground," I said.

She laughed. "You're a dork."

I nodded.

"What do you listen to?"

"Not music you would know."

"You might be surprised."

"I have been before."

"I can't imagine a world without music. It can say things you can't say any other way," she mused dreamily.

"Some people think it's just bubble gum. That it's only for the young."

"That's just stupid."

"I didn't say I think that."

"It's one of the few ways we can communicate across time," she said.

I didn't respond.

"I bet people who decide to drop bombs don't listen to a lot of music," she said.

"Or commission a lot of murals," I said.

She smiled and gently fingered a leaf of an Anaheim pepper.

"Do you want to help pick beans?" I asked.

"Sure, why not?"

"If there are enough, I'll send some home with you."

"That would be interesting. My mom's like the queen of take-out."

"It's hard to ruin beans."

We moved over to the long lines of bean plants. I liked to harvest when they were still pencil thin and tender. The pods had been producing well for some time and were growing sparse now. We bent to our work.

"So you were a Queen fan."

"Among others," I said. "I appreciated their whimsy. Choruses of bike bells. Revving engines. Orchestras and operatic voices. Theater. Vaudeville. Those are the things Mercury understood best, the way music could be theatrical and how laughter could poke fun at something just below the surface. They were great fun in concert."

"You saw them live?"

"A few times. For a while I think I was addicted to the particular sound of Brian May's guitar."

"That's so cool."

"It was a long time ago. Good old gap-toothed flamboyant Freddie is long gone and buried."

"The music is still alive."

"I find it kind of funny that you listen to it."

"Why?"

"It's just that you think the past belongs to those who lived it. They say every generation is defined by their music."

"There's plenty of new music I love too."

"You'll always love it. One day it will make you feel reattached to your youth."

"I'm not sure I want that. High school blows."

I knew all too well about the dangers of memory, musically inspired or otherwise. We worked quietly for a time picking beans. The sun was out and the skies clear.

"What are you thinking about?" Monika asked, unable to sustain the pleasant silence.

"Oh, nothing."

"Can't fool the foolish. You were way out there."

"I was just remembering concerts I've been to," I said, side-stepping other memories that were always nearby. "You might appreciate this. I remember seeing a huge graffiti depiction of the Queen logo on the Berlin Wall in 1984. I wasn't much older than you. I remember thinking that the wall was the perfect sort of place for graffiti. It was right next to an iron viewing stand where you could look over the wall to the East, which was like looking at a film-frame in a documentary that employed archived footage. There were tenement houses that still showed bomb damage from World War II. The East Germans had erected barriers on their side, like huge anchors, that were intended to stop fleeing vehicles. We'd been told that they had mines buried in the no man's land between the walls, and you could watch the East German guards inspecting you from their towers, sometimes even pointing their guns at you, menacing, like all they had to do was pull the trigger. Meanwhile, on our side we had kids with cans of spray paint and time on their hands and they listened to Queen and Motorhead and Youth Brigade and The Dead Kennedys, and it was like we lived where there was color while they lived in a world that was forever black and white."

"The wall came down. We won," Monika said.

"And then the wall came down," I repeated. "Can you begin to fathom what that meant? You weren't even born."

"I had a teacher last year who was from Poland. He told us a lot more than the books. It wasn't in the actual curriculum. With that you're lucky if you even make it through World War II. He got me reading about my parent's time. I forget the year though."

"1989."

"Pre-Monika."

"I can't believe a whole generation has passed already."

"Did you ever think you'd see the wall come down?" she asked.

"Honestly, no. I grew up in the Cold War. In elementary school we practiced drills for when the missiles came. By the time I was a teenager I was thoroughly convinced I would not live to be an adult. I knew we would blow ourselves up."

"What sort of drills? I mean, it just sounds kind of stupid, thinking you could escape a nuclear bomb because somebody thought to pull the fire alarm. Pretty typical of your generation, I must say."

"It was stupid," I agreed. "They had us sit in the halls with our backs to the walls. It was the classic bend over and kiss your ass goodbye posture."

She laughed. I hadn't heard her laugh before. It was more of a girl's giggle. "I'm sorry," she said. "But herding little kids to the hallway while a giant mushroom shows up on the horizon."

"I remain surprised nearly every day that we survived. Having the two biggest guys on the planet standing on the street with the two biggest guns they could carry, daring the other to shoot first. Doesn't exactly seem like the wisest foreign policy strategy ever invented, now does it?"

"No, it doesn't," she said. "But I guess we're still here. I mean the missiles are still in their silos, right?"

"True, though frankly we should probably be more scared now. A few drunks with guns of their own watching the bullies from the sidewalk and a few psychopaths taking the extra bullets apart while they play with matches. A few more stalking the rooflines. Maybe a crazy bastard cooking with chemicals in the kitchen, cooking for the bullies, that is. In my day you had the illusion of control. Now we're blind to where the next shot is coming from. We don't even know where to look."

"Wow," she said.

"What?"

"I just never thought when I came here today that I would make it from Queen to the Cold War to contemporary international affairs."

"Me neither," I admitted. "Why did you come?"

"I just saw you out here working, so I thought I'd give you an update."

I groaned. "What now? Rocks through the windows? Molotov cocktails?"

"Misdirection," she said.

"Do tell."

"You know how I had old Frodo rolling around in the trunk? I got to thinking. Not only was I transporting evidence with me, frankly he was giving me a headache. You should hear the way he thumps when you take a sharp corner. I didn't know what to do with him. As much as I like the idea of filling an entire storage shed with garden art, it just doesn't seem practical and it's not exactly within my budget. So I had another idea yesterday during math."

"A productive use of your time."

"Whatever. It was math that made me think of it, thank you very much. That and remembering your poor owl. There I was, reducing an equation and it dawned on me: relocation. See, so instead of stealing yard art, I'm just relocating it. A gnome for a deer. A cement squirrel for a fairy sundial, that sort of thing. There's more humor in it. Whimsy, you could say."

"You could say."

"The problem is some of that stuff is really heavy. I mean you can't exactly sprint across somebody's lawn carrying a concrete grizzly bear."

"It's asking for an insurance claim."

"Like I'm going to sue the people I'm stealing from."

"Relocating," I corrected.

She ignored me. "I'm developing a theory about yard art. The first part of the theory is obvious, that size is proportional to the fragility of the ego. Kind of like short man syndrome. Second, there's a definite gender bias. Men go in for your game animals and your carnivores, your silhouettes of cowboys. Women go for the bunnies and turtles and flamingos, the cut outs of the farmers bent over in the garden. Gnomes seem unisex as near as I can tell. Third, it's evident that income doesn't buy you taste, just weight."

"Careful. Someone might award you a PhD if you keep this up."

"My goal is to go for subtlety," she said.

I have to admit that she had me intrigued.

"Say I find a gnome sitting on a toadstool. Let's say he's wearing a green vest. If I could only exchange that gnome for one that's sitting on a pot of gold or one that's wearing a red vest that would be rad."

I must admit that I liked her style, though of course I couldn't give her the satisfaction of telling her so. Instead I said, "Maybe you should carry paint."

"I thought about that. It would solve the whole weight problem. It's just not honest though. Plus, there's the time factor. Staying at the scene of the crime and all that."

"Of course not."

"But I don't like being restricted by what I can carry."

"You haven't recruited any of your psychologically damaged friends?"

"I wouldn't trust friends," she said, gesturing spastically. "The friends who would help wouldn't get it. They wouldn't see the bigger picture. Besides, they'd talk. Then where would we be?"

"Indeed."

"So that's why you should help."

"I beg your pardon."

"I mean, I'm doing this for you in the first place. Besides, it's kind of an adrenaline rush. You could use that."

"You're joking."

"I couldn't be more serious."

"You're insane."

"I'm not the one who lives in a hole in the ground."

"It's not a hole."

"Whatever."

"Besides, the city was here. All they did was walk the property and ask if I was harboring sheep. I'm clear."

"If you really believe that's the end of it, I've got some swampland in Florida to sell you—as my father likes to say." She cleared her throat awkwardly. "That's just an expression. I don't have any swampland. My dad says it all the time, part of a regular repertoire of one liners. I'm just suggesting... Oh, never mind." She appeared to be having an argument with herself, then she looked directly at me, her eyes sharply focused. "This is just the first salvo. I've met the people who volunteer for neighborhood association boards. I live with one of them. Can you imagine what the ones are like who run for city council? You're fooling yourself, amigo. You may want to believe it's over, but you're smoking crack."

I couldn't admit it, but the moment she said it I was certain she was right. I remained silent. We had reached the end of the row.

"There's this one gnome I've had my eye on from the start," she said. "He lives by a water feature. He's sort of spot lit. It's all very quaint, very upscale, aside from Mr. Pointy-feet-I-have-no-penis hanging out by the waterfall."

I groaned.

"I'll pick you up at 10:30," she said.

"I promised you beans," I said by way of reply.

"So, I'll pick them up then," she said, and then she walked to her car without looking back.

8

The half hour was marked by the sound of steel-toed boots abusing my front door like a militant cuckoo clock. I was more surprised at her punctuality than at her presence. I considered ignoring the knocking. Reluctantly I rose and climbed the stairs to the door.

"Why is it you insist on trying to kick a hole through my door?"

"Maybe you should try a couple of cans and a string," she said. "Complete the whole play-fort theme you've got going here."

I ignored the remark.

"You think you could have dressed properly," she said. "Jesus, there's not much moon, but what, are you trying to glow in the dark?"

I looked down at my attire. I hadn't changed out of the plain white T-shirt I'd worn all day under a dress shirt.

"I assumed you were joking."

"You don't know me very well," she said. "Go on and get changed, buckaroo. I've still got homework to do. You might want a jacket. It's getting cold."

I started to protest and she pantomimed zipping her mouth closed. I motioned for her to stay put and went back downstairs and added a black hooded sweatshirt to my attire. So this is what I'd become—speaking in mock sign language and joining in teenage vandalism. I followed her to her car without a word. I had no idea what I was doing. I waited until I was in the car to speak. "This is absolutely crazy. I'm not going to be part of teenage pranks."

"I decided we should use code names tonight," she said. "You'll be Mr. Badger and I'll be Secret Agent Makesyourheart-pound."

"Mr. Badger?"

"Yeah. They're ferocious, you know. Don't mess with the badger. Plus, they live in holes in the ground."

"Monika, look—"

"Use my code name."

"I'll do no such thing."

"You can make it an acronym if you want. Call me Sam."

"I don't really—"

"Sam."

"Sam."

"Sam I am."

"Are we going to do a *Cat in the Hat* routine now?"

"If it helps, you can pretend it's raining. It's been raining all the live-long day and I'm the bad influence, or what you think is a bad influence when in reality I'm just going to show you how to spice up your life a little."

"I've been kidnapped by an insane person."

"Vivid imagination. That's what my teachers always wrote on my report card comments," she said. "Actually, it would be better if it was raining. Not the carrying heavy objects part, but the general atmosphere. Have you noticed how in espionage movies it's always raining? And it's always dark. I hate those kinds of movies. Besides, if it was raining, we'd leave mud tracks and then the cops would do the whole *CSI* thing and match our footprints to our shoes and trail us right back to our secret hideout in the woods."

"What are you talking about?" I wondered if by talking so fast she cut off vital air supply to her brain.

"Relax," she said.

"And what's *CSI*?"

"Are you kidding me? Where have you been? Do you live in a hole in the ground?"

"How long have you been waiting to say that?"

"Sorry. Couldn't resist. But seriously, you don't watch *CSI*? My parents are obsessed."

"It's a TV show?"

"A worldwide phenomenon that's been going on for like, well, forever. There must be a billion spin-offs. *CSI New York*. *CSI Las Vegas*. *CSI Miami*. Next up will be like *CSI Aberdeen* or *CSI South Bend* or something."

"I don't own a TV."

"Good for you. You're not missing a thing. It just goes to show you how complacent the whole world has become, because I mean, you'd be hard pressed to find a show with more stupid plotlines and worse acting, and yet people huddle around the TV like it should win an Oscar."

"Emmy," I said.

"Huh?"

"You said Oscar. Those are for movies."

"Oh, right. Yeah. Wait, you don't even know what *CSI* is but you know the difference between an Emmy and an Oscar?"

"I'm not dead."

"Okay. Hey, look sharp. We're about there, coming up on the right. We'll do a drive-by and then park in the next block."

"You said it's heavy."

"It is."

"Then wouldn't it make sense to park closer?"

"We need cover. I mean, it's a pretty recognizable car."

"Yeah," I agreed, "what with the rifle and the paint supplies."

We crept past a two-story Cape Cod 1,000 miles from the nearest ocean. The house straddled the crest of a little hill on a curving street. Yard lights lined the driveway casting small puddles of light. Near the front entrance a small waterfall cascaded through imported boulders, the flow of falling water mesmerizing under a spotlight. The water feature looked like it belonged at a hotel that regularly hosted Avon conventions. A two-foot-tall gnome leaning on a shepherd's crook stood sentinel. Monika continued past the house and then made a sharp left onto the next street. Something heavy clunked in the trunk. She pulled to the curb in the dark shadow of a spruce grove facing the wrong way on the street.

"I reconned earlier. I figure we get Frodo out of the trunk, cut through these trees where it's dark, and then it's a diagonal shot across the street."

"Oh, good, so they've already got you pegged for the police lineup."

"Negative thoughts create negative outcomes," she said.

"Did your crystal ball tell you that?"

"No, my therapist. It might be the only intelligent thing he's ever said to me."

"You know you're just inviting a ticket by parking backward."

"But this way the trunk is closer."

"We're a block away. You really think six feet is going to matter?"

"Mr. Picky."

"Are you trying to get the whole neighborhood's attention? Are you just crying out 'catch me'? Was your therapist Catholic?"

"Mr. Picky Badger."

"Now we're really being mature."

"Mature," she said, laughing. "We're here to steal a gnome."

"Why am I here?" I asked.

"This will be good for the health of your inner child. Come on." She got out of the car and opened the trunk.

Stupidly, like an adolescent dared into taking a drag off my first cigarette, I joined her.

"We exchange Frodo for our new friend there. Put him right in the same place and see how long it takes them to notice."

Frodo was worse for the hostage-in-the-trunk routine. A jagged edge of broken cement showed where his nose used to be and there was an empty hole in his mouth where, I assumed, there had once been a pipe. The fingers of his left hand had broken such that he flipped a perpetual birdie and the general scratching and blemishing of his paint made him look like he chose his attire from the discards behind the Salvation Army.

"You really should take better care of your victims," I said. "You're going to get a bad rep."

"I feel really bad about that."

"At least give them a blanket."

"That's a good idea."

"Don't you carry a winter car kit with some supplies and a blanket or an extra coat or something?"

"No. My dad's always telling me that I should, but he's never done anything about it. He's always saying 'we ought to do this' but what he really means is he's not going to do it so somebody else should, meaning me, so it never gets done."

"You need to plan ahead. I don't think your drill rifle is going to save you in a blizzard."

"What things am I supposed to carry? Canned goods and jet fuel?"

"Common sense things. You know, tire chains and a flashlight. Some food. A blanket. Some idiot must have published a list. It can't be that hard."

"I really should. My car's not that reliable."

"You should. You could put it all in a plastic bin or something."

"Like you can buy at Target?"

"I guess. Anything will do. You could use a five-gallon bucket."

"It's just that Target probably has designer colors."

We stood looking in the trunk as if by picturing a safety kit there the world would be thrown into proper balance. Instead the trunk's only contents were a garden gnome, a loose tire jack, and what appeared to be an open bag of bird seed.

I asked about the bird seed.

She shrugged.

"Why?"

"Birds deserve to eat too."

"You just trail it wherever you go?"

"Something like that." Apparently, she saw my disgruntled look. "Not all the time," she added. She bent into the trunk and grabbed the gnome by the shoulders and attempted to roll him toward her. "I had a bitch of a time getting him in here," she said. "Getting him out ought to be fun, even with two of us."

Without thinking I reached to help her, taking his feet. We lifted him out of the trunk. "How far did you carry this thing?"

"Not that far. Maybe the length of a house."

"Here," I said, "set your end on the bumper and trade me places. You've got the heavy end."

"And Momma said there aren't any gentlemen left," she said in an exaggerated Southern accent. Still, though, she complied and we exchanged positions.

"Maybe we don't want to stand on the street all night," she said.

I nodded and we shuffled into the relative darkness of the adjacent pine stand. "Here, set him down," she said. "I'm going to shut the trunk."

"Keep it inconspicuous," I said.

"That's right."

"How about we just leave him here," I said. "He'll think he's in the forest. Besides, all his gnome friends won't have to see the brutal way you've scarred him."

"Don't you dare chicken out on me now." She left to shut the trunk. I heard it slam, and then slam again as if it had failed to latch the first time. I tried to picture what I must look like, a grown man standing in the dark corner of someone's yard with my hands resting on a gnome's pointed head.

"Ready?"

"I've lost my mind."

"That entirely possible," she said. She bent to grab his feet and I carried him under his arms as if he were a real body. We passed through the stand of trees and stopped just short of the next street.

"I figure we cross at an angle here," Monika whispered, "go up through the neighbor's yard where it's darker up to the corner of the house, then across the driveway to the pond. We get Frodo as close to their guy as we can and then we snatch him."

"You're a genius, Sam. When do we destroy the world?"

"Don't be an ass, Mr. Badger."

We dashed across the street, or we approximated something

as close as possible to dashing when two people try to run sideways while connected to a heavy piece of statuary. We reached
the cover of a tall hedge. I could feel my heart beating in my
chest. We slowed momentarily and then Monika continued at
a low crouch toward the house. I either had to follow her cue
or drop the gnome, an action that would surely break the poor
guy or, more likely, crush my feet. When we reached the house,
she bent and set her end on the ground. Even though I pride
myself on being in shape, I was relieved for the break.

Monika was smiling. Beaming is probably the more appropriate word—her smile brighter than my white tennis shoes, as
if it gathered all the available light to it. "Motion light on the
garage," she whispered, pointing to her eyes and then at the
light like a bad action movie. "It points out toward the street. If
we stay close to the wall, we shouldn't trigger it. Ready?"

"Monika, this is crazy."

"I know," she said. "Isn't it great?" She lifted his feet, and
off we went again.

When we entered the circle of green light that accented the
waterfall, I expected a soundtrack to start. For a small yard feature, the cascading water made a surprising amount of noise,
sufficient that if a deranged gnome owner shouted a warning
before firing the first shot, we wouldn't hear it.

Monika set her end of our gnome friend down immediately
next to another specimen, this one half a foot taller, noticeably
stockier and pristine when compared to our trunk-travelling
companion. I felt bad for our little guy and suffered a tiny pang
of guilt on behalf of its unsuspecting new owners. I looked at
Monika, who was bent over clearing a space in the landscaping bark, and the angle was such that I looked directly into the
green-lens of the spotlight. Looking quickly away, I saw dark
spots floating in a green haze.

"Okay, move him over here," Monika said. I lifted our gnome
and pointed for the place she indicated, but I remained visually
impaired and tripped on a rock. Stumbling with the weight, I
nearly stepped into the pond at the base of the waterfall before

I regained my balance. The water shimmered an inch from my toe. "Stop clowning around," Monika said and then giggled. She guided me to the space she had cleaned in the mulch. "Bye, Frodo," she said, patting his pointed head. "Okay, mister." I didn't know if she was speaking to me or to our next casualty. He was considerably heavier than Frodo. I nearly tripped again as we stepped from the garden bed onto the sidewalk and the three of us did a tricky little dance step as we regained balance.

As we neared the driveway, we heard a car engine and saw a flash of headlights sweep across the face of houses at the curve of the street a block away. "Go, go," I implored, and we shuffled in a sole-scuffing scurry into the shadow of the hedge. As if by involuntary muscular reaction, Monika dropped her end of the statue the moment we reached the shadow and dove into the hedge's base. The gnome's cement feet thudded into my shins before I could arrest its fall and I stumbled sideways into the relative darkness cast by the hedge where I set the gnome on the grass and crouched behind it, my shins aflame. The car approached. I heard the vibration of bass in a rap beat from its stereo system. It was a Jeep Wrangler and it had lights affixed to the top of its windshield and magnetic signs advertising a security company clinging to its doors—the neighborhood rent-a-cop. "Go straight, go straight," I muttered, trying to will the vehicle from turning left and stopping to investigate the rust-bucket parked illegally facing traffic one street over. The jeep heeded my mantra. I wanted to cheer.

"Sorry," Monika whispered from her hiding place within the hedge. "I sort of panicked there. You okay?"

"Nothing amputation won't fix."

"My bad."

She crawled out of hiding. Leaf debris clung to her jacket and hair and webbed her boot laces. The gnome continued smiling, mocking us.

"Come on, let's get out of here before we get caught," I said, placing my hands on the gnome's shoulders.

We shuffled through the neighbor's side yard and started

across the street. My shins ached and my fingers were growing stiff. This gnome's paint was unmarred and slick as a result, and I thought he might slip from my hands at any moment. Somewhere nearby a dog barked.

Just as we neared the opposite curb, we heard the thump of the jeep approaching again, and we sprinted into the cover of the trees. Monika held on this time, and we lowered the statue together. The vehicle drew near. Its industrial-strength stereo offered an ominous beat. We crept deeper into the shadows, momentarily abandoning our charge. The approaching vehicle turned down the angled street where Monika had parked. The pine grove was rooted in a kind of peninsula between the curving intersection of the two streets, and we watched through the trees as the jeep pulled in behind Monika's car. The driver cut the engine but did not turn off the stereo, though he toned it down several notches. A spotlight mounted on the side mirror clicked on, swept up from a downward pointing angle, wiggled a moment, and finally illuminated the interior of Monika's car. A full minute passed. The driver appeared to be eating something; either that or he was contemplating the danger afforded by the drill team rifle and the bomb-making capacity of a carload of paint. I could feel my pulse in my head.

When the security officer finally stepped from his jeep, I saw that he wasn't much older than Monika. He was as thin as a fence picket and wore high-water pants above black tennis shoes. An oversized police-style blue jacket hung from his bony shoulders. He walked a full circle around the car, shining a long flashlight into the already illuminated passenger compartment with his left hand while his right hand never left the handle of a Billy club slung through a loop on his belt.

"Shit, shit, shit," Monika whispered from our hiding place in the nearby trees.

I shushed her like a TV librarian.

"We're in the shit," she said.

"I told you not to park that way." We spoke in whispers. We each hid behind a thick pine tree trunk and snuck peeks to see what Mr. Rent-a-cop was up to. We'd abandoned the gnome some six feet behind us and he lay on his back as if he were sunning on a beach. I scanned for escape routes.

"How'd I know?"

"You might as well have posted a sign saying 'Occupants busy committing criminal offenses.'"

"Shut up already," she hissed.

Although the jeep's stereo masked the sound of our whispers, the rental swine turned our direction and shone his flashlight into the trees. The light swept a few rapid arcs. He moved back to his vehicle and cut his stereo. He seemed to freeze for a moment and concentrate on listening, his light absently pointing into the branches well above our heads. I listened too. I heard the movement of the tall pines swaying ever so slightly at their tops and the hum of a nearby electrical transformer. Mostly I heard the clicking sound of the jeep's engine as it cooled, releasing an occasional *ping* and the dripping sound of fluid draining back into reservoirs.

Apparently satisfied, he returned to his vehicle but left the door open. He sat for what seemed a long while, and I searched the environs for the best escape route from my shelter behind the tree trunk, certain that the real police would arrive at any moment. The tree sap smelled like vanilla. Whenever Monika looked my way, the moonlight illuminated her good white teeth. I thought about telling her to clamp her lips closed but resisted the temptation. At last our Barney Fife impersonator emerged from the jeep with a sheet of paper in hand. This he folded in precise thirds and placed under the windshield wiper of Monika's car. When he returned to his vehicle, he stood again outside its door and scanned the area, his head pivoting on its axis, and then he clicked off the spotlight before getting in, starting the engine, and driving away.

We watched his taillights disappear before speaking.

"Let's get out of here," I demanded.

"Maybe it's a trap. Maybe he's just going around the block and parking."

"A sting operation," I said. "To catch all those backward parkers." I stood. "Come on. Let's go before he does come back." I started toward the car.

"Wait. We can't just leave him there."

"Leave who?" I asked, already knowing the answer. Our gnome looked like he was asleep. I envied him.

"Besides, we've only completed half the exchange," she said. I groaned.

"That will be the payoff. You'll see," she said. "I'll get the head this time."

For the nth time that night I, stupidly, complied like a thirteen-year-old facing a bully. We carried him to the edge of the road, scanned the street, and shuffled to the rear of Monika's car where we loaded him into the trunk. "Give me your rifle," I said. "We'll jamb it under one side so he can't roll." I pushed him tight against the back seat. Before we got in the car, Monika removed the paper trapped beneath her windshield wiper and handed it to me. It was a typed form featuring a letterhead from the Covington Knolls Homeowner's Association. Covington Knolls, I wondered. Had I been transported to England? Was I still comfortably asleep and dreaming this adolescent comedy routine? The letter opened:

Dear Property Owner:
As declared by the jointly agreed upon regulations established by the Covington Knolls Homeowner's Association, hereafter referred to as CKHA, a regulatory body established by neighborhood property owners to protect their common interests, you have been found in violation of the following CKHA code:

In the white space the letter provided, the security guard had entered, using a sloppy, leaning hand:

Illegal parking
Car in street after PM / backward

Monika's license plate number was scrawled below that, as was the address of the nearest house. There followed a long paragraph of legalese and then a single sentence to close the letter:

> Failure to correct the violation cited above within 24 hours can result in your required presence at a hearing before the CKHA governing board and may result in fines, censure, refusal of Association privileges, or further legal action including filing for property seizure or eviction from the Association.

The salutation read: "Neighborly Yours, The CKHA Board of Directors."

"You're in the shits now," I said, refolding the letter.

"What?" Monika asked, appearing panicked.

"You're on the neighborhood association blacklist."

"This isn't my neighborhood."

"They're in cahoots," I said. "Obviously they speak to one another. It's a conspiracy, an axis of regulatory prudes that regularly measures hemlines and the height of the Kentucky bluegrass."

"Don't joke. They probably do talk to one another." She made a fast U-turn and then took a right at the intersection such that we passed the scene of our crime. I looked at the immaculate two-story house we'd visited. Spotlighted, looking for all the world like he smirked at his sudden catapulted rise in economic environs, Frodo raised his middle finger in salutation.

Monika drove out of the neighborhood and through two others before turning at a sign advertising Sunflower Meadow, this one a wooden sign with painted lettering framed by poorly watered trees rather than the enormous stone declarations set within manicured beds we'd passed through at Covington Knolls. Still, the houses remained nice, if less grand in scale, constructed from more fake wood and less fake stone. They were knotted more closely together, and there wasn't a meadow or a sunflower in sight. After a series of turns I could never replicate, she parked next to the side yard of a simple, ranch-style house where the neatly trimmed grass seemed as evenly textured as the neutral-toned synthetic stucco of the house exterior. The back yard was encircled by a six-foot privacy fence that was in turn bordered by neat garden beds, the sort that focused on low-maintenance shrubbery and yards and yards of cedar bark chips.

"This is the place," Monika declared. "Come on, let's give them a little present," she said, exiting the car.

This time I didn't hesitate. Get it over with, I thought. At least we were on a dark street, adjacent a side yard with no houses facing our direction. We opened the trunk and removed our liberated prize. "Right over here," she whispered. "As easy as pie."

Given her declaration, I expected prison flood lights to flash on and sirens to erupt. Instead we had only to carry our kidnap victim some twelve feet. There, next to a golden elder, I saw the empty circle of landscape fabric cleared from the cedar chips. I wondered if his owners had even noticed that their charge was missing. The thought that they might not have noticed his absence made me a little sad. Monika widened the circle with a quick sweeping motion of her boot and lowered the gnome's base. Then she stooped and brushed the bark neatly back against his feet. I thought perhaps he was leaning ever so slightly as if he were car sick from riding in the trunk or had inhaled too many gas fumes. "Mission accomplished, Mr. Badger," she whispered, and we ran back to the car. The door closed with its usual protesting groan. It all felt a bit anticlimactic.

We drove a few blocks in silence before Monika said, "I know it seems foolish, but I sort of like the rush of adrenaline, you know."

I didn't respond. I certainly didn't want to admit that there was a kind of tightening, a tingling in my legs and I thought perhaps my heartbeat had quickened slightly, that I felt—was there any other way to express it?—a little high.

"It's stupid, I know," she said, "but I feel like…like, I don't know, like we accomplished something."

"The free-gnome movement."

"I know. It is stupid."

"No, it's not. Don't say that it is," I protested, surprising myself.

"No, it's dumb," she said. "There's no correlation," she added, and I expected her to say more but she didn't.

"No correlation to what?"

"To anything."

She seemed to deflate. We drove in silence until we reached my place.

"Here we are," she said. I felt like a teenager at the end of a date. I didn't know what was expected of me. There was no etiquette guide for post-vandalism bonding. "Thanks for helping me," she said. "You have to admit, it was kind of fun, more fun than anything you'd be doing down there in your little cavern."

I made no such admission. I got out of the car and paused before closing the door. I could see a great many stars. The moon was but a quarter full. I inhaled the crisp night air and then I leaned back into the car. Its engine idled unevenly, as if the car were caught in a series of small waves. "Why me?" I asked.

"What do you mean?"

"You know."

"Because I thought you needed help," she said.

"Help," I said, enunciating the word such that it stopped somewhere between a statement and a question.

"This morning," she said matter-of-factly, "several thousand people died in the Congo. Yesterday there was another bombing in Pakistan. Fifteen thousand people around the world will contract AIDS in the next twenty-four hours. Five thousand teenagers in this country, in the richest, most developed nation on the planet, will kill themselves this year."

"You keep such statistics on a cheat sheet somewhere?"

"They're all accurate. You can look them up."

"But why me? Out of a world so full of people in need, why did you pick me?"

"Because I had a great-uncle die in Vietnam, a cousin die in Iraq, a former classmate die in Afghanistan. Because last November, the closest thing I had to a best friend got drunk and drove into a bridge abutment doing about ninety." She paused, staring out the windshield.

"Exactly," I said. "So why me?"

She turned and looked at me. "Because I didn't know how to help any of them, no more than I know how to stop AIDS or keep people in Africa from killing each other or convince politicians not to kill soldiers. I'm not even old enough to vote, and if I could, no one would listen to me."

"Okay," I said softly and closed the car door. I started across my property. My front door was silhouetted against the night sky, looking like a portal into the darkness. I heard Monika's car door open and I turned. Just her head appeared above the roof.

"I'll stop by sometime during the week," she shouted.

I stabbed my hand into the air. A wave? An obscenity? It was a noncommittal gesture if ever there was one.

"You should get a doorbell," she shouted.

9

I'd be lying if I didn't admit there are times that I am lonely. Maybe, subconsciously, that's a part of why I go out so little. I know that sounds backward—that, if one is lonely, the solution would be to spend more time among people. But such thinking doesn't factor in coming home to an empty house. And it doesn't factor in memories. A past. A life lived before this one.

Now, if Monika were here and could enter this little discussion I'm having within my head, no doubt she would be quick to point out a flaw in the sequence of my logic. She would remind me that one of the elemental instincts of our species is to remain social beings. Like gorilla troops, we evolved in complex social groups. We congregate, not just living within our family units, but within larger communities. We build, of course, communal units, be they villages or cities or high rises. As such, she might argue that my very isolation is unnatural, that my decision to remain alone goes against our evolutionary encoding.

It is unnatural, I suppose. I've been a member of society before. I lived among others according to the normal patterns and expectations set forth by modern culture for the first four decades of my life. See where that got me.

In the end this is all just a vastly tangential way of saying that I was restless that night upon my return from the juvenile antics of gnome relocation. It was well past my bedtime and yet I couldn't sleep. I wasn't ready to take up a book, which typically is the last thing I do before sleep. I felt remotely hungry, but I'm not the sort who eats before retiring. I put some Shirley Horn on the turntable, wanting the silky calm assurance of her voice, and heated some milk.

The milk, well, the milk tasted like heated milk and I ended up pouring most of it down the drain. As much as I love Shirley Horn, my feet wanted something to move to. I lifted the needle off Shirley's voice. In the sudden silence I suffered a deluge of the feelings for which I regularly wish I could find expression. Perhaps writing offered me that once, though I remain uncertain about the accuracy of such a belief. Such emotions are something I still attempt to expunge through the pen but writing cannot parallel the physicality of movement. Even though the lives of countless musicians and writers and actors should have taught me otherwise, I still want to hold to the belief that if an artist can express feelings through the medium of his or her talent, they might find release, maybe even healing.

The harsh reality is that I write on subjects in which almost no one has interest. Specifically, these last many years I have been writing a book that examines American cultural regions and the evolution of music. I live in a world of confronting dualities. Perhaps we all do. The things that rub together within my head and send up garbled smoke signals are not abstractions. They are literal. Like the fact that one half of the premise for the book I am writing is geographical yet I refuse to travel and I do not own a computer to access the internet for research. I have, however, traveled extensively in the past and I have what my teachers used to label "an extraordinary visual memory." What does that mean to me? I cannot get images out of my head. Not even if I want to, which comes in handy when summoning memories of places where I have spent time. And there is the world of books, thanks to this country's sustained belief about the value of libraries. I see the irony of my dualism, of course, the creature that seldom leaves his den fixating on images once encountered in the world beyond.

Images. And sounds too of course, for the other half of the book's premise is entirely about music. Perhaps I need not enter a diversion here on the uncanny power music holds to trigger memory.

I am plagued by memories.

Sadly though, I have no vehicle to vent memory. Perhaps

if I were musically talented, then I'd only be another sad case of a selfish, bloody suicide, the old shotgun to the mouth bit, or perhaps I'd be one of those track-marked, marble-mouthed bad haircut types who refuse to go quietly into that good night.

I know that I write about music because I am incapable of performing it. All my life I dreamed of being a musician. I haven't a lick of talent, and desire simply isn't enough to carry one into such enterprise. Despite the piano lessons and junior high school band and the numerous attempts at picking up guitars, there remains a gap between desire and ability. As a result, I've been stuck in the role of fan, which is where all music critics begin, and that inevitably leaves one a bit bitter or certainly feeling expendable, something that is probably true for all of us who make our livings off the larger music industry in one capacity or another. For it is, like all industries that make their income off creative enterprise, one that simultaneously makes and brutalizes the very artists it is dependent upon. Perhaps there was a time when writing about music offered some release for me, some fulfillment that could curb a bit of the restless energy generated by the inability to perform. Standing within the shadow of musicians I felt a distinctive adrenaline. While envious of the performers, sometimes when I maneuvered close enough, a thin sheen of their potency felt as if it slipped up on me.

Alas, proximity fails to offer catharsis, but there can be something so palpable in the search for healing that it can prove enough to remain on the hunt, like a junkie jonesing for the needle. So what does one do without such a release, without a habit that emits the sought-after rush?

When I left my former life behind, it is fair to say that I was running from anything remotely familiar. But among many problems with running, there's the sizable difficulty of not having a destination to run toward, and absent a clear destination, one eventually collapses and then the years slip by, one after another, a life falling into its conventions.

What happens when the routines don't work? And how is it

that so minor a forced look to the periphery could throw me so hard? A knock at the door and I am examining my life in a way I've comfortably avoided for years.

It is a surprisingly unexamined life I lead. Given my isolation and the time on my hands. I find introspection dangerous. I actively attempt to avoid ruminating. Never dismiss the power of self-delusion.

Of course even the delusional self struggles when caught within the relentless grip of insomnia, when a single light spilling beyond the window offers only a mirage, an image of a mirrored room beyond the glass. I see my reflection in the window and fall into the belief that I am sitting outside and I want to wave at myself as if offering an invitation to come inside where it is warm within the earth, but stupidly, my mirrored self waves back, beckoning me, each of us alone.

10

I never made it to the bedroom, drifting off—once I did—
on the couch. I awoke stiff and out of sorts.

I broke with morning routine and went for a walk down
in the ravine bottom where the various grass varieties had that
hunched-over exhausted end-of-season look to them and the
few birds present were simply stopping over on journeys south.
A *V* of Canadian geese flew overhead, honking like they were
in traffic, and I glimpsed one lone heron standing sentinel at
the edge of one of the ponds, his body as still as the log near
which he stood. But rather than remain in the relative wild of
the ravine, I climbed out into a neighborhood after less than a
mile and walked among the homes of my would-be neighbors.

Among those winding streets and seemingly innumerable
dead-ends (though these were more politely signed as "No
Outlet," bearing some wish not to offend the dead, I surmised),
I passed one jogger pushing a space-age baby contraption. Otherwise, the neighborhood was remarkably quiet. Any noise and
movement belonged to hired help: several landscaping crews; a
carpet-cleaning van looking like it was under attack from an oc-
topus of water lines and vacuum hoses; and several nondescript
sedans with open trunks that revealed buckets and mops and
vacuums and other cleaning supplies and with their owners'
religious leanings made public by plastic statues of the Virgin
Mary glued to dashboards.

I wondered about these neighbors who had arrived in the
years since I built my home. I'd never met any of them. Looking at the sprawling, immaculate lawns and the soaring, intricate
rooflines, I tried to imagine how they might see me. Once, in
what seemed another lifetime, I'd lived in a neighborhood not
so different than this, if a bit less grand. Embarrassingly, I had
felt a sense of pride upon arriving home each night, one that

manifested itself in trimming the hedges and keeping up with the painting and building a new patio, work that not only built a life but suggested the scrimping and saving to buy into such a place and such a dream had value. How might I have reacted if I thought outsiders threatened the lives we had fashioned or mocked the lifestyle we had poured work and money into realizing?

I walked block after block looking at the homes of my neighbors. The more I walked, I found, much to my annoyance, that I couldn't get my bearings among the residential twists and turns. An innate sense of direction is something on which I pride myself. My wife used to tease me about having a magnet in my head taking up undue space where I would have benefited from more gray matter.

I've often believed my directional ability is related to the strange gift I have of a nearly photographic memory, which I have translated into an obsession for drawing, in meticulous detail, the cityscapes of all the metropolitan areas of which I have firsthand knowledge. This project fills many empty hours of my days. I would be misleading if I labeled it anything but a compulsion, for it is work I feel I absolutely must do each day despite knowing I have no artistic merit or any designs to share my creations. I have found that large rolls of butcher paper suit my task best. The typical drawing spans the six-foot range. Many completed cityscapes line the topmost edges of my walls, and I must admit I get a small satisfaction looking at them, for often I feel I am granted renewed entry to those cities I once knew, although it is entry on my own terms—the city without the smell, if you will.

My magneto had failed me and I felt lost among illogical, curving streets. I kept expecting a familiar landmark, a house or yard or landscape I recalled from the night before. Such is one of the risks of being a passenger in a car in the dark and one turn melds into the next while the eye is caught trying to focus in the brief sweep of headlights. It was a neighborhood with vast swathes of bluegrass that rolled right to the edge of the asphalt, as if the residents wanted to dissuade pedestrian traffic in the belief that sidewalks by nature invited solicitors and riff-raff. I was forced to walk at the edge of the street, an action that leaves one feeling vulnerable and exposed.

At last I stumbled by accident onto a block where the houses looked mildly familiar. I walked until I came opposite the house that had been the target of our escapades and slowed my pace, though I kept moving to avoid appearing overtly guilty. I was nearly surprised to see Frodo there alongside his waterfall, offering the world a perpetual indecent gesture. A part of me thought I had dreamed the night's activities. I experienced a strange and unexpected rush of what I must label joy at seeing the scarred gnome standing where his larger cousin had once commanded the scene.

I slept better that night and the nights that followed, though I dreamed more frequently than I typically do and when I woke, often I worried about what actions the city or my neighbors might be planning. I clung obstinately to familiar schedules in the belief that consistency might promote internal harmony and an ability to forget. My schedules gained such regularity that government entities assigned with the task of overseeing weights and measures could have used them as time standards.

Late one afternoon I heard loud knocking at my door. I was working on the Philadelphia skyline. After years of effort I was at last becoming skilled enough in my use of contrast that I'd learned how to make the presentation of windows opaque and was maddened by the interruption.

Two men in matching polo shirts stood before my door. Both had smoker's teeth. One wore an enormous belt buckle, a ridiculous silver affair larger than the belt it was tasked with fastening, the leather overmatched for a frame too small to accommodate the pants it secured or the buckle it featured. His partner had the opposite problem, a man who appeared to have given birth and never lost the pelvic weight. They addressed me as "Sir" and told me they were with the city and were here to complete an inspection.

"I've already had a city inspection," I told them.

Such a simple factual statement clearly threw them into disarray and they responded with a flurry of paper shuffling, each exchanging identical clipboards.

"That's impossible," Pregnant Man said at last. "No one has signed off. You must be mistaken." A radio clipped to his belt squawked as if in agreement.

"Two guys who could have been your twins spent the better part of an hour walking the property two weeks ago."

"Oh, that. They're responsible for an exterior property review. We're with code enforcement. We're here to"—his head swung around as if looking for something he had misplaced—"to inspect the house," he said. "Where exactly is the house?"

I pointed down the stairs behind me.

"Oh yes, of course," he said.

His partner shrugged and attempted to hitch up his pants. He looked like the sort who took a lot of laxatives. "Neighbors been decorating?" he mumbled. He sported a thick untrimmed mustache. The hair drooped over his upper lip made it sound like he was chewing cotton balls.

I turned to see where he was looking. The closest neighbor's trees were flocked with toilet paper. There had been heavy dew and the wet paper drooped and clung to the branches.

"There's been a lot of that sort of thing happening around here lately," the bowling-pin-shaped man said. "Kids," he said.

"I'd string 'em up," Mustache Man said, pantomiming hanging his own scrawny neck with a noose. "You're lucky," he said. "Nothin' here to vandalize."

"What is involved with this inspection?" I asked, directing my question at the one shaped like a wine bottle and feeling paranoia rise within me.

"We just have to verify that everything meets building code."

"But I had every step of the construction inspected when it was built."

"Well, it should be a breeze then," he said. "This is a city-ordered review, just kind of to make sure everything's kosher, you know. No big deal. This parcel was in the county at the time of construction. Different jurisdiction and all that. County's notoriously lax. Now that you're in the city limits, we just need to have a look-see. Codes change."

"But it's been in the city for years now."

"Yes," he said, offering nothing more, like he was practicing for a poker tournament.

"Is this really necessary?" I asked. "I filed all the paperwork. I had all required inspections. The house has been complete for years. I think you're overstepping here."

"Just doing what we're directed."

"By whom?" I asked. Hearing myself, I thought *whom* held the tone of a haughty Englishwoman. I felt my cheeks reddening and a rumble in my stomach.

"Everything goes through the planning and zoning department. You've received notices."

"What exactly are you inspecting?" I demanded.

"Oh, the usual. Electrical, plumbing. Make sure everything is properly vented and that you have a backflow preventer. That sort of thing. Check the load spans. Inspect your panel. Just make sure everything is safe."

"Make sure you're not roasting chickens from the 220," Belt Buckle said. "No sharks in the toilet and such, you know. No bats in the attic." I thought he smiled as he said this, although it was hard to tell for the mustache.

"I apologize for not calling first and scheduling something," Pear Man said, "but we couldn't find a phone number for you."

My anger rose and I tried to squelch it with a new tactic. A familiar one. "Phone's underwater," I said. "The whole place is underwater. I've turned it into a swimming pool."

"Huh?" Pear Man replied.

"The phone line picks up interference from the smelter."

I had fallen into an old proclivity to meet stress with sarcasm. Mustache Man had given me the opening as I saw it. Compatriots in humor. This tendency to deflect fear and anger with comedy was a trait my wife had objected to many times over the course of our marriage. She told me once she'd nearly stopped dating me on grounds of comedic failure alone. I was in now; I couldn't stop.

"What?" Pear Man asked.

"He said the radiation whacks out the signal for his phone," Mustache Man said, picking up my lead and grinning conspiratorially. I saw Las Vegas performances in our future.

"That, and I want to preserve the ambiance of the stalactites," I added.

Mr. Weeble-Wobble reddened and his mouth curled into a frown. "Can we stop the clowning and get started?"

I felt bad. Moreover, I hoped I hadn't harmed my position by angering him. Obviously, he could not see my own masked anger. "After you," I said, indicating free passage down the stairwell.

"They told me you were a strange bird," he grumbled.

"Who are *they*?"

"People."

"I don't know any people," I snapped.

Mustache Man laughed at his partner. "Lighten up, Fred. You should feel privileged. Everybody around the shop is jealous you get to see this house." I hadn't intended a joke. Such are the minefields.

"Bat cave," I said, deciding I had better run with it.

"Pardon?" Mustache Man asked.

"You said house. Let's call it the bat cave, shall we?"

"Righty-O." He looked at me askance. Maybe the Vegas act was dead before it started.

"My own little crime-fighting headquarters."

"Is that your gig?" he asked.

"Am I wearing long underwear?"

"I don't know," Mustache Man said. His companion looked at him in confusion.

"Let's keep it that way, shall we?" I said.

At last I got a laugh out of my new bowling-pin-shaped companion. I gestured that they should come in and followed them down the stairs. The stairwell ended at a small landing, and I stopped them there momentarily. Down one step to the left opened onto the central living space, the great room, as a real estate agent would label it. "Through the door to your right is the mechanical room, along with a storage room/pantry sort of thing," I said. "Most everything you should be concerned with is there. Washer and dryer. The domestic hot water is solar heated. Those panels are built into the backside of the berm opposite where you came in. Water heater, water shut-off, furnace, and electrical panel, all that is in there. The boiler pumps hot water through a radiant heating system in the floor. The door is fireproof, as is this one," I said, indicating the door that could be closed on the stairwell. "Outside, there is a separate chamber for the backup generator. Bedroom and bath are behind the kitchen," I indicated, pointing to the kitchen portion of the open room. On the wall where we stood at the bottom of the stairs hung one of two art pieces I owned—a life-size portrait of Roger Waters in neon standing against a black and white depiction of his famous brick wall. I'd acquired the piece in the nineties, an extravagant birthday present from my wife. I indicated the room to our left with a sweep of my arm. "Everything else, aside from the bedroom and bathroom, is pretty much a what-you-see-is-what-you-get affair," I said.

They stopped and took the place in. I looked upon my living environment as I imagined they must have seen it, and while I was pleased at the morning light streaming in through the french doors and their surrounding wall of windows, I knew the place still looked cluttered and unconventional. There was an undeniable weight to the room caused not by the bulk of the furniture—more given to tables for work surfaces than couches or chairs—but by crate upon crate full of albums and entire

walls lined with shelves of compact discs. I'd filled all the wood-
en orange crates I'd ever acquired with albums and had moved
on to plastic milk crates years ago. The shelves that lined the
walls I'd built from wood gathered from old pallets. Circling the
tops of the room's walls were my completed cityscapes thumb-
tacked in place. The room looked more like the music room of
a radio station than living quarters.

I knew my imagined renderings of their perceptions were
accurate when Mustache Man whistled and said, "Sweet Jesus,
you some kind of musician or something?" How wrong he
had it, I thought, aware that not a single musical instrument
inhabited the room. Embarrassment threatened to spill over
into anger.

"I'm prepping for a garage sale," I said.

Mustache Man started laughing. "You don't have a garage,"
he said.

Fred, his little pear-stem neck craned upward, stared at one
of my cityscapes—Detroit, in this instance. "These are amazing," he said. "The detail. A real eye for architecture. I've never
seen anything quite like it. Who's the artist?"

An expression must have crossed my face that gave me away,
for at my lack of response he scanned the perimeter of the
room and then his eyes settled on the work-in-progress on the
long table near the kitchen. "A complete unknown," I said.

"Wow. You've even got the lettering at the building entranc-
es. Addresses. Amazing. I always wanted to be an architect. If
only I'd done better in school, you know, then maybe…" His
voice trailed away.

"And miss all this," Mustache Man quipped. "Making con-
tractors and homeowners miserable," he said, winking at me.
"Forcing housewives to cry." Conspirators again, maybe Vegas
remained in our sights.

"I think I would have been good at it," my man shaped like
a vintage milk jar said.

"I expected it to be dark down here," Mustache Man said,

changing the subject. He stepped into the room and bent over the nearest crate full of albums, then stood and read compact disc titles. "Good thing you're on the ground floor," he said. "There's got to be some serious weight here." He reached up to touch one of the steel beams spanning the ceiling. "Expecting a nuclear holocaust?"

I shrugged.

"Come on, Freddie-boy, let's get to work," Mustache Man said. "We'll start with the mechanical stuff if that's okay," he said, turning to me.

"Fine by me," I said.

"No bats," Mustache Man said fifteen minutes later. I was standing in the kitchen trying to provide the appearance of having something important to do. I don't know the proper etiquette for behavior for uninvited strangers. Wine Bottle stopped at the nearby table and stood examining Philadelphia's skyline.

"You must have the patience of a saint," he said as he bent over the table. "I can't imagine how much time this must take."

"All I have is time," I said.

"Can you loan some to me?" Mustache Man asked.

"Time comes with a heavy price tag," I said.

"Ain't that the truth," he said. Pausing at another long table that was piled with books, albums, and discographies alongside tablets of hand-scrawled notes. "You some kind of professor?"

"No. Just a hobbyist."

"You use the woodstove much?" he asked with precisely the same tone he'd employed while asking his previous question.

"Some in winter for additional heat, more for ambiance, more still for processing the drivel," I said, picking up one of my tablets.

"We'll have to measure hot surface clearances and have a look at the flue," Bowling Pin said, mostly to himself. "You said bed and bath are back this way?" he asked, pointing toward the corner beyond my weight bench and treadmill.

"Yes, I'll get the lights for you."

"Keeping it simple. I like that," Mustache Man said, stepping into the bathroom. "It's not a bat cave, it's a submarine."

I am something of a stickler when it comes to bathroom cleanliness. It is not necessarily a compulsion I carry over into other parts of my life. My bathroom, however, reveals a quirk of my nature, and indeed the building inspector was accurate when he drew a comparison to a submarine, for I had the entire room fashioned from brushed steel: the sink, commode, shower, the walls, the cabinet, virtually the whole room. The floor is one large textured concrete pan with an over-sized floor drain—with an eye on the ability to hose down the entire room in one fell swoop. The interiors of the vanity drawers were constructed in the same fashion and for the same purpose, and they were divided such that everything had its place. As a result, the only objects interrupting the smooth, polished flow of steel were a lone towel, shampoo bottle, and a bar of soap. I think it an intelligent design.

On the other hand, I must admit a certain pang of embarrassment when my visitors entered my bedroom. Like my bathroom, there is a Spartan efficiency and practicality to my bedroom. After all, I am only in the room when I sleep. It is a room not significantly larger than the bed it houses. The bed and a lone table with a reading lamp and space for a book comprise the entirety of the furniture. There is a walk-in closet full of drawers and shelves. To be frank, it is more than I need, so really I could as easily get by in a Japanese comfort room. Indeed, I might enjoy the confines of such a morgue-like chamber.

My visitors offered no comment on my sleeping quarters though I believe I saw a look pass between them. At last Fred, the pear-shaped man, said, "There should probably be a point of egress back here."

Mustache Man said, "What do you propose, a ladder and an escape hatch?"

"I'm just saying."

"He's probably under the square footage requirements and there are two points of egress on opposite sides of the structure."

"Yeah, but one is on another floor, if you could call it that."

They spoke as if they were doctors debating my medical condition while purposely withholding key details from me. I had to wonder if such a requirement could be sufficient to condemn the place, and by doing so, condemn me.

Fred continued. "You know, if you were back here in this room and something happened—"

"Roast toasties," Mustache Man said.

"Yeah. Or fumes. You've got to consider fumes."

"Because all this concrete, steel, and tile are going to go up like a sack full of fireworks on the Fourth of July."

"There's drywall. Insulation. Kitchen cabinets. Trim," Pear Man said.

"True. Hard to avoid that."

"Do you know if the wall studs are wood or steel?" Mustache Man asked me.

"Steel," I said. "All copper pipe, no PVC. Steel and concrete in the ceiling. Twelve-inch reinforced concrete walls." I had decided it was high time to opt for seriousness.

"Were you building a bomb shelter?" Mustache Man asked.

"Something like that," I said.

The inspection passed without any findings they cared to share with me, which left me suspicious. They recommended that I clean the flue. "What happens next?" I asked as we climbed the stairs.

"Who knows," said my pear-shaped architecture lover. "We turn our finding over to the property review board. What they do with things is a mystery to me."

"Are there problems?"

"We just report the findings. Not up to us to decide what they mean."

"But that's it for the review?"

"The review? Well, that's politics. I work for the city. The fine people you elect, they're another breed."

"So where does that leave me?" I asked, exasperated.

"Beats me. Somebody will be in touch. Have a nice day," Mr. Pear Man said, lumbering toward their car.

Mustache Man hitched up his pants. "Good to meet you, Batman. Love your cave." I ignored him. It felt as if the beams that held the earth above my head could not bear the weight.

11

I watched the inspectors drive away. The day was pleasant, absolutely still, in opposition to my dark mood. The dew-dampened toilet paper at the neighbor's house looked like a botched attempt at papier-mâché.

I stopped at the bottom of the steps as if to shake hands with quirky neon Roger or to add another brick to his wall. It is difficult, when one is unaccustomed to visitors, not to see the trappings of one's life anew from their vantage point, like confronting what resides beyond the crime scene tape. I am reminded of those times when my mother-in-law used to arrive for visits when we were young parents, and suddenly in her presence, the chair I so enjoyed during Sunday NFL games looked shabby, the shelves I'd constructed looked like garage sale fodder, even my job seemed work for an adolescent. A house that always felt clean and orderly suddenly gathered dust along the tops of baseboards and heater vents, the drapes disclosed their slow submission to the sun's insistent rot, and the kitchen towels had all begun to fray. What had Mustache Man and Pregnant Fred assumed upon seeing my humble dwelling?

I naively thought I was beyond worrying about other's assumptions. How quickly the sham of my confidence was revealed.

I took in this room where I had passed the last seven years. A thing my mother used to say each time she demanded that I clean my room came to mind: "Cluttered room, cluttered mind." She always said this with a look as if she'd just smelled dirty socks. What I saw now was not a space that had been "lived in" as a real estate agent might describe it, but the sanctum of an obsessive. The cityscapes appeared as if they might collapse under the sheer volume of ink. The racks of compact discs and crates of albums looked like exactly what they were—

holdovers from a bygone era. I was surprised that, looking at myself from the outside in, I hadn't taken to adopting stray cats. I reacted to what I now saw as I have always reacted to difficult times: I left.

I walked blindly. Out of cursed habit, my steps took me on the familiar route into town. Past cracked asphalt parking lots cluttered with spent cigarettes and fast-food wrappers, across vacant lots knotted with tumbleweeds piled in windrows. Past tired strip malls sprouting upstart businesses that advertised with vinyl signs. Past spray-painted gang signs. Through the fumes extruded by countless exhaust pipes. Through the noise of cars spilling their radio waves, which gathered into a stew not unlike the collective spillage of their leaking auto fluid joining the asphalt in a once-fossilized dinosaur gumbo.

I moved where my feet took me. The weather was flirting with change and a cold wind blew from the north, the kind of wind that slips inside like a mallet sounding the skeleton as if its bones were keys. I walked faster. Passersby who paid me any mind would have thought I was late for an appointment, though apparently the only appointment I had was scheduled for me by fate—if I were the sort who believes such things— and thus, perhaps I could not have reacted had I seen the car that struck me. I did not see it until after I was sprawled on the ground. Only later did the driver help me understand what had happened as she told me, repeatedly, that she was so intent on finding a gap in traffic she had never seen me. No more than I, entranced in my self-pity, had seen her.

It was no brake-screeching, remove-the-victim-from-his-shoes encounter, yet even at ten or fifteen miles per hour a couple of thousand pounds with momentum exposes frailties in the unwitting human body. I think I blacked out for a moment. I was out for long enough at least for the driver, a hysterical woman of thirty-five, to exit her car and kneel over me, sobbing profusely and declaring endless apologies in a voice that rattled and hiccupped. My head throbbed. The worst pain was concentrated in my left knee. Still, I waved her off, which only added to her hysterics. An awkward bevy of strangers formed a half-circle around us. A large man asked me if I wanted him to call an ambulance. I asked why I would need an ambulance.

"You've been hit by a car, man," he said.

"I don't own a car," I said.

"No, man, this lady hit you," he said. His shirt looked like one bright swath of blood. I wondered if he was bleeding. He knelt down next to me. Evidently, I was trying to get up, for he said, "You should stay still, man." I saw then that he had a huge head of curly black hair. I saw that he wore a red shirt. He reminded me of a Samoan friend I'd had in my previous life, a happy guitarist. He smiled at me and said, "You're going to be okay." He had an infectious and reassuring smile.

"Of course I am," I agreed.

"I never even saw him," the driver declared, a new river of tears streaming. "I don't know where he came from."

"I'll be all right," I said, trying to reassure her.

"I'm so sorry," she said. "I didn't see you at all."

"I wasn't watching where I was going."

"I'll call an ambulance," the man said.

"I'm fine," I said. "There's no need for an ambulance."

"I think you should," he said.

"Did I damage your car?" I asked.

"My car?" She looked confused. "You were walking," she said. "I must have been looking the other way. I'm so sorry."

I thought we had established her sorrow by this point. "I'm fine. Just a bit shaken up." I heard traffic noise that seemed uncomfortably close. I peered beyond where the two knelt beside me and saw an SUV a few yards away. From where I lay on the pavement, it looked like a predator prepared to defend its most recent kill, the tall, deeply grooved tires with tread like claws.

"You couldn't have driven an economy car?" I asked. This prompted new tears.

I tried to get up. The pain in my knee objected. The driver handed me a handkerchief. "You've got some blood on your face," she explained. The driveway surface was filled with loose gravel. I felt granules embedded in my palm and saw cuts and scrapes there when I reached to accept her handkerchief. It had a purple flower embroidered in one corner. I didn't want to get it bloody.

"I'm calling an ambulance," the big man said.

"I don't want an ambulance."

"You need someone to look at you."

"I don't want an ambulance," I repeated.

"Big mistake," he said. He looked at the driver, then at her car, and then back at me. "She tagged you pretty good. I saw the whole thing."

"I never saw him," she declared again. She might have been pretty. I couldn't tell for the mess her tears had made of her make-up. Mostly she looked tired. She wore a skirt and suit jacket. Lying on the pavement with her kneeling beside me, the angle of my vision offered an embarrassing glimpse under her skirt, and I immediately tried to get up.

"Let me help you, man," my new friend said, and he moved behind me and lifted me easily. My head felt as if its contents sloshed forward. The big man held me until I gained my balance. I felt dizzy for a moment and then the feeling passed. My knee protested. I became aware of an ache in my side among my lower ribs. I saw that my pants had torn.

The driver took the handkerchief from me and dabbed at my left cheek. Then she gingerly brushed gravel and a twig from my hair before handing me the handkerchief again. "I'm so sorry," she said like a toy doll with a sound box stuck on repeat.

"It was an accident," I said. "I'll be fine."

"You're hurt."

"Nothing that a couple of days rest won't cure." My head was clearing.

"You really should see a doctor," the man said.

"Are you Samoan?" I asked him.

"By default," he said. "My dad is. I was born in Hawaii."

"If I was in Hawaii, I'd be walking on the beach," I said.

"No SUVs to contend with on the beach," he agreed.

Now that I was on my feet, the rest of the small group that had gathered around began to disperse. A driver in a red pickup behind the woman's SUV honked his horn. He looked angry. Looking at him I felt myself becoming impatient too. Briefly I wondered if he might allow me a ride. Just then he put his truck in reverse, backed away from the SUV and exited another driveway with a squeal of tires. Everyone turned to watch his departure.

"Good thing you didn't get hit by him," the Samoan said.

"Can I at least take you to the hospital?" the driver asked.

"I'm fine, really," I said. "I live close by. I'll just go home and get cleaned up," I lied. "A little soap and water and some aspirin and I'll be as good as new."

"I'd really feel better if I knew you were okay," the driver said.

I wanted only to get away from her and the attention. I wanted away from the gas station and its fumes. Convenience stores seemed hopeless places, the haven for cigarette addicts and liquid sugar junkies, the target of criminals too lazy to plan a proper crime.

I offered the driver a ludicrous stiff bow and stepped away. I tried to offer a handshake to the Samoan and was met instead with some sort of knuckle-punching gesture I flubbed.

"At least give me your phone number so I can check in on you," the driver said.

"No phone," I replied, muttered my thanks once again, and crossed in front of the still idling SUV, seeking my departure.

12

My knee hurt with each step. Instinctively I clasped my right arm to my left side where my ribs pulsed. I lurched down the sidewalk concentrating hard on maintaining a straight line.

I was not precisely sure of my location. I watched street signs and scanned for a familiar landmark. This isn't the sort of city to boast landmarks. It is a city, like most, that spreads outward on the horizontal like a middle-aged belly, one cloned neighborhood after another bordered by a repeated strip mall.

I made certain that I was several blocks removed and out of sight of the accident location before I stopped to rest and get my bearings. I longed for a bus stop bench. Or better yet, a bus. My head throbbed behind my right eye. It felt as if perhaps I swayed a bit as I tried to gain my breath. Of all the places to stop, I realized I had chosen another gas station. I might as well have walked a circle.

I tried to will myself forward but truly needed a rest, so I crossed between the gasoline islands and walked to the building where I wedged myself between a pay phone and a newspaper vending machine. I needed just enough time to collect my senses. Someone had scrawled a profane joke in black ink down the side of the phone enclosure and a sticky puddle covered the top of the newspaper machine. A cluster of cigarette butts was piled at my feet and I could smell their stale release. I stood as still as possible, taking purposefully shallow breaths to try and minimize the pain. I leaned against the wall and felt as if I had a target tattooed across my forehead, like a victim awaiting a mugging.

I don't know how long I stood there. I know I closed my eyes for a time. I wondered if perhaps I had dozed off while standing, like a horse. I only know that after a time I became acutely aware of car sounds coming and going at the gasoline pumps, their sound reaching me the way voices creep into consciousness when awakened upon a beach after a sound nap. I know nothing about cars, yet it struck me that an unusual number of the engines I heard did not sound healthy. There idled quite near me a vehicle that emitted both occasional high squeals and an incessant clicking noise.

I needed to get home. I opened my eyes. I saw parked before me a pea-green and primer-gray Toyota Camry absent pieces of its grill as if missing teeth. The driver's and passenger seats were empty but two teenagers occupied the back seat, and they appeared to be passing a magazine back and forth. One of the teens leaned forward, adjusted a knob, and suddenly bass beats overwhelmed the squeal and click and almost immediately the teen's heads began bobbing in unison. The beat invaded my head like a pulse. A summons to move. I reached the sidewalk, and while movement was not without pain, my head had cleared. I was thinking again. As I stood trying to orient myself, the Toyota pulled alongside. Great, I thought, hit me when I'm down. Instead, the music stopped abruptly and the driver rolled his window down. He couldn't have been more than sixteen and he sported shaggy hair the style of which I hadn't seen in twenty years. "You okay, man? You don't look so hot."

"I'm fine," I muttered. I must have looked drunk, one arm clasped to my ribs, my pants torn, my shirt dirty.

"Can we give you a lift somewhere? I don't think you should probably be out walking around."

"Just a little run-in with an SUV," I said. "Nothing I can't handle."

"Seriously, man. Hop in and we'll get you wherever you're going." He turned in his seat and addressed the boy behind him. "Joey, let the man take a load off."

"I'm used to walking," I said. "Thanks for the offer."

"Come on. It's freezing."

Just then a chill coursed through me. I was likely in danger of shock. The boy, Joey, got out of the car. I saw now that he was probably only fourteen, and while his hair wasn't nearly so long as the driver's, it was cut at an odd, apparently purposeful angle. He motioned for me to get in. Against my better judgment in what had apparently become a new habit, I complied.

There was a time in my life when I would never have hesitated to accept such an offer, a time when I fell headlong from one spontaneous moment into the next, passing time among strangers offering me drinks or a toke off a pipe, a ride, a meal, or a place to flop. Such was the world of concerts and backstage passes. Perpetually smiling stoners with reddened half-closed eyes, swaying to music they craved, pacifists, a brotherhood and sisterhood of those seeking good times. If ever I need a handout and I'm faced with a choice between a bleary-eyed stoner who likely slept in his clothes and a bible-citing straight-lace in a starched shirt, I'll take the stoner every time.

"I'm Stu," the driver said. "You look like shit."

"So I've been told."

"What happened to you, dude?" Joey asked. "You look like you got hit by a car or something."

"I was hit by a car."

"For the reals?"

"Yeah."

"What'd that feel like?"

"What kind of stupid question is that," the blond in the passenger seat asked. "How do think it would feel?"

"It's just that the dude is up and walking and shit, you know," Joey said. "A car hits a dude and I think the guy would be on a stretcher in his socks."

"The car was coming out of a driveway," I said, by way of explanation. "She just wasn't looking."

"What kind of car?" Joey asked.

"Again with the stupid questions. It's like a ton of metal coming at you any way you look at it, bro."

"I'm just trying to picture it, dude. I mean was it like a sports car and it hits you below the knee or like a Mack truck and all you see is grill?"

"It was an SUV," I said.

"Like some bitch in an Escalade or like some grandma in a Honda CRV?"

"I think it was a Suburban or a Tahoe. Something like that. Big."

"Damn."

"So you got a home to go home to," the driver asked, "or somewhere we can lift you to, man?"

"Yes," I said. "I don't really know exactly where I am now or what exactly I was here for, but I live on the west side of town." I proceeded to give him a major intersection and some landmarks to identify the general locale.

"We're sorta headed that way," the driver said. "Got a buddy over that way we were thinking of dropping in on. Word has it he has the makings of a party. We could drop you."

"I'd greatly appreciate that," I said. "I just want to get home and lie down. Maybe take some aspirin for this headache."

"Here, man," the other boy seated next to me said. "This will help take your mind off your head." He handed me a cigarette lighter and a small pipe loaded with a tight bud. I must have looked hesitant, for he said, "Go ahead, man. It's cool."

I hadn't smoked in years. Hardly at all since my daughter was born and not a single toke since I'd left my position at the magazine. Still, a lot of my memories, a lot of good times and unique experiences involved being stoned. Finally, I said, "If it's good enough for cancer patients," and I took a long toke, the smoke hot in my throat and the memory of the sweet smell of the bud glowing orange shuffling me back to the past. Apparently, I was no more successful at standing up to peer pressure than I'd been in my youth, or for that matter, with Monika. I passed the pipe back to the boy and held the smoke in my lungs despite my body wanting to explode with a coughing fit. The lung expansion hurt my ribs.

"Cheers to cancer," the boy said, adding some flake to the bowl and passing it to the driver.

"Did you know," the blond in the passenger seat said, "that

if we lived long enough, everybody would eventually die of some sort of cancer? Like we'd all have prostates the size of pears if we made it past a hundred."

"It starts with your mother's milk," the boy with the effeminate haircut said. "There you are, a sweet little baby just looking for your first suck on a real tit, crying your eyes out 'cause you're so hungry and she's giving you your first dose of cancer 'cause she's got it all locked up in her body from all the heavy metals that they're pumpin' into her in processed food and vinyl seats and shit."

"Car windshields too," the blond said.

"Huh?"

"Car windshields. Some film they put on them. Totally carcinogenic."

"Oh," the boy said. "And nylon, I think. Or polyester or something."

"Like there's anything that doesn't cause cancer," the blond said. "Shit, even fish have cancer now."

"And mercury," I said, trying to fit in.

"That's right," he said, "and that shit will tear you up."

Stu, the driver, handed the pipe to me. Situated where I was, I had to be the go between for the front and back seats.

"How do you want to go out?" the boy with the effeminate hair asked of no one in particular.

"On top of some beautiful bitch," the blond said. "Like those old men who die sweatin' and humpin'. Go out with a big old shit-eatin' grin on my face."

"I'd want to go out in a spectacular crash," Stu, my driver, said as he cut into a new lane. "Like from a movie. Set a record for longest air or highest speed at impact. Just ashes and dust, baby."

The dreary lullaby I was beginning to feel from the hit off the pipe shifted abruptly to a paranoid frenzy. The engine pinged in protest to Stu's hard acceleration. I was pressed against Joey's elbow as we turned a corner and the pain in my side intensified.

"Or maybe hang gliding or parachuting," Stu said. "Something memorable but so extreme there wouldn't be any pain."

"No one remembers," I said, "even when you think they would."

"You'd make YouTube though," Joey said. I had no idea what he was talking about.

"How about you?" the boy on my other side asked. "How do you want to buy it?"

"Not by getting hit by a Suburban in a gas station parking lot," I said.

"I'll smoke to that," he said, and then he did.

I felt like maybe I'd drifted off. Stu and the blond in the front seat seemed to be arguing over where they were supposed to turn. They spoke of a house they were trying to find. I wondered if it was my house they were looking for, but I didn't remember giving them my address.

"I've only been there in the dark," Stu kept saying. "If it was dark, I'd drive right to it."

"Shit, you can't find your way outta your own back yard."

"At least I don't have to go the back yard to take a shit," Stu countered. "Oh, wait, your trailer park doesn't have yards."

Their argument continued in this fashion, and all the while Stu kept turning random corners. I had no idea where we were. My head still hurt and was further fogged by the pot. I wished I could stretch my leg. The Toyota took a hard left, feeling as if it might fall off its skinny tires. "I told you," Stu shouted joyously. "There's Steve-o's truck, man. Sounds like a party to me." Indeed a decrepit postwar house blasted music as loud as a concert, as if it were the music's volume that was causing the weathered paint to fall away from the siding in curling strips.

Stu swung the car to the curb, parking in a fashion that blocked in at least two others. "Dismount," he shouted like a Calvary officer. Turning to me, he said, "You're free to join the party, bub. We can give you a lift later. Or there's probably a phone inside. Oh, duh, you could have used mine," he said removing a cell phone from his jeans pocket and shrugging. Joey did the same. The blond carried a phone as well. "Whatever you want," Stu said. "Feel welcome, man."

I wanted to be home in my dark bedroom.

"Thanks," I mumbled weakly. I'd forgotten that as much as I liked stoners and as good at heart as most were, they are an entirely undependable group.

"Don't mention it. Should be a good time in there." Through the front window of the house I saw a small group gathered around a skinny kid sucking on the end of a beer bong. I wondered briefly why none of these kids were in school.

Stu and the rest disappeared, and I struggled from the cramped backseat. The house did not look the least inviting. Nothing appeared familiar. Somewhere nearby there had to be an arterial street and there I might or might not recognize my surroundings, but here amidst countless blocks of nearly identical homes constructed in a rush to meet the return of World War II veterans, I had no idea where I was. That I'd have better luck finding someone who could repair a broken car than a broken body seemed certain.

My knee hurt but felt capable of supporting my weight. My head still throbbed, though the waves of pain accompanying my pulse had calmed to a slowly rising tide rather than whitecaps slamming the shoreline. I felt I had already entered the party and drank my share of its offerings. I remained indecisive about what action to pursue and instead slumped against Stu's car while I tried to gain my bearings. The warmth of the engine offered small comfort.

13

When a familiar voice awakened me from my stupor, it seemed small and far away. "Mr. Badger?" I heard Monika say. "What are...what happened to you? You need to sit down or something."

"Code names should change with every mission," I said.

"What?"

"I can't be Mr. Badger today," I said. "You need to call me something else, like Crash Test Dummy." I understood that I sounded delirious. I could not decide if it was the result of injuries or pot.

"What happened to you?"

"I was a crash test dummy."

"Mon, you know this guy?" another voice asked. I forced myself to stand straighter.

"I'm just resting," I mumbled.

"Help me get him to my car," I heard Monika say, and then I saw that she was speaking to two other girls, a blond and a brunette in jeans and light jackets in feminine colors sporting identifiable logos.

"What's the matter with him?" the brunette asked. She was shorter than Monika and her expression made it look as if she'd just tasted something that hadn't agreed with her.

"Come on, give me a hand," Monika said, pointing to the blond, who was tall and athletic.

I felt arms converge around my waist from each side. I struggled to remember the last time I'd had human contact. The lyrics to Joe Jackson's "The Human Touch" appeared in my mind without being summoned. "What are you doing here?" I asked Monika.

"Party," she replied.

"Oh," I said, as if she'd offered me new information.

"It's lame-o," she added. "I tried to tell my girls, but they think any party with a beer bong ranks up there with a Hollywood after-Oscar affair. After-effect-vomiting is my prediction. I'm not sticking around."

"You just don't know how to have a good time, Mon," the girl helping support my weight said.

"What the hell are you doing here?" Monika asked, ignoring her friend.

"I know where all the parties are," I said. "It's a gift. Like radar."

"Who are you?" Monika's friend asked.

"He's my neighbor," Monika answered for me. "This is Rachel. And bitch-eyes back there is Ashley."

"The pleasure's mine," I said.

"Is he drunk or something?" Rachel asked.

"Serial killer," Monika said. We'd walked half a block. I recognized Monika's car two car lengths further ahead.

"Almost there," Monika said.

"I'm fine, really," I said in mild protest.

"Seriously, Mr. Wiggles," Monika said, "what happened to you?"

"There was a little incident with an SUV."

"You got hit by a car?"

"Soccer moms hate me. I must put out an anti-nuclear vibe."

"Are you some kind of protestor?" Rachel asked.

"With every breath I take," I replied.

"You need to get to a hospital," Monika said.

"Really, I'm fine. I just want to go lie down. My head's a little foggy. I might appear to be rambling."

We had reached the car and Monika opened the passenger door. She helped ease me into the seat as if I were an invalid. "Thanks, Rachel," she said. "Call me when you need a ride. Whatever you do, don't overextend your stay. The beer-induced limp dicks will be out in force today."

"Thanks, Rachel," I muttered, wishing I had some party wisdom to offer as Monika closed the door.

"How'd you wind up here?" Monika demanded even before she placed the key in the ignition.

"I hitched a ride, apparently with some of your fellow scholars."

"You smell like weed."

I shrugged.

"Were you seriously hit by a car?"

"Just a glancing blow," I said.

"Stop being sarcastic."

"I was crossing a driveway. The driver didn't see me and I wasn't paying attention. She was going something like two miles per hour. It's not really a big deal. A couple of days' rest and I'll be as good as new."

"You should see a doctor."

"Nothing's broken. I'll sleep it off. I really appreciate the ride home though."

"What if you have a concussion?"

"Then I'll have a headache. Really, I'll be fine."

"You could go to sleep and never wake up."

"Not going to happen," I said.

She still looked skeptical but started the car and began driving. "I'm probably at greater risk as a passenger in this rattletrap," I said, smiling.

"Want to walk home?"

"No."

"Then zip it."

"Yes, ma'am. Shutting up."

When we'd driven three blocks, I asked if I could turn up the heat. She clicked a dial into the red and adjusted the fan. "I'm freezing," I explained.

"You're probably in shock. People can die from shock."

"It's cold out. I'm not dying."

She gave me another look, arching her eyebrows.

"I'm surprised to see you at this kind of party," I said. "Doesn't seem your style."

"You should talk."

"I wasn't going to the party," I protested. "I was at the whims of the ride I accepted."

"I wasn't going to the party either. I was just dropping off those girls."

"Your friends. I'm sorry to take you away."

"They're not really friends, just people I spend time with."

"I figured you for the social maven," I said.

"You'd be wrong."

"But you're so nice to people. A regular taxi driver."

"Friends are more of my brother's terrain. Everybody loves Danny. Me, not so much. I'm just the weird sister."

"What's not to like?"

"I'm a little too much for most people."

"Imagine that."

"Don't joke. I'm serious. I've always had trouble making friends. It gets lonely sometimes."

"Why?"

"Why am I lonely? That's a stupid question, Mr. Rocket Scientist."

I was fairly confident I'd just heard the real explanation for her constricted social circles. "Why do you have trouble making friends?"

"People don't like me."

"Why?"

"What is this? An analysis session? Because I spent too much time in the birth canal. Because my parents refused to allow me access to breakfast cereal and cartoons. Because they provided me a car seat that failed consumer safety tests."

"Your peers don't appreciate sarcasm?"

She made a face at me like a two-year-old and then turned away. "I've never been able to relate to kids my own age."

"And why do you think that's the case?"

"I don't think they like smart people."

"They don't mind that you're smart—" I started but Monika interrupted me mid-sentence.

"Yeah, when I'm their partner on a group project and I do all the work, they love me."

"They just don't like it when you rub it in their faces," I said, finishing my original thought.

She frowned. She sighed. A short flurry of erratic movements appeared to supplant what she wanted to say. She relaxed and then frowned again. "Some of my teachers used to say that I was too 'academically' competitive. It was like their go-to phrase in parent-teacher conferences. They said that I needed to give other kids the opportunity to learn in their own ways."

"How'd that go?"

"Just peachy," she said.

"You didn't follow their counsel?"

"Teach to the lowest common denominator? Now there's a system for success. Maintain the bell curve. Reward failure."

"Maybe you haven't handled your own failure so well," I offered, my condition apparently making me invite attack.

"I must need to come study at your feet, Wise One. You appear to have mastered the art of failure," she snapped.

"My, my," I said. "And you claim to suffer from delayed comeback syndrome." This time she stuck her tongue out at me.

"How come you're not in school?" I asked, intent to start down another failed conversational path.

"Early release day. Every week someone starts a party. Half the school's drunk by dinnertime."

"What day is it?" I asked.

"Thursday, Sharpshooter. You really did crack your head."

"I didn't know what day it was before I got hit by a car."

"That's kind of pathetic."

"Occupational hazard."

"But you don't have an occupation, do you?"

"Exactly."

"Check it," Monika said a minute later, slowing the car.

"Pardon?"

"Check it out," she said, pointing.

I followed the line of her finger to a tacky, aging ranch-style bungalow with a flock of three plastic flamingos standing at the edge of a neglected flower garden.

"You're scarily obsessed," I said.

"I consider the pink flamingo the classic of all lawn ornamentation," she said. "Understated in size, graceful in shape, gaudy in color. Hideously colored you could say. With the wonderful irony that they always seem used in climates where you could never—not in a million years, not given the craziest extremes of global climate change, not accepting bird navigation foul-up, not even in the case of a severely compromised flamingo—never, ever see the real thing. I mean they're not like duck decoys. Sticking them in your lawn isn't going to draw the real thing out of the sky and offer you a ready dinner."

"You have that gleam in your eye."

"I can't help myself. Besides, I just said foul-up. Get it?"

I groaned audibly. "Have you continued your campaign without me?" I asked.

"Temporarily suspended."

"How come?"

"Mom's been on the warpath lately. Saw my grades. They're not where they should be."

"I thought you were the smart girl who values original thought."

"I am the smart girl."

"Then why the grade mishap?"

"I just kind of don't turn things in all the time. Funny, teachers seem to hold that against you."

"Imagine that."

"School bores the hell out of me. Always has. Most of my teachers use the curriculum created back in the Stone Age. Some of them just aren't that smart."

"So your failures are actually somebody else's fault."

Her anger was rising. "I didn't have to pick you up, you know.

I could dump you out right here, let you die in the street. You're probably bleeding internally."

"I'm just trying to understand."

"I'll stop the car."

"No, really. I mean it. I'm trying to get it. I bet you do the homework. Probably more than what's assigned. You just don't turn it in. I've got that right?"

She shrugged.

"Clearly the actions of a genius."

"Screw you."

"Debate team is apparently out. You being so eloquent and all."

"Have you always been an asshole? Or is that a trait you've cultivated living down there in your hole."

"I don't get a lot of practice, so I have to take it out when I'm up here among the living."

"It's too bad that car wasn't going a lot faster."

"Would you be satisfied if my assailant dragged me a few blocks? I could be dying."

"You said you're okay."

"I am okay."

"What the fuck, man?" she erupted. "Did you already have brain damage before you were hit by a car? I mean who gets hit by a car? And who walks anyway? Then, showing all the wisdom of your years, you accept a ride from a bunch of stoners. What's wrong with you?"

"I thought you were trying to help me."

"I am trying to help, you stupid, agoraphobic mule."

"You read the dictionary for fun? You know 'agoraphobic' and still you don't turn stuff in."

She glared at me.

"Stating the obvious?" I asked. "Something you've heard a few million times before?"

She nodded.

"You've already told me about your drill team failures, so

you've got nothing to put on the good old college app, right? Or is that why you're rescuing me?"

This received a protracted glare. She visibly hunched her shoulders. "Eyes on the road," I warned. The car accelerated. She seemed to move closer to the steering wheel, her hands high on its circle and her elbows jutting outward. I don't know why I could not fight off the urge to continue assaulting her. "Awkward in the peer social situations, are we?"

She continued to accelerate and looked intently at the road ahead. "People don't understand me," she said. "They don't know how to relate."

I closed my eyes. I tried to silence the demon that seemed intent on being mean to Monika. "Join the club," I said. I took a deep breath, the action causing pain in my chest. I swallowed hard once and opened my eyes, looking at her. She appeared as if she had forgotten my presence. "I know I'm not in a position where I should be giving advice," I said.

"You think?"

I ignored her. "I know school can be a drag," I continued, "but there's a certain part of the game you have to play."

"This coming from the guy who jumps right into all of society's little games." Her death-inspired look of dark eye make-up and whitened skin suddenly took on a defiant, almost devilish aspect. "You know where you can shove your advice."

"Or life bites you in the ass," I finished, ignoring her. "You want to go to college or art school or something, don't you? You have to keep the grades up or you end up stifling your own opportunities."

"What's so great about college? It's all a big conspiracy. Jack the tuition up. Tax the middle class to death by having the government make billions off student loans and then send the job base overseas so the graduates have nowhere to work. Sell people on the effluvium that college is their ticket to everlasting beauty and happiness, and meanwhile populate the elite schools with the same inbred rich tight-asses who have always run things."

"Do you feel better now?"

"Bite me."

"That's mature. Great consistency there, Monika. You get 'effluvium' and 'bite me' into the same exchange."

"Stop trying to bait me."

She had me there.

She pulled abruptly to the curb but said nothing, brakes squealing. I looked at her. She was steaming, eyes narrowed to slits, hands clutched to the steering wheel.

I made no move to get out of the car, and she took no action. At last, swallowing first, I said, "I'm sorry. I really am. I don't know what came over me. I'm sure you hear plenty of that crap. You're obviously smart and passionate. College just opens doors."

"You've got the whole guidance counselor thing down pat. Where are your khaki pants?"

"Statistically speaking, I mean," I said, trying to lighten the mood.

"I know all the statistics. Higher income rates. Lower unemployment. Better advancement potential. I just don't know if those statistics mean anything to me."

"I take it I'm only adding to the adult annoyance."

"Actually, the guidance counselors have mostly given up on me. I think maybe even my dad has too. Now, Mom's hanging in there. She aced Nagging 101. But mostly anymore she just grounds me to the house so I can be fully exposed to her manic-depression and her constant reminders about all the things my brother will never get to do."

"She really is looking out for your best interests."

"Whatever. I'm just so ready to be done with all this."

"So was I."

"So you dug a hole?"

"No, I mean I couldn't wait to get out of the house. College seemed the ticket. You just haven't seen the diploma hanging on the cave wall. I'm often tempted to use it for fire starter when I've made a mastodon kill, but I've resisted."

"Don't try so hard to be cute. I knew from the way you spoke that you're educated."

"It's just that I seem like a bit of a deranged hermit, so not a great education spokesperson."

"Something like that. I was going for 'recluse.' Trying to be kind."

"I'd have thought the same thing."

"Where'd you go?" she asked.

"A small school in New England."

"Okay, there's only about a thousand of those. Which little chocolate factory was blessed by your presence?"

"It doesn't matter."

"Yet you're pretending to be my college counselor."

"I was one of the little assholes you referenced earlier.," I admitted, looking out the window.

"Which bit of ivy?"

"Dartmouth. It was easier to get in back in the day."

"Yeah, I suppose back then they'd just let anyone into Dartmouth."

"Where are you looking?" I asked. "Tell me you're considering college at least."

"I have no idea."

"Have you taken the SAT yet?"

"Yeah, junior year. I'm supposed to take it again in about a month."

"Have you been studying?"

"Not really. I usually do pretty well on tests despite their bullshit. I did really well on the PSAT, I guess. I have to do those stupid, mind-numbing tests now for the National Merit crap. What a pain. The counselors haven't let go of that one. Only because they think it makes the school look good."

"National Merit *crap?*"

"It's a scholarship thing."

"Yeah, I know. You become a National Merit Scholar and it's like punching the golden ticket."

"Whatever. Tests don't mean crap. It's all a big industry.

One big circle of you-scratch-my-back-I'll-scratch-your-ass."

"Maybe. But you do realize how gifted you must be to find yourself in this position, the whole debate over whether tests demonstrate knowledge aside. Just how well did you do on the SAT last year?"

"I don't know."

"Bull. Give me the numbers."

"In the 1500s I think."

"Dartmouth, remember. Now just where in the 1500s?"

"1580."

"Damn."

"It doesn't mean anything."

"That's why you thought you'd take it again, get those 20 points you missed."

"It just sort of pissed me off. Like I said, it doesn't mean anything."

"No, it doesn't mean everything, but it does mean something."

"Yeah, whatever."

"You've got brains. You shouldn't be embarrassed about that."

"Who said I'm embarrassed? That would just be stupid."

"You can have any life you want," I said.

"What do you care anyway?"

"I just like to see people recognize the opportunities before them."

"Like you've done."

"This isn't about me. You deserve a great education."

"Yeah, I'm a frickin' genius. Like you are. Is that your story? You're one of those off the charts types whose wiring is so screwed up you can't wear socks that match. All your synapses are closed. Your left hemisphere gets in arguments with your right hemisphere. One of those Rasputin clones who wears the same sweater every day for a year." She suddenly pulled the car back into traffic, picking up speed as if to match the speed of her sentences.

"I wish I had a beard and a sweater," I grumbled. "Does the heat even work in this Pacific Rim rust torpedo?" I checked my socks while Monika dialed up the heat another notch.

She was just getting started. "You carry a MENSA card in your wallet," she said, "but you think MENSA is an international spy organization working for aliens. Is that your trip? Or do you build pipe bombs in your little hole?"

"You just stay on the attack, you little angst-riddled brainiac. Too smart to turn in your homework."

"Schizo."

"Wanna-be punkster," I countered.

"Child molesting porn addict."

"New-age hippie."

"Middle-aged dropout."

"Pity princess."

"Coffee-grounds guru."

I chuckled despite my better interests. "Rice eater," I tried.

"Rice eater?" she asked, suddenly bursting into laughter. "Where'd that come from? I mean, what's that? You could have resorted to picking on my mama at least. Rice eater?"

"I got flustered," I confessed.

"I do happen to love rice," she said.

"You know about the coffee grounds?" I asked.

"Everybody knows Underground Man hits the local coffee shops. Carrying your big plastic bucket."

"It's for the garden compost," I explained. "And it's not like I hit all the coffee shops. Only two in fact. And there's competition. Practically a waiting list."

"All the stupid people at school confuse coffee grounds with tea leaves. They say you do some ceremony where you read the grounds. Like you know the stories of the people who drank the coffee and then you fiddle around with their futures."

"Well, that is true," I said. "But the child molester thing hurt."

"Fair enough," she said. "By the way, do you hear me asking for your advice?"

I pressed into the seat and tried to get comfortable. I marveled at how apparently far from home I had ended up and realized there were large portions of this small city I'd never seen. Despite seven years of residency, I remained a stranger to the place. We began to pass familiar streets. I wanted only to be in the safe confines of my home and crawl into my darkened bed.

There was a time in my former life when I'd been a frequent sufferer of migraines, and my headache had begun to resemble those unwanted memories, so I tried to keep still. I knew that when I moved to exit the car, standing would be accompanied by a tsunami of pain.

When we pulled to the curb near my door, Monika said, "I really think I should be taking you to the hospital. You're really pale."

"I'm trying out your death pallor look," I said.

She frowned.

"I just need some Advil and my bed."

"Remember, if you end up dead in the night, I advocated for medical care."

"Duly noted," I said.

She got out of the car and came around and met me at my open door. She offered a hand and I accepted it. The wave I'd expected arrived precisely on cue, and I staggered a step. I am a tall man, one often prone to light-headedness if I stand too quickly, and for a moment I thought I was going down. A kind of gauzy curtain dropped over my eyes and sound disappeared. I wanted to ease back into the car seat and fumbled until I gained a grip on the open doorframe. The feeling passed, although a pulsing pain in my head remained. Monika tried to steady me with a hand at my waist.

"You're not all right," she said, her voice matter of fact.

"Just a bad headache and a sore knee. I stood up too fast."

"It's called a concussion."

"And how does the esteemed medical profession treat a concussion?" I asked.

"I don't know."

"They tell you to take it easy and warn you not to hit your head again. I'll be fine if you just help me inside."

"How about I help you to a hospital instead."

"I am not going to the hospital," I said, more forcefully than I'd intended. I pictured the hospitals I'd known, chaotic places filled with dread. Harried places where even the staff looked like jumpy combat veterans.

"Okay, okay," she said, slipping one arm around my waist and guiding my left arm over her shoulder. "You don't have to throw a tantrum."

I wanted to protest. Instead I accepted the rebuke and the help and together we crossed the field to my door with the grace of strangers chosen to partner in a potato sack race.

The short walk was exhausting. I tried to recall my ancient Boy Scout first aid training to treat shock: rest, warmth, elevate feet. There may have been something in there about "seek medical attention." While I still thought the extent of my injuries relatively minor, clearly my body was preserving its energies for combating distress and wished no more exertion. I leaned heavily upon the railing and on Monika as I descended the stairs.

"Bedroom," I muttered once we reached the landing at the bottom of the stairwell. Roger Waters leveled his neon gaze at me impassively. I lurched toward the bedroom, Monika scurrying to assist.

I abandoned her altogether at the bedroom doorway, reached instinctively forward in the dark and gathered the spread off the made bed, withdrawing it just enough to crawl within, comforted by the interior darkness of the small room.

"You said you had Advil." She sounded as if she were underwater.

"Bathroom, left top drawer," I grunted.

I vaguely remember the touch of a cold glass, of pills inserted, the offer of water, which once tasted, I gulped ravenously before collapsing back onto the bed. I thought I heard music in my dreams.

14

I had no idea how long I'd slept. I momentarily suffered that strange sensation I used to experience regularly in hotel rooms when work took me to new cities and I would lie in bed uncertain where I was. I heard music. I perceived but the faintest melody, so faint I could not identify the song. I wondered if I had died and neared some judgment place that possessed a soundtrack.

When I padded toward the bathroom, I was initially surprised to see that it was light outside. My knee remained stiff and had swollen but seemed stable. Movement aggravated the pain in my ribcage, but my head had cleared. When I emerged from the bathroom, I found Monika seated on the floor near the fireplace with headphones on and a stack of albums and compact discs before her. She was reading liner notes.

Evidently, she sensed my presence, for although I remained behind her, she removed the headphones and scrambled to stand up. "The dead have awakened."

"I should invest in a burglar alarm," I grumbled.

"This collection is the most amazing thing I've ever seen. It's like a museum." Fidgeting as per usual, she looked like a child who needs to pee. "I ate some of your food. Hope that's all right. You're going to need more crackers."

"What time is it?"

"One. It's Friday. You've been asleep for nearly a day."

"Aren't you supposed to be in school?"

"Biology."

"Did you stay here all night?"

"No. I gave you more Advil before I left. You don't remember?"

"No."

"Obviously my mom would have killed me if I didn't come home. I didn't know if you'd be dead when I came back this morning. I've got to tell you, coming down those stairs was scary, Batman, like *Blair Witch* scary. I pictured you all blue and cold. I almost couldn't do it." She paused. "I mean, what would I have done if I found you dead."

"That would be something of a predicament. Not an easy explanation to the ole parents or the authorities."

"I hadn't thought about that. I was still pretty hung up over the whole dead thing."

It suddenly occurred to me to wonder if she had found her brother. I felt like a chump.

"I hope it's okay that I'm listening to your music."

"Music belongs to everyone. It's the great unifier."

"I meant for getting into your things."

"Monika," I said. I would do nearly anything to stop the odd tremors of her nervous energy. I looked at her. There was real fear in her eyes. "Thank you," I said. "You didn't have to help me. Listen to all the music you want." Then I turned and headed into the kitchen. I was famished, something I took as a good sign for my health.

I made her lunch without asking, and she accepted it without argument. Perhaps we had crossed some threshold where every exchange didn't demand a comedy routine. I ate a hot ham and cheese sandwich and we shared homemade vegetable soup I'd made earlier in the week.

As she accepted the bowl of soup, she said, "You seem a lot better. How are you feeling?"

"Like I got run over by an SUV."

"Smart ass."

When we were finished, without asking, Monika filled the sink and did the lunch dishes. She asked, "So what were you, a DJ or something? How'd you get all this great music?"

"I'm just something of a collector," I said.

"I've never seen this much music in one place, outside a

music store, of course. It's *like* a music store, only one with good taste. You're are all over the place though."

"You won't find much bubblegum here. Let's just see what you've been into." A stack of albums stood next to a smaller stack of compact discs on the floor where she had been seated. "So you figured out how to work a turntable."

"Yep, I fed the squirrels to keep it spinning," she retaliated.

"You didn't bust out any rap moves did you? No scratches on my Etta James," I said, eying what currently occupied the turntable.

"Yeah, I'm a total gangsta girl."

I sat on the floor. Bending down so far brought pain to my ribs. I had to sit with my leg straight in front of me.

"You should probably ice that," she said.

"Thanks, Mom."

She frowned.

I looked through the compact discs and albums she had out. She'd been reading liner notes for the James when I'd interrupted. I was pleasantly surprised at the eclectic mix she'd chosen. Some Motown. A bit of English punk. A good deal of '70s rock. Old Van Morrison. On the jazz side there was an old Dixie Dregs disc that was a personal favorite. Lots of Marley. Almost all were musicians I hadn't listened to in years but ones I loved.

"I wrote about music for a long time," I said, picking up the Morrison.

"Like a critic?"

"I've written my share of reviews. Mostly I focused more on feature articles about artists, tours, recording sessions, that sort of thing. The backstories. I was fixated on the narrative behind composition and on the stories that came with balancing the creation of art and sharing it. Some interviews. Later on I got into the scholarly side and wrote liner notes and historical accounts of bands and musical movements. I like to think of my best work as tracing musical DNA."

"That's sweet. So like you've met some of these people."

"A few."

"Like who?"

"Well, these guys for instance," I said, holding up the Dregs disc. "I got to talk to them backstage at Montreux. And I interviewed Morrison, maybe twelve years ago," I said, returning him to stack of discs. "A lucky chance. He's notoriously reclusive…"

"Something you know nothing about."

"He was a dynamite interview because he's smart and soulful, if eccentric and zealous about his faith, but he sticks to the music. An honest musician."

"Oh my god. You're totally telling the truth," Monika said. "I can see it in your face. You really have done all these things."

"Why would I lie about such a thing?"

"That's outrageous. You're my new hero."

"Aim higher," I said, and when she frowned, I added, "I want to be more of a superhero."

"Do you have copies of things you've written?"

"No."

"Oh, you must have."

"Nope. My wife…I used to save clippings. I got rid of all of them years ago."

"Why?"

"Because the music is what matters. I was just one of the parasites living off my hosts. What you have in your hands, that counts. What enters your ear and touches you. Nothing else matters."

"Is that why you left? Why you don't write anymore?"

"Music is constantly evolving," I said. "People evolve too, but mostly as a species. Individually we tend to stop somewhere along our evolutionary curve. Music will always keep changing, growing, and I wasn't prepared to change with it."

"You had this dream life and you walked away."

"Sometimes life throws you curve balls."

"That's it? A bad cliché? Maybe you weren't much of a writer."

I nearly took her bait and said something cruel. Instead, I merely said, "Probably not."

"If you're such a bad writer, are you a good musician?"

"Only in my dreams."

"Me too," she said. "I've tried to learn guitar a few thousand times. I think I have retarded fingers."

"I know the feeling. I have no voice. No rhythm. All I wanted growing up was to be a musician. I had to settle for hanging out with them instead."

"That's not such a bad deal."

"It was great. But I reached a point where I was forced to look around and realize I was still writing about pop culture while the larger world was going through one crisis after another. I watched places I traveled turned into war zones and killing fields. I wasn't even producing meaningful journalism."

"I believe music can heal the world," she said.

"Music will forever have a stranglehold on my heart," I said. "The world would be a much sadder place without it. But I had friends who were covering stories where people were dying, and I was writing about whether Nirvana would lose their edge once they landed on the Billboard charts."

"Who are you saving hiding down here?" she asked.

"Garden gnomes," I said, deflecting.

"And maybe pink flamingos," she added, laughing.

"Is there something you need to share?" I asked.

"Not really."

We remained silent for a while. Monika seemed to scan the overflowing shelves stuffed with compact discs that lined the walls.

"So seriously," she said. "What made you give up on saving the world?"

"I found out it wasn't worth saving."

"I should probably get going," she said later.

I had struggled to get up off the floor. Monika had assisted me, and I now sat at the table, my books and things open before me, untouched for days. She had returned the albums and compact discs to where they belonged and stood reading titles, her head tilted like a librarian reading shelves. "Do you think I could borrow some and put them in my iTunes?"

"Help yourself. In fact, you can keep what you borrow," I said. "I haven't listened to any of it in years."

"For the reals?"

"Try using English."

"You're a weird one, Mr. Grinch," she said, headed for the stairs. She paused and grabbed another disc. "I'll check on you later."

"Are you my nurse?"

She disappeared into the stairwell, but I still heard her when she said, "Therapist." The word sounded in the same register as the clomping of her boots on the stairs.

15

I went back to bed. When I woke next and entered the main room, I was surprised to see it was dark outside. I turned and made for the bathroom. When I reentered the main room, I turned on the light switch and was startled to find Monika seated on the floor in front of my recliner.

"You should close the door when you pee," she said. "It's really loud."

"I live alone," I said. "I don't even have a dog to offend."

"Maybe you should rectify that."

"What?"

"The dog."

"Dogs have to eat and piss and be walked."

"You should still rectify the door."

"The door?"

"Closing it."

"So that my non-existent dog doesn't have to hear me?"

"Good manners."

"Given how much time I spend at state dinners and high tea."

"Manners are manners."

"Like the etiquette rule that suggests you shouldn't let yourself into someone's home."

"I needed to check on you."

"What are you doing sitting in the dark?"

"Thinking."

"I'm so glad I could accommodate you."

"I liked it better with the lights off."

"This is why I live alone," I said, and in anger I shut the lights off with a swipe of my hand at the switch. I bulled forward into the sudden dark in the direction of the kitchen. My good knee contacted sharply with the table edge and a book hit the floor with a thud. I cursed and drew back from the collision. The sudden movement hurt my ribs.

"You'd think you'd know your way around better," Monika said, her voice like an invisible balloon floating in the darkness. She must have heard my labored breathing or I had emitted some painful sound against my will, for her voice lost its sarcasm when she asked, "Are you okay?"

"Damn it," I seethed, trying to take shallow breaths.

After a bit of fumbling, she turned on the lamp near where she was seated moments before.

"I'm fine," I stammered. "Did you make coffee at least?" I asked, willing myself to move on to the kitchen.

"Coffee. It's exactly the sort of monoculture crop that takes advantage of growers in developing and underdeveloped nations."

"I just wanted a morning cup of coffee, not a beatnik geopolitical platform."

"It's nighttime."

"Pardon?"

"You said morning cup of coffee. It's Saturday night. You slept all day again."

"What time is it?"

"Like ten. Ten-thirty."

"Oh," I said. I felt oddly defeated.

"Sit down. I'll make your coffee."

"Without a lecture?"

She was opening cabinet doors. She frowned when she removed a canister of the grocery store shelf variety. "You really should buy organic. And you should look for free trade brands," she said. "It's a new century, man. There are organic whole bean suppliers that cut out the middleman and provide the growers better profit margins. They reinvest locally where the beans are grown."

"How do you know all this?"

"I read things."

"Just not textbooks."

She looked angry. "*More* than textbooks. I don't sleep that well, so I read a lot. And I don't drink coffee."

"What do you drink?"

"Mostly water."

"I'm sure I'm in good hands then," I said as I watched her pouring coffee into the filter without measuring. "What are you doing here on a Saturday night?"

"I told you. I was thinking."

"Oh, right. Employing my little sanctum for some meditation. What were you thinking about?"

"Lots of things."

"No music tonight?"

"I like quiet when I think."

"You can't think at home?"

"Not as well."

"Why is that?"

"Because someone's always hovering, asking annoying questions."

"Oops. Sorry."

"Have you ever noticed how people ask lots of questions but hardly ever listen to the answers? My parents have answers they want to hear and answers they think they will hear. They're so busy listening for the answers they think they will hear, they don't really listen to what I say."

"There's a difference between what they want to hear and what they expect to hear?"

"A world of difference."

"What do they want to hear?"

"That I'm fine. Only they'd never believe me if I said I was fine. They want to hear that I'm doing well in school, that I'm fulfilling my potential. That's a big thing around my house. They want to hear that I am planning ahead, thinking about college. They want to hear that I'm happy."

"What do they expect to hear?"

"That I'm turning into my brother," she said and stopped.

"Tell me about your parents."

"You have to understand. They feel they failed. My parents are both smart, successful, driven people. They like to be in control. My dad's a software engineer. My mom has two Masters and runs a community health clinic. Dad runs marathons. Mom started her own charity. They just don't always have time to focus full attention on their kids." She paused, frowning while she scooped coffee. I didn't know if she frowned at the coffee or at what she was telling me. "I don't mean that like it sounds," she said. "They aren't neglectful or anything. Just distracted. They're good parents. It's just that, we'd… Well, there's lots of guilt at my house."

I had forgotten about the pain of my bruised ribs or the brief flash of anger. I stood at the opposite side of the kitchen counter listening. "Guilt," I said. "For not being able to prevent what your brother did."

"Yeah, of course. They think they could have stopped it. I think the same way. Like, I should have known. Only I didn't know. I mean my brother was no angel. He liked to test people. He pushed limits. But I never expected this. My parents were blind-sided. I guess with suicide you always are. Maybe we shouldn't have been. It's hard not to be suspicious of what you think you should have known. Looking backward you think everything's a sign. So like my mom thinks, well, Danny got his ears pierced without permission, so that should have been a sign that he was experimenting with identity. Just showed up at dinner one night with these huge plugs stuck through his ears. The shit hit the fan. I'm talking go looking for a bunker. Dad went ballistic. Accused him of being on drugs. Mom was convinced she'd failed as a parent. All she could talk about was how he would regret it in the future. That's a big theme with my mom—regret. Only now Mom thinks she should have seen the earrings as him calling out for help, like earrings are the natural precursor to trying to off yourself by whirling around the room with your neck tied to a ceiling fan."

I winced at the nonchalance of her description. "Now they scrutinize everything you do and say."

"It's like they think if they listen just right, they'll hear when I'm formulating my suicide plan. Like listening to a song backward for the secret message. You know, 'The Walrus was Paul.' Monika's going to slit her wrists in a Jell-O bath. They're so busy listening that they don't actually listen at all."

"Thus the hovering."

"The hovering. Mom likes to pretend she's behaving like a mother bird. Only she feels more like a vulture."

"Have you told her that?"

"Like a bajillion times. Only she can't hear me."

"Your dad?"

"He moves freely through the stages with no order. He's in full-on denial right now. His gig is acting like everything is normal. Like Danny will wake up one day and we'll have him back. Sold his Audi and bought a frickin' Subaru wagon. What's that tell you?"

"Denial can be very real. Palpable even."

"Have you ever been around someone who is suicidal?" she asked.

"Suicidal? No."

"It's different than other kinds of death."

"You have lots of death experiences?" I asked, sounding meaner than I wished.

"Three grandparents. A great-uncle and cousin. My friend in elementary school in a car accident. Another car accident and another friend last year. Two dogs, one that I witnessed. It ran in front of a car when I was supposed to have it on a leash. I was eight. It took him like ten minutes to die. Right there in my lap, panting."

"I'm sorry," I said.

"You?" she asked, apparently taking no offense at the tone I'd used when asking the question.

"I've not been a stranger to it."

I saw her look instinctively to the one other piece of art I owned, a framed family caricature we had done on a beach vacation that hung above the end table next to my recliner, but to give her credit, she offered no comment and asked no questions.

"I'm sure you're right," I said. "Facing a suicide by someone you love must be altogether different than any other kind of loss."

"Let's just say there's no suicide section in the greeting card aisle. People seem uncomfortable when your Christmas card photo shows the family gathered in the old hospital vegetable patch."

"How long ago did he…?" I didn't know how to phrase the question.

"Enter the patch? Last summer," she said flatly. "Not long after he and his friends trashed your garden. I thought we should have an anniversary party but we couldn't agree on the proper party theme. My vote was for clowns. They're festive, you know, but a little creepy. I don't know where a clown party fits into Kübler-Ross, but I'm sure it belongs there somewhere. If not, it should."

"In the grand scheme of grief, a year isn't a very long time, even if it seems an eternity."

"Yeah, well, I think I'm supposed to be nearing the acceptance stage but apparently I'm stuck at pissed-off-voice-your-emotions-through-sarcasm. I'm not sure that's one of the official Kübler-Ross categories."

"I'm not sure real acceptance ever comes," I said, ignoring her sarcasm.

"Yeah, well, anywho," she said. "None of this has anything to do with what I was thinking about."

"And just what was that?"

"About your art."

"My art?"

"Yes, your art."

"I'm no artist."

"Then what are you? What would you call this if not art?"

"I do it because I find it relaxing."

"I think they're beautiful. People are too quick to dismiss the power of simplicity. The detail is amazing. You've spent time in all these cities?"

"Yes."

"When you worked as a writer?"

"Yes."

"There's something so stark about them that makes them compelling. But it's funny," she said. "They feel lonely. I think that's why they are so moving, more than their simplicity."

"Lonely?"

"There are no people," she said. "You draw entire cities without people."

"I don't have the talent to draw people."

"I think you don't want to."

I said, "It's just how I see cities when I think of them."

"There must be people in the pictures you draw from."

"I don't use pictures."

"Then how...?" she started. She eyed me suspiciously. "You draw from memory?"

"Yes."

"Entirely?"

"Yes."

"That's insane."

"Like I said, busywork."

"Most artists are afraid of scale like this. Too much space to fill. Too much room for the mistakes to show. I know what I'm talking about. In murals, it's all about scale. It's like going out in public naked, like to the mall or something. But I struggle to get detail into my work."

"They're line drawings," I said. "Really they're not detailed at all."

"Oh yeah," she said. "What city is this?" she asked, pointing to a cityscape that stretched six feet along the tops of several shelving units.

"Chicago."

"Close your eyes," she said.

"What—" I protested.

"Close them," she demanded. I complied in what apparently was now a bad habit. "What's the heavily shaded building with the two spikes coming out of the top?"

"The building with the X braces?"

"Yeah."

"Your spikes are radio antennas. It's the John Hancock Center," I said. "Anybody who has ever been to Chicago knows that."

"Don't peek," she said. "How many floors have you drawn here?" I could hear her counting under her breath.

"One hundred," I answered without hesitation, seeing the building again perfectly in my mind. "You can't see them all in this view because some are blocked by other buildings. Well, you can see bits of them. There's a restaurant on the ninety-fifth floor. The two spires are white and they contain more than fifty radio and television antennas. On the ninety-fourth floor there's a section of windows that have been replaced with wire mesh so that visitors can hear the city traffic and the wind coming off the lake."

"No details, huh?"

"I wanted to be an architect as a kid."

"I thought you wanted to be a musician."

"Tell me you don't have competing interests."

"Competing interests," she said, with a grunted dismissal. "My teachers tell me I don't have any interests at all. You should hear my school counselor talk about the emptiness of my college apps."

"Maybe you just have trouble staying focused for the long haul."

"Like I should be listening to you, Mister 'I've got the building details down cold and no people.' Jesus, who draws an empty city?"

I shrugged.

"All these windows and no one looking out any of them."

"If there were people, you'd want to know what they were

looking at. You would wonder what they were thinking. What their lives were like. You'd want to know why they were looking out a window instead of working or eating. I see the city as its own personality. I'm interested in the buildings. That's enough."

"That's the bitch of people, huh? They have lives and relationships and pasts."

"And agendas," I added. "Politics. Idiosyncrasies. Secrets."

"Such a pessimist," she said.

"We can't all be such myopic little optimists."

"I'm not."

"Right. You just want to save the world, one gnome at a time."

"We can't save the world," she said. "I think we're doomed for sure. I mean, wake up and smell the coffee. Am I right? We're screwed. I'm really not an optimist. But I'm not a nihilist either. I can know we're toast and still believe there is such a thing as morality."

"Hence saving neighbors who don't ask for saving."

"Just human decency."

"You assume humans are worth showing decency."

"Maybe I'm just willing to admit I'm in denial. Unlike you."

"What am I in denial about?" I protested.

"I'm not the one taking the time to draw the things humans construct."

I shrugged.

She moved about the room with her head tilted to view all the other cityscapes I'd tacked high on the walls.

"How long does it take you to complete one?"

"Three or four months, typically. Sometimes more."

"No one sees them?"

"I do."

"Some of these I know. I mean, some are obvious. New York. Seattle. San Francisco. I don't know this one," she said, stopping.

"Houston," I said.

"And this?"

"Denver. Atlanta, Charlotte," I said, my eyes moving down the line.

"No LA."

"It's an incredibly boring skyline," I said.

"What are you working on now?"

"Philly."

"Nothing international? You should draw Paris. You've been there, right?"

I nodded.

"If you drew Paris, you'd have to draw people. You can't draw Paris without Parisians."

"See, there you go," I said. "I guess I'll have to stick to the homegrown."

"Because American cities don't have people."

"In the historical sense, that's practically true," I said. "Some barely have identities. They are still inventing themselves. They can still be viewed as abstractions."

"Is that what you are doing?"

"It's mindless doodling."

"I don't buy it," she said.

"You think you know what this reveals. You've got some window into my soul now," I said.

"Cities viewed from a distance. It's not rocket science. People give way too much credit to psychologists when it's all really pretty apparent if you pay attention." She sighed and looked at me, then turned away. "All those windows and not a single face. You do the math."

I turned away from the drawing of Philadelphia, intent on the coffee I'd still not gotten.

"What I can't figure out," she said, "is what happened to make you so afraid of people." She followed me toward the kitchen, stopping at the incomplete face of Philadelphia spread across the table. "Did you grow up in a city?"

"Boston," I said.

"Ah ha," she nearly shouted. "You try to hide your accent.

That explains New England. Dartmouth, all that. But there's no Boston," she said, scanning the room from where she stood at the table.

"No Boston," I said.

"Didn't you like it there?"

"I loved Boston."

"Then why haven't you drawn it? You know it better than any place, right?"

I let the comment go. I tried to change the subject. "You ever live in a city?"

"No," she said. "Born and raised right here. Smallsville. White milk, white bread. I want to live in a city. I'll leave when I graduate."

"What city?"

"Oh, I don't know. Anyplace I can go become another person." She was studying the parts of Philadelphia I had completed. There were big gaps in the skyline still, like a second grader's smile. "Just look at all those places to hide," she said absently.

"Around every corner," I said.

"And behind every window."

Monika left a short time later, worried that her mother would soon be checking up on her. "If she didn't give me a cell phone," she'd said, displaying the device she kept in a hand-knitted bag, "she'd probably never let me leave the house."

"Just where are you now?" I asked.

"I'm at a friend's," she said. "Even though she worries about what kind of influences they might be, it makes her happy to think that I have friends."

"You don't?"

"Sure, but most of the time they annoy me. There's so much drama in high school. Now my mother, she was a cheerleader and in student government, on prom committee, the whole queen dork thing. She can't understand why I'm not just like her. She thinks I'm some sort of evolutionary throwback. She probably checks for gills when I'm asleep."

"Maybe she was abducted and you're not a mutant but an alien," I offered.

"Thanks a lot," she said. "I suppose you loved high school, Mr. Dartmouth man. You probably were class president."

"I was in chess club. Need I say more?"

"No, that covers it."

"High school will be over soon. You should try and enjoy it."

She looked at me skeptically and seemed to take in her surroundings once again before mounting the stairs. "Don't decide to become an advice columnist," she said, skepticism turning to assault. Then, halfway up the staircase, she said, "By the way, you look a lot better."

"I might survive," I said.

"Maybe you will after all."

"You'll forgive me for not showing you out."

"You should call me if you need something. I wrote my cell number on a piece of paper on the kitchen counter."

"No phone," I said, holding my empty hands before me.

"Are you sure this isn't a cave?" she said, waving her arms in her usual frenzy. "I can't check on you tomorrow. Sundays are off limits. Family time. I get to watch my dad watch football."

"No harm, I didn't ask you to."

She looked hurt and started up the stairs, her big boots clomping.

16

I fell asleep in the living room recliner. I awoke with a jolt that flamed the pain in my ribs and then sat in the dark for two hours before forcing myself to go to bed.

It was well after noon before I awoke again. I sat before the Philadelphia skyline and did not pick up a pen. An hour passed. Two. I stared at the incomplete city. Every window, every ledge seemed little more than a sniper perch, every shadow a place the sun would never reach.

The handwritten manuscript remained untouched as well, the tablets stacked in a nest of books riddled with sticky notes. Twice I started for the woodstove before the sheer time behind the manuscript's development stopped me. I traded it for a library book and soon found I'd read the same page three times. What next? I wondered. An abscessed tooth? An aneurism? Another visit from city officials bearing a letter of condemnation?

My head crowded with unbidden memories. Faces hovered in my mind, bringing a tug of fresh pain that centered on my bruised ribs. With the return of faces from the past came the voice I could not quiet. My own. I've become sick of my voice. It comes at me monotonously, like a voice-over for a poorly filmed home video. I suppose it is illogical that, troubled by a cacophony of cluttered thought, I should seek silence, when silence only amplifies the sounds within my head.

I forced myself to rise, determined to retreat to the garden. I was not in the kind of physical condition to accomplish any real work, still the simplicity of fresh air and late afternoon sun offered a useful prescription for both mental and physical health.

The garden's condition mirrored my own, that early fall appearance of plants weary under the weight of recent production, their chlorophyll beginning to fail with exhaustion. There would soon be a great deal of cleanup required and the dead bodies of plants would need composting to enrich the future for living ones. I found refreshment sitting among the plants and watching the movements of birds on the ponds below the house. I remained outdoors until after nightfall, walking among the ponds in the ravine bottom, each step offering renewed but manageable pain from my bruised body and the promise of healing for my battered mind.

17

Days passed with eerie symmetry. I tried but could not face ink in either medium. I spent undue time simply sitting without movement. Occupying space. Ruminating.

On Thursday, in an attempt to place attainable obstacles for my new convalescent life path, I decided I would attempt the stairs and depart through the front door. I needed to check my neglected mailbox. Mounting the stairs, I saw that a note or letter of one sort or another had been taped to the glass of my front door. An unsummoned tremor rolled through my ribs. Was this announcement of more action by the city?

Reaching the top of the stairs, the glimmer of sunlight passing through the document taped on my door, I saw that it was no official correspondence but a note scrawled with handwriting. I opened the door and retrieved the note, only to discover, to my dismay, that it had been attached to my door with used chewing gum. "Monika," I muttered aloud. The note was written on the back of a completed sheet of calculus homework. I saw no corrections and no grade indication—another failure to launch, I assumed.

> Stopped by to check on you. Didn't answer my knocks. (Guess you know that.) Door locked. Hope you're not dead. Actually, come to think of it, that really is concerning. What if you are? Dead. What am I supposed to do? Hope you are out. Or you decided to go to the hospital. I'd like to know you're not dead.
>
> Will check in on you again later. Have appointment after school or I'd stop then.
>
> Monika

She certainly had fully embraced the sentence fragment. Perhaps the writing section of the SAT would haunt her. The note was, typical I thought, undated. I felt a bit bad I was causing her worry. If I were in her shoes, it would be disconcerting. But then I'd never asked for her shoes. And she'd passed time inside my home, she'd seen the french doors, had it never occurred to her to venture to that other portal of my domain?

How long ago had she written the note? I began to picture the arrival of firemen and rescue personnel. A SWAT team taking a battering ram to my door. I guessed that I somehow needed to assure her that there was no body in need of retrieval. Grumbling, I descended the stairs for a pen.

The second trip up the stairs felt like a North Face ascent. The pen chose not to write on the vertical plane of the door, so I had to remove the note. A rock approaching the proximity of flatness offered the closest thing to a writing surface I could locate, and the resulting response made my reply appear like the handwriting of a six-year-old. Perhaps my regression was complete.

M,

I have rejoined the living. Thank you for checking on me.

I spent undue time contemplating the proper salutation and ultimately decided on the option of not using one at all. Better to not invite an extended correspondence. Yet then, in the most counter-productive of fashions, I added a line:

PS: Turn in your homework!

I moved to return the note to the door, but it appeared the gum would require new moisture if it were to work again as an adhesive. Frustrated, I closed the corner of the page in the door and locked it. I immediately had second thoughts on the postscript, but what was I to do, scratch it out and complete the arc of childhood regression? Worse still, I had violated one of my own steadfast writing rules and had used that most annoying of all pieces of punctuation—the exclamation mark! Clearly the SUV should have been going faster.

My body was responding to the benefits of movement. I experienced one of those glorious fall days where it seemed summer had briefly revisited and the skies were crystal clear and the air temperature was ideal for exertion. I remained hopeful that the weather and the exercise were proving restorative and my life could return to something approaching normalcy.

Upon my return, the agent of correspondence on my door had moved back near its original position, annoyingly reposted with yet another wad of gum. Where was a truancy officer when needed? I noted the time: 11:30 a.m.

Glad you are alive. Feeling better? Will come by after school.
Monika

Great. Visitors. Just what I needed. I tore the note from the door. A big piece of it remained stuck to the gum. I'd have to climb the stairs—again—with a scraper and some glass cleaner.

Determined to kill two birds with one stone, at five minutes before three o'clock I ascended my stairs, scraper in hand. After completing the task, I felt conspicuous waiting by my door. I wished I had something to lean on and remove some of the weight from the sore knee, knowing all the while that such a wish only augmented the pathetic portrait. What was I doing, I wondered, waiting for a seventeen-year-old stranger with a penchant for vandalism? It took twenty minutes of pretense at being occupied after cleaning the glass, but Monika arrived as threatened. I made a show of making one last round of glass cleaning.

"He lives," she said as she approached. "Took you long enough to respond to my note."

"I was convalescing."

"I was worried sick. For all I knew, you were dead down there. I couldn't decide if you were dead or just avoiding me."

"Now why would I want to do that?"

"I almost called the cops but I couldn't smell anything."

"Pardon?"

"Aren't dead bodies supposed to put off a smell? But then I guess I don't really know what I was supposed to smell. I read a story once, like freshman year, about a woman who killed her lover in her wedding bed. They sprinkled something around her house to cover up the smell."

"Lime."

"What?"

"The townspeople sprinkled lime around the house foundation."

"Oh yeah, that's right. It's like the people were protecting the lady. They didn't want people to talk about her, so they were covering up her crime. Only they didn't know it was a crime yet."

"The story is by Faulkner," I said, refusing to go down her misguided garden path.

"There you go. Dartmouth would be so proud of you."

I shrugged.

"I was really worried," she said.

"I'm sorry," I said, and I meant it. "I didn't know you would be checking on me."

"I told you I would. Besides, who else is going to do it?"

She had a point.

'You really should invest in a phone," she said. "Or maybe an intercom, like in an apartment building."

"I'm really not looking to encourage solicitors."

"Oh, right, the hermit thing."

"I'm not a hermit."

"Then what are you?"

"Monika!" I stopped her with a harshness that surprised me and inflamed a jolt to a rib.

"Right. Sorry. I forgot. You're the gregarious one. A regular bon vivant. An epicure."

"Practicing vocabulary for the SAT, are we?"

"Possibly."

"Good for you."

"See, there you go. You should help me study, Mr. Dartmouth Man."

"Thanks. I'll pass."

"Oh, come on. I need someone smart to talk to."

"To? At."

"That's mean."

"See, I'd be a poor tutor. Or sparring partner, as the case would be."

"You can at least quiz me tomorrow."

"What's tomorrow?"

"I'm taking you inside a piece of local history."

"Excuse me?"

"There's an open house tomorrow at a historic home that's scheduled to be torn down. It's never been open to the public before."

"I think our one little adventure together has filled my quota."

"No gnomes involved. You like art and architecture and history, right?"

"Certainly, but—"

"This place could be gone as soon as next week. Bulldozer city. You might not get another opportunity."

"I appreciate the offer, however—"

"The university wants to tear it down. You can guess what they want to build."

"I have no idea."

"Sure you do. Guess."

"I'd prefer not to."

"Oh, come on. It's practically obvious."

"I don't know. A football stadium."

"Really, that's your guess? In a historic district?"

"I didn't know it was in a historic district."

"But it's a historic home. Where else would it be?"

"Monika, I really don't have an interest—"

"They want to build a parking lot."

"A parking lot?"

"Yes, tear down beautiful architecture, a piece of living history, for a parking lot. You should be outraged."

"Why don't you fight to preserve it rather than wasting your time with me?"

"Oh, I am."

"Of course you are."

"You'll want to join me once you see it. I'll pick you up this time tomorrow." She turned to leave.

"I'd really rather not."

"Be ready," she said, walking away. "I'm not taking no for an answer."

I had moved here thinking I would build a life. In my moments of greater self-honesty, I might admit that I was hoping to build a refuge. But now I feared I'd actually constructed a prison. I was at a loss for what course of action to pursue. Lock the doors and hide in my basement? Be conveniently absent should city officials or teenage do-gooders arrive?

I'd prefer not to, I thought, even as I ascended the stairs at three o'clock the following afternoon. I had resolved that I'd get some gardening in that afternoon, be industrious upon Monika's arrival and beg off her invitation. When she honked her pathetic, ill-sounding horn, I thought I would wait her out, make her get out of the car and approach me and see my industry and accept my preference against house touring. Except she honked a second time, and then a third, so I was forced to walk to where she was parked at the curb.

"Shake a leg, Mr. Green Jeans." She reached over and opened the passenger door. Stupidly, I got in.

I think I was expecting a house out of a horror movie, something once stately but revealing its neglect and suffering under the onslaught of decay and the general disrepair of an aging neighborhood too near the blight of an abandoned downtown. True, the neighborhood showed all the marks of neglect and the frequent blasphemy of old homes having been converted to multi-unit apartments, but the house, like several on the block, still held much of its original charm. A large Craftsman with a huge covered front patio and limestone foundation, the house suggested taste and understated style. The interior, although full of dark wood in the forms of many built-ins and bookshelves, plank floors and wide cornices, was filled with natural light from ample windows. While clearly dated and needing some TLC, the home still exuded the charms of its era.

All in all, it was a pleasant tour. Monika proved surprisingly quiet and moved about the home as if it were a museum. There was not a gnome in sight.

"What'd you think?" she asked as we descended the steps from its front porch.

"Charming," I said.

"Way better than anything you'd ever find in the 'burbs," she said.

"Everyone has their own taste."

"You're not really going to defend homogenization, are you?"

"Homogenization, pasteurization, culturalization. I'm pretty ambivalent about the entire dairy processing industry," I replied, trying to be cute.

She ignored me. "Don't you think it's criminal?" she said.

"Homogenization?"

"The fact that they're going to tear this place down." We had reached her car and she remained at the driver-side door, apparently awaiting agreement.

"It does seem a shame. I thought you were going to protect it."

"I tried. There's a committee. They're trying to preserve old homes all over the city. They promote gentrification."

"I can get on board with that."

"Too late."

"Pardon."

"This one's a goner."

"I thought there was a committee."

"There is," she said, clearly exasperated. "But the bureau-crats have all the power. They're deciding its fate as we speak."

"Who is?"

"The city council. Right now. There's a hearing just a few blocks from here."

"But what about the committee?"

"They filed all the paperwork. Delivered the petitions. Did their thing. But this is a losing battle, my friend."

"And you're the patron of lost causes?"

She ignored me again. "They're probably proclaiming this block's fate any minute now. There will be a protest of course. A small one. A few of the righteous making their feelings known into the din of the ambivalent."

"Why aren't you there?"

"Oh, we're going."

I groaned.

"You mean you're a big fan of parking lots?"

"You said it's too late."

"It is. But we have to be heard, don't we?"

"What's the point?" I said grumpily.

"There will be another house after this one and then another and another."

"Exactly," I said.

"Come hear the decision with me. Maybe you'll be inspired to hold a protest sign or speak out against evil."

"Or what? You'll hold me hostage?"

"Just come along for the ride. We're a dozen blocks away. We'll hear the council decision, the committee will make a for-mal statement, we'll hand out a few flyers so people can be informed about future actions developers are planning. The whole thing will take like fifteen minutes. Your gardening can wait fifteen minutes. You can just sit in the shade if you want."

I didn't see what choice I had, having accepted her ride to downtown, not to mention her help over the past week.

As we passed under a yellow light at an intersection, she tilted her head exaggeratedly to the left and then looked down the street we crossed. "My mural is just a couple blocks down that way," she said. "Maybe we'll drive by on the way home." I think she was making a Monika effort at nonchalance.

I had to admit that I was curious to see what oddities might appear in her work.

We drove the handful of blocks into the old, decaying heart of our city's dated downtown. It had seen a brief surge of futuristic hope in the late 1970's and banks, primarily, joined by a few other businesses, had invested in what they thought was the beginnings of a commercial center. A dozen multi-story buildings, mostly square, uninspired architecture had sprung up, averaging ten stories with the tallest reaching fourteen floors. They clustered in a two-block area, and as businesses fled for malls and then box-stores, the usual detritus had taken over, including all the vestiges of city and county government. Let it be said, this was not a scene to inspire a future drawing.

City Hall occupied the first two floors of a former bank tower, its primary entrance opening onto a half-block concrete square that sported what once may have been a fountain. Quite the heat sink, if you ask me, a square of unrelenting cement surrounded by the tight quarters of rising multi-story buildings manufactured from prefabricated concrete.

We'd arrived, predictably I thought, a fraction too late, and a bespectacled and tired-looking woman with unruly hair was just finishing a statement condemning the city, the university, and "unchecked, uninspired greed in the guise of development." It appeared the local paper may have sent a reporter but this was certainly not the terrain of TV remote crews or rhetoric-fueled throngs. Aside from a few bored-looking workers on smoke breaks, two policemen, and a handful of homeless people, the organizers of the "protest" were the only people present to receive her words. Talk about preaching to the choir. A number of them held protest signs, all less colorful and less imaginative than the two Monika had retrieved from the hostage compartment of her car. She'd thrust one in my hand when we reached the square that read:

PROTECT YOUR PARADISE,
A PARKING LOT COMING YOUR WAY SOON!

I appreciated the Joni Mitchell reference, as well as the image she had painted of a big yellow taxi plowing into a house, the shrapnel of its bricks exploding with cartoonish zeal.

Monika struck up a conversation with two protestors, a couple in their mid-sixties. Together they seemed to form a plan and soon the two dozen protestors had rallied into a circle and began a chant:

MORE PRESERVATION, NOT MORE PARKING!

They marched in a small circle, shouting their slogan over and over. On their third circuit, apparently I'd strayed too near and Monika grabbed my elbow, dragging me into the line of marchers. Somewhere a megaphone appeared and the woman who had read the statement launched a steady stream of invectives against development. A drum appeared as mysteriously as the megaphone had and it began to beat out the chant.

At some point I found myself looking up, my head craned to see straight up the enclosing exterior walls of the surrounding buildings. I saw a blur of windows and ledges and overhangs. Perhaps it was the awkward angle of my tilted head, or maybe it was dizziness brought on by turning a circle. Perhaps it was latent effects from the injuries I'd received or perhaps I'd simply not minded my water intake, but I felt suddenly nauseous and heavy perspiration flooded down my sides and from my hairline. I tried to lower my gaze and control the dizziness, but it seemed as if I'd lost muscular control and I continued the neck-aching tilt, examining the buildings around me, which then began to swirl.

I tried to step out of line but someone touched my shoulder and redirected my path. I stumbled. The sky that appeared between buildings shrunk, as if the buildings had begun to lean into the space. I stumbled again and sunk to one knee—the good knee, so I still had some sense of self-preservation.

I became aware that I heard a kind of howl. It occurred to

me that the drum, like the chanting and the megaphone had all stopped.

The howling did not.

And then I realized that the howl emanated from me.

I was still looking above, taking in a particular darkened window where a washing platform was anchored, the glass opaque and reflecting the late fall sun. I forced my gaze away. Lowered my head. The little circle of protestors all stood motionless.

Monika stepped toward me, her arms extended. It looked like she wanted a hug. She seemed frozen in the stance. I shut my mouth on the foreign sound that arose from my throat. I forced myself to my feet, shook my head, and stepped backward, away from her. I continued backing until I felt the hard, rough surface of a wall. I touched its solidity, my fingers behind me tracing the mortar lines and the uneven brick face.

Monika's hands remained extended, palms facing out. She was speaking, but it took me some time to comprehend what she said. If a portrait of concern existed, her face was its model. The spinning I felt had slowed but not ceased. I held my hands against the brick, looking for anchor.

I realized that Monika was trying to soothe me. I wanted nothing of it. Embarrassed, confused, I only wanted to make an exit. Yet I was dependent on her to leave.

"Get me out of here," I managed. "Please."

To my surprise, she didn't say a word, simply reached out and grabbed my hand, turned me, and, releasing my hand and grasping my elbow, guided me along the wall and out of the plaza.

When we reached the car, she opened my door and waited as I got in the seat. She could have been waiting upon a toddler or an elderly person—a study in patience. Once behind the steering wheel, she signaled and quickly entered traffic. She'd not spoken. More surprising, her usual fidgeting, the movements that often coursed through her like tremors, were not present. When she at last spoke, she simply asked, "Do I need to take you to a hospital or something?"

"No, take me home please," I said, my voice barely rising above a whisper.

She looked at me, sizing me up. "Are you hurt?"

I shook my head.

We drove in uncomfortable silence. Monika's driving appeared to lack her usual aggression. I watched her work the gears as we departed from a stoplight, still trying to make sense of what had happened. Glacially, it occurred to me that Monika was frightened. Why wouldn't she be, trapped in the company of a howling maniac?

"Thank you," I said, eventually, feeling I needed to remind her that her passenger was human.

She did not reply.

"For rescuing me," I said.

She turned to look at me. I could see the wariness in her eyes, the way one looks at a large dog that seems calm but with whom you've suffered past moments of aggression, like experiencing your calf in its clenched mouth. "What happened back there?" she asked after a long bit of scrutiny.

"I think maybe I'm dehydrated," I said feebly.

"Right."

"I really don't know what happened," I admitted. I felt the moment deserved honesty.

"That was really freaky."

I had to agree with her.

She spoke with a hesitancy that I'd not witnessed within her before. "Was that normal?"

"Normal? Outside of institutions featuring padded walls? No, I don't think 'normal' applies."

"You don't have to be snarky. You know what I mean."

I did, of course, know exactly what she meant. "No," I said. "That was a new one."

She looked at me with renewed suspicion, and we drove the rest of the way home in silence.

When we pulled to the curb before my front door, I hesitated before getting out of the car. I felt I owed Monika something, an explanation, a reassurance that I wasn't insane or dangerous. I fumbled but could find no such reassurance. I hadn't lied to her. Whatever had seized me during the protest was an entirely new and quite unsettling experience. I scrambled for something to say, at last landing upon this: "We didn't get to see your mural."

"What?"

"You said that we were close to your mural, that you'd drive by. Because of my little episode, we didn't."

"Oh, that."

"I'd like to see it sometime," I said.

"Really?"

"Really."

"Okay." And then, as I got out of the car, she asked, "Are you going to be all right?"

I nodded.

"I'd tell you to call if you needed something, but you know," she said, shrugging.

"I know," I said. "I'll send up smoke signals or something." I shut the car door, turned, and started along the path worn to my door, wondering if I shouldn't shut it behind me permanently.

18

At three o'clock on the following Monday afternoon, I was working in the garden. The weekend had felt like it lasted for decades. I had passed an unhealthy amount of time in my bed. Physically, I was feeling moderately better, although much of my left torso was badly bruised, as if a poorly trained tattoo artist had attempted a relief map of Africa. My work day, if one should call it such, had remained a struggle, although I'd forced myself to take notes from some musical historiography texts and from interviews with musicians whose very manner of speaking belonged in another age. Philadelphia, however, remained a city under quarantine.

Really, the garden required almost no work. It was the time of waiting for the first hard frost and all that dying. I retired down the stairs.

Yet, at 3:10, when I heard the sharp knock on the glass of my front door, I could not suppress a smile.

"Were you serious when you said you wanted to see my mural?" Monika asked without an attempt at greeting.

"I was."

"Do you think you can manage to not freak out? No anxiety attacks or whatever that was?"

"I'll do my level best."

"'Cause I'm really not down with that brand of nuts. I mean, I've been around plenty of crazy, but that doesn't mean I like it."

"I hear you. Loud and clear," I said, all the while wondering if I were in a position to issue any sort of promises.

"Okay, well come on then."

"Now?"

"You've got someplace to be?"

I shrugged, closed the door, locked it, and followed her to her car.

Once we were in, she nearly shouted, "Seatbelts." I complied. Satisfied, she asked, "Was asking about my mural some awkward attempt at being nice?"

"It was."

She turned the car off abruptly. "Sorry to disappoint," she said.

"You haven't yet," I said. "Now let's see this art."

She eyed me suspiciously. "You're a strange one."

"Look who's talking."

She shrugged and restarted the car, pulling away from the curb with her usual vigor. "I can't believe you haven't seen it. It's kind of hard to miss."

"As perhaps you've noticed, I don't get out much."

"Just teenager's parties, accident scenes, and public protests."

"Exactly."

"You're a strange one, Mr. Magoo," she said while accelerating. The engine responded with the sound of BBs hitting a tin can.

"I've never said otherwise."

"Is it a clinical condition? Does it have a label?"

"Does what have a label?"

"Whatever this is. This whole fear of the outdoors. Do you have a diagnosis?"

I laughed, not knowing if it was an appropriate response. She looked at me as if annoyed. "I was just thinking about that word 'outdoors' the other day," I explained. It's a funny word, don't you think? I mean, did the person who built the very first door come up with the word? Was he sitting there in his cave with his brand-new door closed to keep the heat in and the predators out, admiring it, thinking I should go outdoors now?"

"He?"

"Huh?"

"You said he. What if the first door was invented by a woman?"

"True, although we could have the whole debate about prehistoric social groupings and evolutionary development as differentiated by gender, but that's all beside the point."

"What is the point?"

"That when we created an indoor world, our thoughts about the rest of the world changed, so our language had to change too."

"So why'd you chose to live indoors?" she asked.

"It's not so much indoors as under-doors really."

"Okay. Even weirder. Why are you afraid?"

"I'm not."

"You're not?"

"Not of the outdoors. I just don't do well around people. I actually spend a lot of time outdoors. I like walking around the ponds. I get nervous around a lot of commotion."

"I've noticed."

I shrugged.

"Why?"

"It's really just become a habit, I think."

"Then why didn't you become nature boy. Live in an actual cave. Catch your supper every night. You could have gone to Alaska. You could live in a cabin and play with dynamite like that one guy. That one in Montana."

"What guy?"

"That guy. What's his name? Kazakhstan or whatever his name is. You know, the guy who mailed people bombs."

"Kaczynski? The Unabomber?"

"Bingo."

"It's precisely people like him I wanted to get away from. Please don't make that comparison."

"I don't mean that you're like him. I just mean he intention-ally lived away; he wanted to become a kind of recluse, con-vinced that the world is a nightmare."

"The world *is* a nightmare," I said.

"There you go. You have a habit of making my arguments for me."

"Your usage of the word recluse seems rampant with negative connotations."

"Well, what other term would you use?"

I thought a moment and didn't answer.

"Name five of your friends," she commanded.

I stared out the windshield.

"Three," she said. "Name three friends." She paused.
"When's the last time you spoke to your family?"

"I wrote my mother a few weeks ago. Within a month." I felt
mildly vindicated.

"You wrote her. When is the last time you saw her?"

I remained silent.

"I'm serious," she said.

I sighed. "It's been a number of years. It was difficult. We
had trouble being so near one another without slipping into old
roles or trying to avoid certain uncomfortable memories."

"Your other family?"

"My father's dead. One brother I've seldom spoken to since
I moved here. My sisters and I exchange cards on holidays."

"I was serious earlier," she said. "Have you been diagnosed?"

"For what?"

She frowned. We drove in silence for a while. "I'm not
judging or anything," she said after another mile. "It's just that
there's help. My mom was diagnosed bipolar years ago. She's
been on meds that have helped, but she won't take them anymore. I think she's in love with the manic episodes. She won't
even go see her therapist, yet she makes me see one."

We parked in a block of retail businesses, one- and two-story
storefronts all constructed of differing colors of brick, boxy,
matter-of-fact upright buildings erected in the 1930s or 1940s,
all now undergoing their second- or third-generational cycle,
a block of thrift stores and coffee shops and homespun art
galleries. A throwback to the past, there was a seed shop on the
opposite side of the street. We'd parked directly in front of the
door to the Christian Scientist Reading Room. "It's on the other
side of the building," Monika said.

"What is?"

"The mural."

"Oh," I said and opened the car door. "By the way," I said as the car door squeaked. "I know my diagnosis. Mourning." If she heard me, she offered no acknowledgement.

I wasn't prepared for the mural. The intention, of course, with its location and sheer scale and its narrative qualities, was to offer full effect to the driver or passerby approaching from the street opposite the way we came. Instead, we entered a coffee shop where Monika waved to two college-aged women working the counter, crossed worn wood flooring through clusters of simple tables and scattered, comfortable-looking couches and chairs, and exited through a set of double doors opening to a patio. Outside were metal café tables and the pleasant surprise of a flower garden. It seemed the rare sort of public space where I could feel comfortable. A sort of pocket garden. Two sizable old trees, an oak and a maple, offered shade. Enchanting, all in all, for a constructed environment.

I had slowed upon my surprise at entering the patio, but Monika had not, and having crossed to stand against the opposite wall, she glared at me impatiently. She wore bulky cargo pants and a neutral-colored long sleeve shirt as if she were planning on a backpacking expedition. She looked vaguely militaristic were it not for purple striped socks pulled over her pants legs. She stood glowering at me. I moved to where she stood and did not turn around to face the mural until I had reached her. Then, for a moment, the old cliché "it took my breath away" suddenly proved literally true and I audibly gasped, a sound that received a wary bit of inspection from Monika.

Boldly imagined and vividly colored, her mural filled the two stories, from patio brick to sky and from alley to sidewalk. The brick face on which she'd painted the scene was unbroken save for a solitary two-paned window that featured an iron planter box at its base, one overflowing with colorful flowers and trailing vines. Monika had duplicated the window exactly, making its two panels appear to be four, only her created window was open and a woman leaned from it as if contemplating something below and far away. She seemed from another age and perhaps another place, as if the window and its occupant had been transported from Brooklyn in 1943. Monika had achieved the kind of third dimensionality that made the woman's body appear as if it penetrated the flat surface and leaned beyond the flower box duplicated at the window's base. A cigarette dangled from her left hand and looked as if it might be forgotten and allowed to fall at any moment. The created sky offered a permanent dusk that suggested the threat of a storm. A street scene framed the bottom third of the mural, the normalcy of the lives depicted there detached from the woman's and her far distant concentration. There was a kind of resignation in her posture and the line of her body, and she seemed entirely lonely despite the appearance of others passing in the street scene below her. The talent in the construction was astounding.

"Holy shit," I said, turning back to Monika.

"That bad?"

"That good. This is beautiful," I said. I took it all in again, mesmerized. "Why is she so sad?"

"She is longing for her past," Monika replied.

"She's so lonely," I said.

Monika did not reply. I watched her carefully. She had a look of quiet satisfaction. I turned again to the mural. It seemed etched as a relief against the sky. "It's stunning," I said. "Remarkable."

"Thanks. I thought you might appreciate it."

"Your parents must be so proud. I bet they drive by here every day. I know I would."

"They've never seen it."

"How is that possible? How could they have never seen it?"

"Don't hold it against them. I've never told them about it."

"This must have taken months."

She nodded.

"Where did they think you were all that time?"

"They thought I worked here, so see, in a way I never lied to them. Although in reality they probably thought I was out smoking crack or something."

"Children always think that kind of thing about their parents. It's almost never true."

"You don't know my parents."

"You need to show them this. It's downright cruel not to."

"They wouldn't get it."

"What's to get? It's beautiful. Anybody can see that."

"I hoped there's something more to it than being pretty," she said, looking glum.

"That's not what I meant. There's so much more."

"Tell me what you see."

"It's not just what I see but what I feel. I can feel her sadness. I can sense how detached she is. She's removed herself. Something, some circumstance or some longing has isolated her. She's afraid it's forever. There's a threat on the horizon. She feels it."

Monika chewed absently on a fingernail.

"I might have to come here and sit every day and keep her company," I said.

Monika shrugged, but I could see satisfaction in her expression. "Just doodling. Isn't that what you said about your cities?"

"My stuff belongs on butcher paper. Your work will be in galleries and museums one day."

"Most people think anything on a wall is graffiti."

"They'd be fools."

"You want a cup of coffee?"

"I thought you didn't drink coffee."

"I don't. But I'll have some tea."

"Only if we can drink it out here."

"It's awfully cold out."

"I don't care."

"Okay. You're buying. I'll help you pick out some beans too. You got a coffee grinder?"

I shook my head.

"Guess it's time to part with some of those millions you've got buried."

We ordered from a woman whose dreadlocks might have harbored several small animals. She proved pleasant and knowledgeable. Soon we were joined by another woman who wore a series of bangles on her arm that clicked and rung like music as she spoke. The warmth of her personality was nearly infectious. Soon she practically had me crawling inside barrels to smell and touch roasted beans. By the time I walked away from the register carrying my purchases in a bag constructed of hemp or used rags or some combination thereof, I'd received an encyclopedic (and stereophonic, with Monika chiming in regularly) lecture about coffee roasting, cultivation, South American micro-climates, and the economics of fair trade. I'd bought a grinder, two kinds of beans, a cup of steaming coffee, and a glass of some tea concoction for Monika. Once we returned to the patio her arguments were offered renewed credibility at my first sip.

"You like it?" Monika asked.

"You've converted me. The perfect accompaniment to the scenery," I said, raising a toast to the mural.

"I told you," she said. "Every dollar you spend is a decision. You can help feed a family or line some CEO's silk pocket, your choice."

"Pollyanna."

"God, you're such a pessimist. You see the ugly side of everything."

"This from the Miss Longing-for-a-distant-past artist."

"You're an asshole."

"Look, I'm not saying that trying to save the world isn't worth trying. It's just not realistic."

"Have you always been so paranoid?"

"Paranoid? Who said anything about paranoia? What are you talking about?"

"Paranoid in the belief that everybody's out to do harm. Your belief that no good can come of anything."

"Bone up on that vocabulary. I think skepticism is the word you're looking for, not paranoia. Welcome to your twenty-first century."

"And you don't believe there's a single thing you can do to make it better," she said, pointing a finger at me.

I shrugged.

"You're afraid to participate." She continued to level her accusatory finger. "Only you do, we all do. We cast our votes with our bank cards. You didn't get all those CDs lining your walls for free."

"Put your finger away."

"I'm just saying."

"I'm not disagreeing with you."

"*Your* solution is to crawl into your rabbit hole and disappear. Well, you're still here, buddy."

I shrugged like a teenager.

"What happened to make you such a pessimist? What was so awful that you walked out on your family?"

"Excuse me," I said, much louder than I intended. "I did no such thing."

"I just assumed."

"Don't assume. It's not becoming."

"I've seen the picture of your family."

"What do you mean? Have you gone through my things?"

"The painting. The caricature. I told you you're paranoid. Who else would it be besides your family?"

"And you naturally assumed I must have left them."

"I'm not making accusations. I just thought, given your lifestyle and all."

"My lifestyle."

"I assumed you chose to live alone."

"That will teach you to make assumptions," I said.

For the first time since I'd met Monika, she looked embarrassed rather than fidgety. Her face, usually abnormally white, had flushed. And still, in her typical fashion, she pushed forward. "What happened? The great American divorce?"

"They died," I said flatly.

"I'm so sorry," she stammered and grew redder. She patted my hand where it lay outstretched on the table top next to my cup of coffee. It seemed the sort of gesture I would expect from an old woman, someone regularly accustomed to death, not a seventeen-year-old wearing engineer boots and purple striped socks.

"So there you have it at last," I said. "Your crazy recluse has a tragic past."

"I didn't know," she said.

"How could you?"

"They were beautiful," she said. "I mean, the people in the painting. Your wife and your daughter. They were both very pretty."

"Stop trying to be nice. It's a caricature."

"What were their names?"

"Susan. My wife was Susan. Our daughter was Renee."

"How old was she?"

"Fourteen. Nearly fifteen. All she could talk about was getting her learner's permit. Well, that and this fixation she had on wanting to sing. And boys of course. Fourteen-year-old girls like to talk about boys."

"How long ago did they...they die?"

"Seven years ago. Renee would be older than you if she were alive. Twenty-one. An adult."

"Can I ask what happened?"

It was as if I had a cut that kept trying, with limited success, to form a scab, and Monika could not resist the temptation to work her fingernails under the edges. I knew the temptation well. There was some cruel satisfaction in plucking the scab away and seeing the emergence of fresh blood, some satisfaction too at rolling the remains, the blood-thickened, cratered skin between your fingers.

I looked at the mural instead of at Monika. I stared at the

woman she had created. The woman seemed like someone who understood loss. A person who understood loneliness. Monika's imagined woman held her lips parted as if she wanted to say something. Worry lines appeared on her forehead. Her eyes, frozen in a slight squint, gazed into the distance. I reasoned that her creator must know something about loss too.

I addressed myself to the mural. It was the best I could do.

"Do things ever seem desperate to you," I asked.

"Personally?"

"No, generally. I mean, what with the recession and the wars and a faltering democracy. All the people out of work. The ugly politics. Doesn't it seem like dark times?"

"Of course," she said. "People are dying all over the planet. I'm part of the first American generation that will earn less than our parents. Desperate is easy."

"I've been feeling it for a long time," I said. "Years." I sighed, thinking. Still sidestepping too. "This really has nothing to do with your question, but how old were you on September 11th?" I asked.

"Ten."

"So, you probably don't remember a whole lot. Or rather you remember the planes hitting and the towers coming down but not much else."

"I suppose that's fair," she said. "I remember my mom shrieking. She dropped a plate. She was unloading the dishwasher. She had the TV on in the kitchen. I remember running to see what had happened," she said, sighing. "Your family was in the towers?"

"No. No, I didn't mean to imply that. I don't wish to be misleading. It's just that everything is connected for me. In my mind it all starts there. It probably starts years before, actually, but that's the day when things seemed to shift permanently, when I became aware. Before, it seemed life was easy. Maybe before we'd been living in a dream world. Ever since it's felt like hurricanes and stock crashes and body counts."

I took a breath. The past seemed far away. "We were living in

Boston. We were happy. Successful. I was in love with my wife. I was proud of my daughter." I paused again.

"You were living the American dream," Monika said.

"I was."

"Before September 11th."

"And after, too. That's just a date. A marker. I had no direct connections to September 11th," I said. "We saw it all pretty much the way you did. The way most saw it. There were Bostonians on the planes of course. I knew people who knew people. My closest connection was a photographer I'd worked with once or twice on articles. We had kids about the same age. He was supposed to be flying that day—on one of *the* flights— leaving Boston for an assignment, but his daughter had been in a fender-bender with his car the night before, and he'd decided at the last minute to postpone his trip by a day, stay behind and deal with the insurance company. Random salvation. Random condemnation.

"I think a lot about randomness," I continued, "that and the collective fear it inspires. After September 11th the whole country shared shock. The attacks revealed our vulnerabilities. That woke us up. We suddenly became accustomed to fear, something we'd never really allowed in our consciousness before. The politicians wanted to talk about togetherness, about reforming a shared American identity but in reality we only shared our collective grief. Fear penetrated everything. We grew paranoid. The atmosphere drew the crazies out in droves. They'd always been present, but we could isolate them. See them as the exception rather than the norm. We could look at the randomness of their acts and take comfort in it rather than find a new source of fear."

The words were pouring out of me. Some seal had ruptured. "What I mean is we'd already witnessed the Oklahoma City bombing. We'd seen Columbine. I could go on. But after September 11th, we lived in another place entirely. We pretended brave defiance but we were merely reactionary. The whole next year became one murky dreamscape." I stopped, frustrated with myself. "I don't know what kind of crap I'm dishing out," I said. Monika stiffened. "I can't speak for a country. But I know something in me changed. I became afraid. But that's a whole different story. I'm getting distracted. That's not what you asked. You asked about my family."

I sighed and took a long drink of coffee. "You're too young. You won't remember this. But just over a year after September 11th, there were sniper attacks all around Washington DC."

"I do remember," Monika said. "My dad used to watch the news every night. CNN. It was his ritual while he did the dishes. Two guys driving around shooting people through a hole in the trunk of their car. One of them was just a teenager."

"Exactly. Lee Boyd Malvo. He'd been recruited by John Allen Muhammad. Brainwashed maybe. I don't know. They killed eleven people, critically injured three others. No one ever remembers the victims' names. But they remember Malvo and Muhammad. They killed people pumping gas. They killed people shopping. For twenty-three days they had three states on edge. They fed on our paranoia. They made a game out of manipulating fear. People were afraid to stop for gas. This was a time when we were told to watch out for crop dusters spraying deadly chemicals, when we were supposed to report suspicious packages on the subway. I remember being searched going into a Red Sox game for the first time." The words raced out of me.

"There were other shootings after Malvo and Muhammad. Some were copycat syndrome I suppose. Two guys in Phoenix from their car. Dale Hausner and Samuel John Dieteman. They shot dogs. Horses. They shot joggers and bikers. Most people never heard of them. There was a guy in Ohio, Charles McCoy, Jr. He shot at cars from overpasses and bridges for months. How easily we forget.

"We forget people like John Sebastian O'Donnell. He killed seven people in Boston a month after they arrested Malvo and Muhammad. Another sniper. He found perches high up in buildings. He broke into unleased offices. Janitor closets that had operational windows. Balconies. He fired exactly two shots each time. Boom, boom. He was very precise. Military trained, special ops. He'd earned his combat stripes in Panama and then Grenada. He left the weapon at his sniper position, clean of prints and with no serial numbers, always the same style of gun, left it right where he'd taken the shots like a dare for the police to find him. He made it a game for the police to out guess what building he would choose next, where in the skyline he might hide. He wore a business suit and rode down the elevator after, as if he was just another desk jockey.

"He shot people waiting to cross the street. He shot people eating lunch outside on a warm November afternoon. He shot my wife and daughter walking in a park after school on the day my daughter had been told she'd won the lead role in the school play."

I heard Monika gasp, but I pressed on. The story came out in a rush, like I'd had the wind knocked out of me. "They called me not ten minutes before he killed them. They'd walked to an ice cream shop to celebrate and then they took their ice cream cones to the park. I was meeting with an interview subject five blocks away. They invited me to join them, only I was *too busy* with work. Renee would have gotten Rocky Road. Always Rocky Road. With Susan it's hard to say. She liked to change things up. She'd been on a health kick, so maybe frozen yogurt. I don't know. They don't tell you those kinds of things in police reports.

"The witnesses said that Renee was hit first. There were only seconds between his two shots. I often wonder if there was time enough that Susan had to see what happened to our daughter. If she had, I know she would have welcomed the second shot, would have begged for it.

"A mother and her daughter walking in a park. Susan Elizabeth Dunbar and Renee Alexandria Dunbar. Those are the names we should remember."

I was startled for a moment to discover I still had a coffee cup in my hand. My other hand lay on the table and Monika's hand remained on top of it. I turned away from the mural and saw that Monika was crying. Huge glistening tears dropped from her eyes silently.

"I'm sorry," I said. "I made you cry."

She made no movement to wipe away her tears.

"I don't know why I told you," I said. "I hadn't intended to. I'm not looking for sympathy. You asked what happened and now you know."

When at last she removed her hand from atop mine and wiped her eyes, darkening her fingers with mascara, I handed her a napkin. I watched as she dabbed her eyes. I'd never spoken of my family with anyone who hadn't known them and rarely with those who had. I'd long ago left that life.

Monika was correct when she assumed that I had chosen my lifestyle. I was never so self-delusional as to believe that by moving away I could forget, but I did believe distance could retard the pain. That belief failed, of course, as any person of average intelligence would have known. Perhaps I had chosen a life that allowed me unblemished focus on my past, to wallow entirely in my grief. Looking at Monika, I only wanted to take the telling back. I had betrayed my wife and daughter by speaking about their deaths.

We sat in silence for some time.

"I don't understand how someone can be so twisted," Monika eventually said. "To kill people. For no reason."

"The randomness has added considerable complexity," I said. "I've spent a great deal of time contemplating the nature of fate. I don't just think about the people O'Donnell killed, I think about the ones he didn't. The person who crossed the street just before my family. Others were spared. Why? In the lack of other explanation, it becomes easy to believe I've done something wrong in my life and I'm being punished for my mistakes."

"I get that," she said. "I don't think most people would. With my brother it gets really confusing because it hurts so bad to see him, a machine breathing for him, food going in one tube and shit out the other. But I get so mad at him. He did this to himself. In the end, that's all there should be to it. Really he's to blame. But blaming him seems wrong. I think I must have contributed. We all must have, right? I want to believe I could have changed his decision, but that's a lie. The truth is I never saw it coming."

"You couldn't."

"I know that," she said. "It doesn't help."

"I know," I said. "Death is senseless but we can't accept senselessness. We're mired in chaos but we still want to believe in order. Placing blame is an attempt at organizing chaos. I've seen John Sebastian O'Donnell. I attended his trial. I've been within fifteen feet of him. I've read his profile, his case history, his testimony, the reports by psychologists. I don't understand him one bit better for all the reading. Susan and Renee were merely targets to him in some game or quest, mere strangers to him. That makes understanding even more difficult. Blaming him isn't enough, so I want to blame everybody. I blame the kid who worked the ice cream counter for being too slow to serve, or too quick, too efficient, whichever placed them in the park at the moment O'Donnell settled his rifle. The timing of the stoplight at the corner that let them cross when it did. The engineer who programmed the light. I blame the culture that created O'Donnell. The military that trained him. The parents who harmed him in some irreparable way.

"He was filled with hate. He said he picked out people who were well dressed. Only whites. Only women and girls. He said that he thought our society needed reminders that they had it easy. He said his mission was to re-instill fear so people could reevaluate their priorities. I've tried blaming everyone and everything. In the end none of it makes any sense, so you're left only blaming yourself because your own life is all you have left."

We again sat in silence for several minutes. My coffee had grown cold. I drank it just the same. Monika had removed the mascara ruins from her face. Without the black etchings around her eyes, she looked younger. I turned back to her mural.

"Is she you in another age?" I asked. It was the first time when in Monika's presence that she didn't lead the conversation. I'd talked enough for both of us.

"She's not me. She's separate from me, but I've crawled inside her. She's shown up in my dreams."

"Have you imagined the room behind her too? The one we can't see."

She nodded. "I have a bunch of sketches in my journal." She paused. I could feel her looking at me. "How did you know?" she asked.

"With great musicians, if you pay close enough attention, you can hear what they decided to leave out."

"Do you know what's inside the buildings you draw?"

"Not at all. Maybe that's why you're the artist and I'm just the guy living in the hole in the ground. I know the facts, the building heights, the support systems, the year of construction, the architect. But what's within those walls, that's a mystery to me."

"The other day at the protest," she said. "When you lost it. You were looking up at the buildings."

"Was I?"

"What did you think you saw?"

"I don't know."

"Is that why you live underground now? Because of what might be hiding above you? Because you can't see what's inside those walls?"

I cleared my throat. How to explain what I didn't understand. "Maybe," I said, "it's because I have seen exactly what is hiding there."

19

otice of Public Hearing" read the folded stationery taped to the glass of my front door. No gum. Because I carried my fiber bag with my coffee purchases and needed the assistance of the stairway railing for my tender knee, I did not unfold the notice until I sat down at the kitchen counter. I felt like a child opening an expected failing report card.

The letter was on official city stationery right down to a raised city emblem in the letterhead. It cited my property address and legal property description and notified me that there would be a public hearing to discuss "the results of the recently conducted property review." It provided a date two weeks away on a Tuesday evening at city hall. The meeting would be open to the public and I was "strongly encouraged to attend." "Encouraged," it read. I wanted to laugh. I was "encouraged" to attend the meeting that might well determine my home's fate. How gracious of them to invite me. I envisioned an auditorium full of neighbors taking their turns at a microphone. Spitballs. Rotten tomatoes.

Two weeks. It would be like awaiting results of a biopsy.

I awoke the next morning with little on my mind beyond the notice. Intent on an early walk, I opened my front door to encounter a sea of pink plastic flamingos. They perched within the tall, natural field grass, each standing ridiculously on one leg, black painted eyes no more than hatch marks. Another piece of folded stationery adorned my front door, this time attached with painter's tape. I was beginning to think it was time to invest in corkboard. The letterhead identified a local church. "You've been flamingoed," the letter declared. It proceeded to explain that the flamingos had been placed on my "lawn" as part of a fundraiser for the church youth group. An anonymous party had paid to have the "flock" take "roost" and a donation on my part would expedite the "flock's" removal. The letter went on to suggest donation amounts but emphasized that any amount was "greatly appreciated" and that no donation was required. It then provided a phone number to call for "prompt lawn de-flock-sation." It did not, to my surprise, make any evangelical advances. At the bottom of the letter was a handwritten note full of familiar long, looping letters and flourishes:

> Thought you'd get a laugh out of this. Knew you'd appreciate the kitsch. Plus, since you live in a vandalism zone, I thought you needed to take the heat off.

This time Monika had signed her name using a flower to dot the "i". She wasn't the sort of person from whom I expected flowers.

I walked into the midst of the flock. Their heads all pointed uniformly east as if scanning the horizon for a flamingo hunter among the opaque windows of my nearest neighbor. A few of the birds revealed their greater age by a sun-faded discoloration of their pink plastic skin. I picked up one of the more aged birds. I held it by its neck and slung it over my shoulder like a baseball bat. The single leg by which it had been planted on my property ended in an arrow-like point rather than a bird foot. "B. Baptist" had been written in permanent marker on its belly. The face at the end of the neck I held offered no expression. I looked from it to the sea of identically expressionless birds surrounding me and laughed. There were easily more than a hundred of them, the flock extending from within ten feet of my door nearly to the street. I laughed louder. Perhaps in lieu of a donation, I'd offer to purchase all of them at double their cost. I'd make the display permanent and decorate the birds accordingly for major holidays. They could sport beads and leis, little hats and swim trunks, Halloween costumes and Easter bonnets, Santa Claus hats, turkey feathers. Let my neighbors talk about me then.

I pitched the bird I carried as if it were a javelin. It stuck in the ground near the door, landing at a 60 degree angle and facing the other birds, making it look like some sort of maniacal conductor. I left it there and departed on my walk, still chuckling at my newly decorated front yard.

20

I walked for a long, long while. My knee remained stiff and I knew it would swell that evening, yet forcing myself to keep it moving felt productive. Where I normally turned right toward town and the library and other familiar destinations, I turned left. After passing what seemed miles of neighborhood developments that could be interchanged one for the next, I reached a large cluster of retail stores. The development appeared new and the building materials conveyed a uniform aesthetic. Landscaping broke up the asphalt expanse. There was an imposing natural foods market and a chain bookstore, an electronics store and an enormous home improvement warehouse.

I entered the natural foods market and was treated with free samples nearly every time I turned down an aisle. I recognized none of the brands and had never before encountered some of the products. The word "organic" appeared nearly everywhere and I kept expecting throwback hippies to appear with leather sandals gripping dirt-encrusted toes. I expected handknit brightly dyed garments and pervasive amounts of body hair but instead found sharply dressed customers sporting good tans, athletic arms, an army of women in workout attire, and cell phones apparently permanently attached like prosthetics. One woman seemed to be speaking to herself, and I gave her a wide berth before seeing some sort of electrical device suspended from her ear. Where I'd once lived for the emergent technology of sound and amplification, clearly I had fallen light years behind the technological curve.

The store was pleasant. The free samples proved delicious. Employees and customers alike seemed unnaturally friendly, which made me suspicious. A little café set into one corner looked so inviting that I treated myself to a late second breakfast of a bagel and coffee—organic, fair-trade coffee, I might add, thinking Monika would have been pleased.

Next, I browsed at the bookstore for a long while. There were comfortable chairs and it was early enough that few customers joined me in the stacks. While I liked the price per item offered by the library a great deal more than the sticker shock the store provided, it was pleasant to be among so many books without the nursing home smell. Yet another coffee shop dominated one wall of the store and it appeared to corner most of the morning traffic.

Then, I found myself walking the aisles of the home improvement store. I strolled among its ceiling-high shelves in something of a daze, marveling at the sheer volume of merchandise. Perhaps I truly was dazed, for in every aisle at least one apron-wearing employee asked if I needed assistance. Where were they, I wondered, all those years ago when I'd remodeled an old bedroom into a home office or when I'd built a play fort and swing set for Renee? Where were they when the plumbing demanded repair and I bought four fittings for every one that proved the right size?

I had strolled into the electronics department. An employee near the middle of the aisle appeared to be sizing me up. He moved toward me. This one was still pimple-faced. His nametag said "Phil" and it identified him as "in training," as if he were a puppy still trying to find the door. As he neared, I could see his mind rehearsing his query. I wanted to cut him off, but he was young and a quick draw and just as he reached the "help" before the end of his question, I responded, "No thanks, got it," and I grabbed an item on a gigantic display before me—a doorbell kit. An omen, it seemed.

Next, I wandered into the gardening section where fall deals abounded as they tried to reduce inventory and make room for snow blowers and log splitters. Knee-sore and suffering consumer overload, I sat down on a clearance-priced outdoor bench. At either end of it stood large, matching planter boxes still loud with blooming asters. I was surprised at how comfortable the bench proved. I was equally taken aback at how fairly priced it appeared. When an employee stopped and asked if I needed help, I further shocked myself when I told him that I wanted to purchase the bench.

"I'd be happy to take it up front, sir. Just let me go get a couple of flatbeds."

"A couple?" I queried.

"It's a set," he said. "The planters go with it. It's a great deal."

"Forty percent off," I said.

"That's right. You're basically getting the planters for free and the bench at a discount. And it was a display, so they're throwing in all the plants too."

"What a steal."

"I'll run get those carts and then we'll get you checked out and I'll help you get it loaded onto your truck."

Now the logical thing would have been to stop him right there. Yet five minutes later I was seated on my new bench on the curb outside the store, having lied to the clerk, telling him that my wife had taken the truck across the way to the natural foods store. It had been an elaborate lie, one that had arrived fully formed in my mind with astonishing ease, a lie about how my wife only bought organic and that we were having friends over for dinner, and how she had a weakness for fruit-filled pastries and how she'd probably stopped at their coffee shop because they often had peach turnovers. He had indulged my lie politely, smiling the whole time and offering to wait and help me load, though he relented at my insistence that my wife worked out and could practically lift the whole truck over her head. My real wife, not the one of my lie, had worked out. She'd been a dancer throughout her twenties, and I wondered, were she alive, wouldn't we like to shop organic? Wouldn't we linger on a lazy morning in the grocery store what with Renee out of the house and away at college? Certainly, the fondness for fruit pastries had been entirely real. The lying had come much easier than to tell a stranger that my wife had died while walking across a park on a Thursday afternoon. And he, of course, had received my lie effortlessly, something that would not have been the case had I told him that another of O'Donnell's victims hadn't been any older than himself, a retail store employee jogging on a Saturday morning, or that Malvo and Muhammad, had killed people in the parking lot of a suburban home improvement center that bore a logo identical to the one on his apron. Such was not the sort of small talk one made. Much better to tell a few lies.

In the end I hired a thirty-something guy I found in the parking lot in a big pickup who had bought nothing more than a new paint brush. I paid him forty bucks for the ride and de-livery.

"It wouldn't fit in the car," I said stupidly, gesturing loosely toward a sea of vehicles reflecting the late morning sun. Appar-ently, I'd grown suddenly adept at lying.

"Nice truck," I said, once we were on the road. "I keep thinking about getting one."

"Comes in handy," he said.

I told him my wife was taking the car and going shopping. "Clothes," I said. "I'll probably have to build her an entire sec-ond closet she buys so many clothes."

"Then you'll need that truck," he said.

"You're right," I said. "See, I might just get something out of the bargain after all."

"Yeah," he said. "A truck payment."

When we reached my place, all he said was, "Nice flamin-gos."

"Yeah, there's a story there."

"I bet."

"You'll have to watch that you don't hit them, but you can pull over the curb and we'll back in right by the door."

He shrugged. Once we'd positioned the truck and unloaded the bench and planters, placing them just to the right of the door and backed up against the foot of the berm, he asked, while examining the door, "Where's the house?"

"We're a bit off budget," I said. I held my arms before me,

a gesture meant to present emptiness. "I'm making progress, like this for instance," I said and bent to retrieve a small bag from where I'd laid it down on the ground. From it I removed my other purchase of the day, the doorbell kit. "See, little steps here and there," I said. "But this will be nice," I said, pointing to the bench. "Can't thank you enough."

He took the two twenties and drove off without another word.

"Nice bench," Monika said as she waded through the flock of flamingos. "Very Martha Stewart. Well, pre-prison Martha Stewart at least."

I looked at her blankly.

"It looks sharp," she said.

"Thanks."

"Enjoying your birds?"

"Immensely. I'm thinking about keeping this one," I said, nodding with my chin to the one I'd chucked closest to the bench.

"I don't think you're supposed to do that."

"I had a peek under the wings. Apparently, they're Baptists."

"So I've heard."

"I was a little surprised. Flamingos don't seem the Baptist type to me. Presbyterian maybe, but not Baptist."

"I would have thought flamingos were agnostic," she said.

"I was a little surprised that you hired out lawn-decorating Baptists."

"It's my parent's church. I used to go to youth group there."

"Really."

"I was never much into the religion stuff, but youth group was fun. In the beginning. Most of the kids didn't really get into the church part. We just had fun going bowling and stuff. You know, hanging out together."

"Bowling. Flamingos. I'm getting a whole new perspective. Bowling?"

"Bowling. It's a sport, you know. Ten pins, really heavy ball."

"Sorry, I was hung up on the monogrammed shirts."

"Bowling, swimming. Skiing twice a year. A camping trip every August. Video game nights. Bad karaoke. It was fun."

"Sounds fun."

"It was. The youth pastor was cool. He was somebody you felt you could talk to without him passing judgment."

"You still participate?"

"Not for years."

"What changed?"

"The youth pastor for one. The kids got older. The religion stuff got serious for some of them. A couple declared themselves reborn. I started to feel judged, so I bolted."

"Are your parents active?"

"Not so much then. They were just looking for a group of friends for us they thought they could trust. The dedication to the church is a post-vegetable thing. Now they serve on church committees and attend prayer groups and bible study. It's a big battleground for us. They argue with each other about trying to get me more involved. My dad spends a lot of time worrying about 'my soul.' We fight all the time about religion, which seems very unspiritual to me. My concession is that I go to church with them on Sunday mornings without a fight. Meanwhile, Dad tries to find evidence that the devil picks out my clothes."

"Does he?"

"Only occasionally. But all my nail polish is clearly devil induced." She held her hands up and wiggled her fingers to display blue fingernails. I looked her over, having grown accustomed to her style of dress such that I didn't really notice it any more. She wore fairly plain jeans with the knees missing and a good deal of writing in permanent marker on the thighs, a pink tank top covered by a pea green shirt that appeared large enough to fit her dad. I stopped my scan at the ever-present engineer boots. "And your footwear."

"Oh, of course. You have to be equipped for walking through boiling cauldrons and over condemned souls."

"So what happened with the youth group? You said you felt judged."

"In my experience, a lot of people with clearly defined religious views expect conformity from others. Don't get me wrong, I'm not judging. But at that age, kids were choosing what they believed and how they wanted to be seen. A lot of the ones who stuck with the group started to take religion really seriously. I mean, these were kids getting ready to go into high school where everybody gets grouped and tagged. The whole cow at the processing plant thing. They attended a church that truly believes it's your job to convert others to your beliefs. There was a lot of pressure on those kids to talk about religion all of the sudden. They're kids, right? Impressionable. Talk about religious belief included clear positions about other things. About lifestyle. About sex and abstinence, virginity and abortion. Family values stuff. My natural inclinations were to lean in other directions. Not only did I have strong opinions, it just looked to me like a lot of other kids were having a whole lot more fun. The more I hung out with other people, the more some of the kids from youth group felt like it was their job to save me. It was super annoying. At one point, one of my so-called friends told me that I couldn't get into heaven unless I followed her god. I told her that if I'd meet her in heaven, I didn't want to go."

"Yet you had me flocked. You must have kept a few friends."

"Yeah, sure. I've got connections all over. I'm just more the lone eagle type, hence the spy-like abilities."

"Apparently you made up with the girl who told you that you couldn't get into heaven."

"Nah. That's a funny thing. She ended up prego and dropped out of school last year. Her parents shipped her off to Virginia. I'm sure wherever she's at, it's just heavenly."

"Her parents being the charitable and forgiving types."

"Bingo."

"I hate hypocrisy like that."

"Ehh," she said, shrugging her shoulders. "Who isn't a hypocrite? It's pretty hard not to be. I mean, like I try to step lightly,
leave a small footprint, you know."

"With those boots?"

"Right, like it's hard. I mean, just by living in this country
we participate in economics that use two thirds of the world's
resources. It's hard not to participate even if you're conscious
about it."

"How'd you start to care about such things?"

"Born that way, I guess. I've always been a bit of a noncon-
formist. Walk me down a one-way street and I'll go the other
way. I was a strange kid. Always reading. Listening to adults talk
and to the news. I like swimming against the tide."

"Like a salmon."

"Don't even get me started on the plight of the salmon.
Dams. Habitat destruction." She stopped abruptly and laughed.
"Seriously though, I want to do the right thing, but then look at
me, I drive everywhere. I try to justify it because I think I have
lots of places I need to be. I buy clothes even when I don't need
them. I may be in love with my phone. Like I said, it's hard not
to be a hypocrite, so I try not to judge others."

"Like by telling people you don't want to attend their heav-
en."

"Exactly."

"So, seriously, what do you do in place of passing judgment?" I asked.

"You try to help somebody who needs help. Only you draw
the line there. Somebody falls down, you offer them a hand up.
You don't tell them which direction to walk as a condition of
helping."

"Even if they are going to trip over the exact same crack that
made them fall down in the first place?"

"Do you really think your pointing it out will make a difference?"

I leaned back into the bench. I contemplated what Monika
had said. "You're right," I said.

"Maybe," she said, changing the timbre of her voice. "I doubt it. What do I know? I'm seventeen, remember?"

"And you don't turn in your homework."

"That's right. I have absolutely no credibility. Nice bench," she said after a pause.

"It is."

"You know you have to give the birds back."

"I know."

"You don't have to give a donation either. That's not why I asked them to do it. I just did it for the laugh. And to piss your neighbors off."

"What do they do with the money?"

"Every summer the youth group goes to Mexico and helps build a house for a poor family."

"And there's no evangelizing while they hammer nails?"

She shrugged. "I'm not saying I advocate it, but what are you going to do? At least there's still a house at the end of it."

"Good point. Is it fun?"

"Couldn't tell you. I never went. My parents are afraid of Mexico. They think that the moment you set foot in the country, you are kidnapped and someone sells your organs on the black market." She stopped abruptly and sighed. "Okay, truth. I'm a hypocrite, like I said. If I'd wanted to go badly enough, I'm sure I could have convinced them."

"You do seem capable of arguing your point," I said.

"Not a total hypocrite. Not an evangelize-on-Sunday-preacher who bones adolescents on Monday. I volunteer locally. Habitat for Humanity. I'm sure there are strings for those families too, but I don't have to hold them."

"Maybe I'll give your flamingo friends some money," I said.

"So you're really not pissed?"

"Pissed?"

"About the birds?"

"The birds, no. The birds made me laugh this morning."

"Good."

I looked out across the flock. "I'm serious about keeping one."

"You'd probably better make a donation then."

"I will."

"And not chump change."

"Okay."

"You can use my phone to call them. If you call now, they'll probably have them picked up before dark."

"Okay."

"I really do like your bench."

"Thanks."

"The flowers are a nice touch. They give you some color."

"The world could probably use more flowers."

"Maybe that should be our campaign. We could be like Johnny Appleseed," she said.

"Spreading invasive species across the land at our whim, killing off native plants everywhere."

"Whew," she said. "You're back. You had me worried there for a minute."

"Sorry to disappoint."

"You didn't."

"I got a notice yesterday," I said. "About a hearing. The whole review thing comes to a public hearing in two weeks. I suppose the neighbors will be there."

"What are you going to do?"

"I don't know. Show up, I guess. See where I stand before I do anything rather than wasting all my time worrying about what I don't know."

"I'll be happy to speak up if you want."

"I know you would."

"That's all the letter said, that there would be a hearing?"

"That's it. Nothing more. I've been thinking. More than the neighbors' rumors or their belief that something is an eyesore, it will all come down to whether or not the city, or a powerful someone friendly with the city, thinks I have something that they want."

"You're kind of dense if you're just catching that one."

"I've never been accused of being a rocket scientist."

"They can't say you aren't improving the place," she said, patting the bench and standing.

"And attracting wildlife. Maybe I can get wildlife sanctuary status or something."

"Become a flamingo refuge."

"A migration corridor."

"We could buy decoys. Change them out regularly according to the seasons."

"We'll buy a few taxidermy animals," I said. "Convince people that the elusive bison have made a return."

"Better yet, you let the real thing loose. A rampage would get their attention. Or maybe some small but feisty predators, a lynx or some badgers or wolverines."

"That would make the neighbors think twice," I agreed.

"Your garden might suffer."

"Everything comes with a price." I stood, then bent and pinched a spent bloom from my new pot.

"True," she said. "By the way, do you think I could borrow some more music?"

"Sure," I said, starting toward the door. I pointed toward the disorderly bird. "Of course, I don't know how well a bird can get along in a basement."

"Basements are where all the whackos live, and after all let's face it, he looks pretty whacko."

"He'll fit right in."

21

As promised, by evening the flamingos had disappeared as quietly as if they'd flown off to Florida. I'd stopped to admire my new bench once more before retiring. It was a night filled with stars.

I hadn't been inside long before my new doorbell rang, startling me so that I nearly spilled the cup of tea I'd just made. When I reached the stairwell, all I could see was a pink flamingo leaning against the glass. I smiled in spite of myself.

Just as I reached the door, the flamingo jumped away as if taking flight.

"Nice doorbell, Mr. Bo Jingles," Monika said as I opened the door.

"Nice flamingo."

She handed me the bird. "Believe me, it took some convincing. Those church people don't let go of stuff so easily."

"There's some historical evidence to support that theory."

"Get your coat," she said by way of reply.

"No more relocation missions, Monika," I said. "I've retired my secret agent badge. It's time I return to being a grown-up."

"None of that," she said. "I just want to show you something."

"That's code for trouble, right?"

"Nothing like that at all. Quit your whining and get a coat."

"You've seen me with crowds. Let's not do that again."

"It's nighttime."

"So."

"That will make all the difference. You'll see."

I protested one more time.

"That's enough. This is more of an education venture, a cultural program if you will. You appreciate culture and art, correct? It's my duty to prove it can flourish right here in No-wheresville."

I groaned.

"Go put your little bird to bed and get your coat." She wore a long trench coat. "It's cold out."

In what had clearly become a bad habit, I complied and followed her orders.

"Where are we really going?" I asked once I got in the car.

"Like I said—to witness some of the local talent."

"Just what sort of vandalism do you have planned?"

"I'm serious. You're going to meet some people who will blow you away."

"Monika, please, no offense or anything, but I'm really not interested in hanging around with a bunch of teenagers."

"Who said any such thing?"

"I'm in no mood to meet people."

"As if you ever would be. Think of this as an adventure."

"That scares me even more," I said. "Seriously, where are you taking me?"

"We're going underground."

I expected a *Twilight Zone* sound-over to accompany the push of her foot into the accelerator that followed.

We crossed railroad tracks twice and then bumped over three more sets of tracks clustered together in some sort of transit yard. We were somewhere vaguely north of downtown surrounded by old warehouses rising among crumbling brick buildings and enormous rusting Quonset huts. Graffiti-painted boxcars stood idle on side tracks. We cut between two vast buildings that looked like airport hangers, took a hard left and suddenly descended a wide concrete slope that resembled a highway off-ramp but which was really a stormwater canal. The slope led into a long curving cement channel with steep sides. Monika accelerated. Weeds sprouted from cracks. I glimpsed what appeared to be a sand bar hugging the geometry where cement bottom met cement wall. She swerved sharply, and looking back through the rear window I tried to see what she'd maneuvered to avoid. It appeared to be a dishwasher. Returning my attention out the windshield, I braced myself for impact as she cornered around a piece of driftwood. A thin film of water now appeared on the surface in front of us, and I heard it spray from the tires. She responded by speeding up.

I realized I was gripping the "Oh, Jesus" handle with both hands and nearly had my knees pinned to the dashboard. Monika looked at me and grinned. Just as I was about to plead for salvation, she braked and swung the car hard to the right. We slid, tires echoing in the concrete canyon like a stunt car. She accelerated again as the back end came around. We shot under an overpass and she turned violently into another spin, this time reaching down and cutting her headlights at the same time. We screeched to a sideways stop.

I was convinced that these weeks in her company had been a long, complex buildup for a kidnapping or some kind of gang initiation rite and that I had arrived at the place where I would meet my demise. It all felt very cinematic.

I looked to Monika, sure she would be holding a space-age weapon like a glow stick with a lethal attitude, and instead I saw that she was pointing out her window not with a weapon but with her finger. I followed its direction.

Ahead some two hundred yards distant, under another, wider overpass, in the dim amber light of highway lamps and two oil barrels with flames reaching above their rims, was illuminated a group of about fifty people, several of whom seemed to be dancing. I could hear a base beat and felt it vibrate the car mildly.

"Welcome to the Underground," she said.

"I thought I lived there."

"You don't even know."

There was a concrete abutment beneath the overpass that formed a kind of shelf. Two figures were atop it at a microphone stand like they stood on a concert stage. At the far side of the underpass, a van was parked with all its doors open, spilling tangles of wires and cords. Large speakers occupied the ground near both bumpers and more sprung from a roof rack.

Monika got out of the car and motioned for me to follow. As soon as she opened the car door, I heard music, not overpowering like a concert but loud enough it carried up and down the storm-water system and reverberated off the cement. I thought perhaps I'd entered an apocalyptic movie set. I joined Monika and we started walking toward the group ahead. "What on earth is this?"

"Karaoke night," she said, a huge smile showing in the dark. I stopped cold.

She walked on a few more steps and then, as if suddenly realizing I wasn't beside her, stopped and turned back toward me. "Oh, come one. Get over yourself. Some of these guys are crazy talented."

"But why are they in a flood canal?" I asked, still not moving.

"Why not?"

Just then a voice that seemed a reincarnation of Janis Joplin erupted, shooting down the canal and past me with animalistic force. The voice was enough to get my feet moving again. We walked to its rhythms, which came in waves like a siren's song.

"Who are these people?" I asked Monika when I reached her.

"A lot of them are the people we step around in the street. A couple rent rooms and live on aid or disability. Some of the teenagers are addicts and live on the streets. Some of them hook. Like the girl who's singing now. She's fourteen or fifteen. Calls herself Raven. Total meth-head. Some of the other teenagers are just ordinary kids, local high school or college age kids, you know, the thespian, literary types, the whole clove cigarette pierce-your-face crowd. The guy with the van is Joe. He's like a social worker for the county or something in the daytime and a DJ, karaoke bar dude at night. One night every couple of weeks he comes here. Except for Joe and a few regulars, it varies quite a bit. There are always drifters passing through, so there are surprises."

"How did you find out about this?"

"Through Joe," she said. "He's somebody my brother knew."

There were more questions I wanted to ask, but I kept silent and we continued walking. Thoughts eddied. As we neared, it was evident that even in this nighttime underworld brought together through some common bond of music there were social stratifications. The local kids, identifiable by the overt hipness of their clothes and lack of hollow cheeks and cratered skin, gathered together close to the makeshift stage and were wrapped in blankets. They laughed and talked within the music but shouted their appreciation the loudest. The older people stood in small clusters, most huddled near the fires. Some sat alone. The other teen crowd, the one that must have represented the addicts, moved among the groups like insects flitting near a light. We encountered one of them immediately as we reached the fringes of the gathering—a self-appointed sentry. "Peace, homes," he said, with a quick upward nod. A ripe smell followed in his wake.

We passed a group of people clustered near one of the barrel fires. They ignored our presence. The fires released an acrid smell, making me wonder what toxic leftovers lined the barrels. The people huddled near the fires' warmth all wore multiple layers of clothing, noticeable by the mismatched colors sprouting at their necklines and sleeve ends and by their overstuffed bulk. Stained ski jackets revealed fluffy fibers at holes. They capped their attire with knit hats and fingerless gloves. Several passed a bottle.

I turned my attention to the stick figure belting out Joplin. Her eyes were closed and her body swayed with her singing. A tall, stringy gray-haired woman in a knee-length wool coat stood next to the singer without moving as if she were part of the act, and I expected her to come suddenly to life and reveal a hidden musical instrument. Eerily, her eyes were wide open and seemingly unblinking, revealing a milky blue. I began to wonder if the woman was channeling Joplin and transmitting her through the girl.

"She's really good," I said to Monika, my voice unable to disguise my surprise.

"Yeah, she's a regular. She's definitely got the whole Joplin vibe down. But there's a guy behind us, sitting alone up against the pillar there in the shadows..." I turned to look. "Don't look," she hissed. "I mean be discreet at least, Music Man, don't look right at him."

I adjusted my reconnaissance and pretended to be taking in the van and all its electronics. "That's better," she said. "You can't just stare at people, particularly that guy. He's a little kooky. He's also the real talent here. I mean, the off-the-charts talent. He does all original stuff, the whole singer/songwriter routine, where the rest of them, even the talented ones do covers. He's trippy though. Probably schizophrenic. Some weeks he refuses to perform, others he practically takes over the whole night and becomes the MC. Once he threw a tantrum and spent twenty minutes hurling insults at the audience. They thought it was hilarious and came right back at him. The whole uncertainty about this guy is part of the entertainment."

"Does he have a name?"

"Not that I've ever heard. I hope he sings tonight. He'll knock your socks off."

"What's the story with the silent partner?" I asked, pointing with a nod of my chin at the woman who swayed on stage alongside the Joplin impersonator.

"Rumor has it that she killed her own children by accident. A fire or something. Stories change. She doesn't talk at all. The other homeless people give her a wide birth. But anytime the Joplin girl sings, she does this number."

"And it's nothing but Joplin?"

"Oh no, she can do anybody gritty enough. Bonnie Raitt, Stevie Nicks, Grace Slick, but clearly she likes Joplin best."

"How long's she been coming here?"

"Little miss anorexic crack head? Probably six months. I'm sure she and her little gang of misfits will be moving along to somewhere warmer soon, unless she's homegrown. She'll be lucky if she survives another six months the rate she's going at it. One thing coming down here reminds you," she said, "is that somebody's pretty much always got it worse than you."

We'd arrived center stage and Monika unfurled a blanket and laid it on the cement. A small soundboard was set up on one side of the bridge abutment and there too, I now realized, was a projector. It really is karaoke, I thought, the stuff of my worst nightmare. And sure enough, following the skinny drug addict and her silent entourage, a trio of the local teens got up and consulted briefly with Joe, the resident soundman. The light on the projector illuminated, and I saw song lyrics shining on the wall in six-inch font, in this case, the words to Michael Jackson's "Beat It."

The teens were beyond terrible, so bad as to prove entertaining. As is my standard reaction to all such exhibitions, I grew more uncomfortable the more they sought the spotlight, for they clearly enjoyed their horrifically off-pitch screeching. I expected their hair to ignite in flames at any moment. At times the only sound they emitted was laughter. The audience started whooping and hollering for more when one of the boys broke into an un-rhythmical dance, throwing his body to the cement and writhing and then jumping in the air. His partner felt inspired to attempt a pathetic moon walk, which looked more like a bad mime attached to the end of a rope. The girl took over all singing duties and at least found the right register. As a show of appreciation, one of the homeless men mooned them. I looked for somewhere to hide.

"Beat It" was followed, predictably, by "Billy Jean." Clearly, they enjoyed mocking their generational inheritance. Next the girl sang, if you could call it such, old Whitney Houston while her compatriots attempted Motown-style backup, which I must admit, made me smile. They were followed by a homeless man who appeared faceless save for a nose, the remainder of his face lost to a thick gray beard and a black watch cap. He sang Sinatra. Respectably, I might add. Like Ms. Anorexia, he needed no karaoke screen lyrics. He was followed by another teen who did a set of show tunes and was then joined by one of his friends for an equally off, off Broadway rendition of a bad ABBA song. By the end I could not tell if they were mocking Broadway, Sweden, their audience, themselves, their parents, or all of the above, but clearly they were having the time of their lives.

Apparently, guitar man back there in the shadows had had enough, for Monika's favorite resident psychotic singer/songwriter rose and walked over to confer with Joe. He carried a battered guitar and walked with a limp. The crowd went silent when he ascended the cement shelf that served as a stage. Before he reached the microphone, he pointed directly at me— and don't think I'm giving way to paranoia here—pointed a crooked, accusatory, condemning finger, and shouted: "Newbie sings or I don't," before retreating toward the van. The audience immediately began chanting, "Newbie, newbie." I resided within a nightmare.

Monika sprang to her feet and offered me a hand up. I ignored her. "You don't want to piss this guy off," she said. "I'll help you."

"Or what?" I asked.

"He's unpredictable. Besides, the crowd might riot."

"There's no way I'm doing karaoke." I turned and began walking away. A particularly menacing-looking street teen stepped out of the shadows as if to block my exit. The crowd's chant grew louder.

"Just one song," she implored.

The audience continued its chant, teen and homeless members alike. Joe began playing the background music to *Jeopardy* over the sound system. Peer pressure with sound effects. Like bullies, the crowd began to exert what seemed an angry tone to its teasing. I had returned to second grade. I took another step and the microphone behind me squealed like an injured animal. I could feel Guitar Man's eyes on me.

"I've got your back," Monika said. "You will want to hear this guy sing. I guarantee it. This is the price."

I took her offered hand and turned toward the stage to the cheers of the audience.

We walked to the van and met Joe, who showed us reams upon reams of lyrics gathered into three ring binders. "We should pick something we both know," Monika said. I was busy scanning the darkness beyond the van, looking for an exit opportunity. Guitar Man paced behind the van as if he'd been locked out of a dressing room.

"What are you looking for?" Joe asked Monika, who flipped through a binder.

"Something from the '70s or '80s, maybe earlier, something back before Mr. Secret Agent man here went underground." She opened another notebook midstream and immediately shrieked, "Got it. Perfect." She turned the page for Joe to see and left me in the dark. Joe smirked, appearing quite satisfied.

Monika took my hand and dragged me to the makeshift stairs—a series of stacked pallets—that ascended the platform. As I'd discovered from our night of gnome relocation, she proved unnaturally strong. The audience cheered and began clapping. Guitar Man appeared behind us at the base of the steps as if to prevent my retreat. The white screen on the opposite side of the underpass wall flashed and the lyrics for the Velvet Underground's "Pale Blue Eyes" appeared. I had to hand it to Monika, if ever there were two singers we could butcher and still be seen as paying tribute in the butchering, it had to be Nicco and Lou Reed.

"Can you see that far, Gramps?" Monika asked, pointing at the lyrics.

"I may have to kill you," I said.

"Save it for later. It will give you something to look forward to." The music started and the audience gave one last whoop before falling expectantly silent. Monika elbowed me. I could hear Lou Reed's voice in my ear as plainly as if he stood beside me. I felt my face flush, and a rivulet of sweat rolled down my side. I contemplated leaping off the stage no matter the peril.

Butcher the song we did. Never had five and a half minutes passed so slowly. "You couldn't have picked the REM version?" I grumped, knowing it was shorter. My voice cracked and wavered. Yet the crowd cheered and applauded and one old man joined in with the singing as if to help carry me when I floundered. I took both satisfaction and buoyancy when Monika joined in harmony on the chorus, if you could label it harmony, for her voice was so bad mine sounded melodic by comparison.

Despite everything, at one point in the song, not needing the illuminated lyrics, I sang with my eyes closed, and as I sang I saw the pale blue eyes of my wife and my daughter. When I opened my eyes on the last chorus, I was met with Monika's brown eyes as she belted out the lyrics beside me, as confident as a rock star. Our pitiful performance was met with enthusiastic cheers from the small gathering of misfits. Even desperate people have a sense of humor.

I rushed off the platform. Guitar Man met me on the makeshift steps and treated me to a high five as we passed and he said, "Nice warm-up act, newbie."

I wanted nothing more than to flee the place despite the back-slapping congratulations of the teen set, and I was striding in the direction of the car without concern for Monika's whereabouts until the first note sounded from the stage. One chord and one perfectly sung note stopped me and made me turn back.

The man stood at the microphone with his eyes closed. Then the guitar exploded at his fingertips. Thick ropy veins stood out on his arms as he attacked the strings. The untrimmed curls of the guitar strings paralleled the fashion of his hair, which hung across his face, obscuring it. He looked like a man writhing in pain. Seeing him mattered not, and I closed my eyes and listened. The song thundered from him. His voice raced toward the surrounding cement and then charged back. The voice and the guitar both sounded bigger than themselves and the song spoke of abandonment and despair. I returned to the blanket and sat down.

He sang through a set of seven songs, a mix of lonely sounding ballads and surging acoustic rock, all presumably original and each one better than the one before. At the conclusion of each song I cheered until my throat hurt. When he finished his set, he appeared spent. No act followed, nothing could. The crowd shuffled off in groups and clusters.

"Worth the price of admission?" Monika asked on our way to the car.

"You probably took a year off my life expectancy," I said. "Maybe two."

"Yeah, but it was still worth it, huh?"

I nodded. Even if I knew better, for a brief moment I wanted to believe that music could save the world.

22

I tried to heed my own advice and not spend undue time worrying about the public hearing. I've been offered the lesson in more concrete fashion than most that if outside forces truly want to exert control over your life, you can do little or nothing to alter their desire. If the city wanted to take action, I would have two choices: live with their decision or hire a good lawyer. It was time to do what I'd learned best in my seven years underground, follow Bartleby and ignore the outside world until the hearing date arrived. Besides, it seemed just possible that unless there was some ulterior motive, they had no real action to pursue despite the neighbors' complaints. Of course, I had no way of knowing how influential my neighbors might be.

I did my best to get back to my work. I'd always approached writing with the same stubborn religiosity as I did everything else, and eking out one slow word after the next, doggedly I tried to write the next page. I stared at the blank paper for better than an hour. I knew instinctively—if only I would listen—that it was past time to abandon ritual. At the ninety-minute mark, I turned the thick pile of manuscript pages over and began to read. The earliest sections were several years old, old enough the pages had begun to discolor. As I started reading it seemed quite possible that my writing style had changed over time and that the tone had shifted and the recent material proved denser, more esoteric. I read the first four chapters with something gnawing at me, some elusive half awareness of fatal trouble afoot. I knew the research was strong. The writing, despite needing revision, was generally of good quality. I believed in the material at the book's heart, an exploration of music, economics, and geography. Yet something critical was off. These were crossroads where the honky-tonk met the church choir loft. The results of plantation song encountering southside

Chicago shift whistles. Of West Virginia coal intermingling with Delta mud. Kansas City stockyards and Florida swamps. And still some impoverishment in the book lingered like a note out of tune.

Trying to identify the error, I read the opening chapters a second time. I thought about pushing ahead in the manuscript, yet I knew that the fundamental error was already exposed, was staring me in the face, daring me to identify it like the muzzle flash from a sniper's weapon.

I threw the chapters down onto the table's surface where they landed with a thud atop the gap-toothed Philadelphia skyline. I stared at the pages piled atop those rigid buildings that, in their mass, obscured the city streets below. I recalled Monika's voice: "All those buildings and no people." No one stood at a window. No one relaxed on a balcony. No pedestrians inhabited the sidewalks. No doormen welcomed entry to grand hotels.

There were no people in the book.

Oh, sure, there were rosters and rosters of names. I wrote long expository passages about cultural patterns and social shifts and their effects on the music. There were, however, no stories. No lives. Music without musicians. Words without sound.

I'd written about honkytonks with the eye of a sociologist. I had not allowed the reader the chance to smell the stale booze or the wet air fueled by the sweat of dancers. There was no bass beat thump in their bowels, no touch from the dust lifting off the dirt dance floor. Intent on academic points about economic stratification fueled by cultural isolation, I'd failed to take them within the country churches where the wood floors shook from stomping feet and birds stopped singing in the trees beyond the church windows. Readers hadn't been allowed to taste the rye and hand-rolled tobacco carried in a note from a blues guitar or hear the anguish of a coal miner's widow's wail in a fiddle chord. I hadn't provided the stories of the musicians who had found notes residing in their bones and in their blood, in their faith and in their grief.

This discovery should, in all logic, have deflated me. How many years had I given to the writing already? How much of myself had I given that yellowing stack of manuscript pages only to recognize I hadn't begun to give enough? Strangely, rather than feeling defeated, I felt elated. The work, if I were to undertake it, would be overwhelming but then what had I but time?

I pushed the manuscript pages I'd read aside. Immediately before me in their absence rose the sixty-one floors of One Liberty Place rising like a glass cathedral. I stared at the empty windows for a long time. I closed my eyes and remembered the Philadelphia of my past, saw again the blue glass of One Liberty Plaza and recalled how the windows would reflect the outside rather than allow penetration, how they revealed passing clouds or approaching storms. Like all cities from a distance, the downtown hub could be an imposing place, a chaotic web of interstate highways circling a glass and steel center, a maze seemingly so full and layered that it appears impenetrable. A place designed exclusively for people, so dense the people become invisible.

I held my eyes closed and saw the skyline again in memory without the gaps of the incomplete drawing. I saw the color I could not render in pen and ink, saw too the clusters of smaller buildings in the foreground, the old seven- and eight-story hotels, the apartment buildings. I concentrated my close-eyed focus there and saw where there were rooftop gardens, where there were balconies and windows that opened onto apartments where music or the murmur of conversation escaped.

I opened my eyes, took up my pen, and began populating a rooftop with patio containers loaded with flowers and trailing vines. I added trees and picnic tables and benches. On one bench I drew the suggestion of a man, little more than an ink smudge. Then I drew another figure, a woman I imagined, leaning as if smelling a rose bush, and between them I drew another smaller figure. I stopped and shook my hand out, flexed my fingers. Then I picked up my pen again and drew couples on balconies sharing drinks, a quartet seated at an outdoor table, a quintet occupying patio furniture. I drew soloists standing at windows, positioned such that I gathered they looked away from the city, perhaps following the line of the river with their eyes or imagining a place of forests or mountains or plains full with windblown grasses, anything beyond the hard edges of asphalt and steel. The people were tiny, nearly microscopic, true to the scale of the drawing, yet I understood that each of them had a story to tell. A story and a past and a future.

23

The next morning, I started with a blank writing tablet. I restacked the manuscript pages, turned them upside down, and pushed them aside to a corner of the table. The previous afternoon I had spent a good deal of time within a book filled with biographical essays on the first jazz musicians and reread several chapters of an early history of New Orleans. As I read the stories of individual lives, I could hear the music that fit their time and experience playing like a soundtrack in my head. I'd been immersed in the music for so long now.

That afternoon I found my old copy of the city bus map and route schedule and saw that I could reach the coffee shop where Monika's mural was located with only one transfer. I arrived at a moment when the shop was nearly empty, and the woman who ran the shop greeted me as if I were an old friend. I was shocked to be recognized. She asked how I'd liked the coffee I'd purchased and suggested a new blend I might like. "So Monika successfully converted you?" she asked, making light conversation. It felt as if the question might apply to any number of things, though of course I knew it really was asked in reference to the purchase of fair-trade coffee.

"Yes," I said. "I do believe she has."

"Good for her."

"It's very good of you to support her work. Not many people would give the exterior of their building over to a teenager."

"You've seen her work. How could you not support that kind of talent? I figure we need all the beauty we can find in this world. Besides, you might have noticed, Monika can be very persuasive."

"Relentlessly so."

"That's the perfect word, relentless. When I first met her,

she approached me about a job and then when I didn't have any openings, she asked about placing art in the shop."

"That sounds exactly like Monika."

"Doesn't it though? Even though I liked her gumption, I found her exhausting until I got to know her. I liked the idea but I imagined some mediocre high school art show. I blew her off. Looking back, I'm more than sorry because I always hated it when adults were dismissive or patronizing. I've come to love Monika, but she was so enthusiastic, so energized, I thought, my lord, what would I be getting into. Here she is, this fidgety teenager telling me how I could provide the space that could give the finger to conservatives and define art for an artless community. I was more than a little put off. But then I saw the work… Have you seen any of her other work?" she asked.

"No."

"You must. The second time she approached me, she brought in these two huge portfolios. I mean dozens and dozens of pieces. She spread them around until she'd covered almost every table in the place. If there were people at the tables, it didn't matter, she just laid her work over their books or reports. No social boundaries in that one. Paintings. Drawings. Short poses. Long poses. Self portraits. Landscapes. Conceptual pieces. Collages. Some were just stunning. Some were disturbing. But every piece took your breath away."

I looked around the coffee shop. Small, mostly framed paintings occupied the wall space between windows and down the hall to the bathroom, below the counter and all along the dividing wall between the shop and the next store. "Is this some of her work?" I asked, motioning to the walls around us.

"Not a one," she said. "When I first said yes to her, we filled nearly all of our space with her work. But within a week she started bringing in the work of her classmates. Every time she put one of their pieces up, one of hers came down to make room. Two weeks later she was bringing in work from a senior center, then from other artists around the area. It's been really lovely stuff ever since, as you can see. Like this guy," she said, pointing to a still life near the cash register. "He's had a one-man show in Chicago, yet she got him to agree to place work here. That piece," she pointed now to a large Cubist-inspired portrait on the opposite wall, "is by a high school freshman. We'd been featuring art for maybe a month before we started having artists—established ones and nobodies alike—approach us about displaying their work here. Who knew there was so much art being produced?"

"It does open your eyes, doesn't it?" I agreed.

"I don't know a thing about art, I just know what I like. It makes the place feel more alive. Now I have nothing left of Monika's, except the mural of course. The mural is how artists find us. I keep begging her to let us display some new pieces, but nothing. Lately she keeps telling me she's working on a project close to her heart but she hasn't shared a thing.

"That's Monika for you," she said. "She was in just the other day. She mentioned you. She said I need to display some of your work. She told me I would need to ask about it."

"My work?"

"Yes. She said you were an artist."

"I'm no artist."

"You're who she calls Mr. Underground Man aren't you?"

"Pardon?"

"I'm sorry. Maybe I'm mistaken. You draw don't you? City-scapes, she told me."

"Yes," I stammered and then I started to retract the admission.

"She said I should ask you sometime if you'd drawn Boston yet. She said that once you draw Boston, you'd have work that had to be displayed."

"I'm not an artist," I muttered.

"If you ever change your mind, bring your work in."

I wanted to protest but didn't know where to begin. This person was a stranger. I didn't even know her name.

As if she were a mind reader, she said, "Oh, I'm so sorry. I don't even know your name. I'm Gabrielle. My friends call my Gabby. Can't imagine why."

I introduced myself and shook her hand.

"It's good to meet you. Officially, I mean. Say, you don't play music, do you? Monika has been pushing and pushing me to start an open mic night. We're looking for performers to get things started."

"Not on your life," I said.

"Oh," she said, disappointed. "I thought maybe Mr. Underground Man was some sort of stage name."

"No, it's just a Monika thing."

"Say no more. Monika's known me for over a year, yet I'm still Coffee Sister One."

"And who's your sister?"

"Coffee Sister Two, of course, which I don't really mind because she's actually older than me. I never get to be number one at anything. Plus, she doesn't even work here—a silent partner who just drinks a lot of coffee."

I thanked her for the conversation and ordered a cup of coffee which I took outside to the patio despite the cold. I took some notes while I drank my coffee. For the first time I was beginning to see the book in images and moving pictures whereas before it had seemed an accumulation of facts. When I took my dirty cup to the dish bin, Gabby was at the register.

"You should come Friday night," she said. "It might get interesting."

"Monika was threatening to start a band," I said. "That might be plenty interesting in itself."

"God, I hope not," Gabby said. "She used to sing along with her iPod while she painted."

"Sadly, I've witnessed that firsthand."

"Then perhaps you'd better stay away Friday and keep drawing. Let me know when you've drawn Boston. I'm saving space. Don't be a stranger," she called out as I departed.

24

I took Gabby at her word. I returned for a second visit to the Coffee Sisters later in the week and again the following Monday. Gabby asked me again about my drawing and asked specifically why I focused on cityscapes. As it turns out, she had completed her undergraduate degree in architecture, and while she had never employed the degree, she was highly knowledgeable about architectural design principles. We had an enriching conversation about design themes and then moved on and shared our mutual fascination with Frank Lloyd Wright. When I told her that perhaps I'd pushed his principles of organic unity to a degree of hyper dedication, we shared an in depth conversation on sustainability. Gabby was passionate about the subject. Politically active, one trying to live by her principles, we couldn't be more different. I admitted that too often my own interests tended toward the academic. When asked how I'd met Monika, I shared her attempt to rescue my home.

"Mr. Underground Man," she said, "now I get it." She then described the street view of my home with precision. "Finally, someone who understands building within space rather than against it. I'm so thrilled to have met you. What you're doing makes so much sense."

I was nothing short of shocked at the unexpected reversal of interest in my home, someone who embraced its simple science rather than condemned its eccentricity.

I left the coffee shop exuberant and went from there back to the natural foods market where I passed a pleasant hour exploring labels. Certainly, I overpaid, but I treated myself to a certified hormone-free steak and what would surely prove the last of the season's locally grown melons, along with some wild rice from the bulk bins and a can of imported olives. I stepped outside into a light rain, and even that did not dampen my spirits.

Walking home from the bus stop toting my purchases in my trusty Coffee Sisters canvas bag, I allowed myself to admit that, oddly enough, I'd left the house earlier in the day purposefully seeking some human contact—not an admission I make lightly. I'd wanted to hear other voices.

It had been more than a week since I'd last seen Monika. I'd tried not to give her absence a lot of thought. Perhaps, I considered, that was it and Monika had exited my life with the same abruptness with which she'd entered it. Given Monika's nature, that I might never see her again seemed an entirely distinct possibility. It was not an easy thing to admit that I'd come to value her friendship.

Friend. It is a word I had not used in a long time. I have not always been without friends. Before Susan died, the house was filled with friends, some of them dating back to our college days. Many had started families at the same time we did and our children had played together. We met new people through Renee, through school functions and soccer and dance classes. And there certainly were colleagues and other contacts I'd made in my working life who had become cherished friends. I turned my back on all eventually, even before I moved away. I knew the offers of comfort I had received daily were heartfelt, but I'd wanted to suffer. I thrived on the pain. Loneliness made the pain acute. Pure. Like a poison clarified. Like all addicts, I'd grown defiant in its defense. To allow oneself to grow close to someone only accentuated the suffering that would accompany their inevitable loss.

When I reached home, I found Monika seated on my new bench. Her form seemed indistinct, as if the outline of her were blurred by the rain. She had her legs drawn up onto the seat and sat with her arms wrapped around them and her head down on her knees. Bunched up like that she looked like a child, and the big engineer boots seemed out of place. She appeared dressed entirely in black, the only color visible in the streaks of her dyed hair.

She looked up as I neared. Her eyes were reddened and swollen. Her hair was limp from the rain. She wore no make-up. The polish on her fingernails was chipped and peeling. She looked at me without expression.

"Monika, what's wrong?"

She looked up again. Her lip quivered. "My brother died."

"Oh, Monika, I'm so sorry," I said, kneeling awkwardly in front of her.

"I thought I would be ready," she said. "It's been like he was dead for such a long time."

"Oh, Monika." I didn't know what more to say. She collapsed forward, leaning her head on my shoulder. Her arms were crossed within the curve of her body. I felt the shudder of her crying. I gathered her into an awkward hug.

"I thought I could handle it," she repeated between sniffles.

I didn't know how to console her.

"I know he's better off. I know this is what he wanted. I mean obviously it's what he wanted. He just didn't get the job finished before. Why can't I accept that?"

"Because he was your brother," I said. "Because you loved him."

"I still don't understand why he did it."

"I don't think we are meant to understand."

She leaned away from me back onto the bench.

"We need to get you out of the rain." I stood and, my hand at her arm, guided her to standing and from there to the door. She moved as if something in her was broken. After I opened the door, she stepped inside onto the landing and stopped. I nearly collided with her as I stepped inside and closed the door.

"What's the matter?" I asked.

"I don't want to go down there." She looked scared, the way she looked in the car the day she drove me away from city hall after witnessing my anxiety attack.

I looked down the stairs. The lights were off but I could see the neon of Roger Waters's legs. "Okay," I said. "We don't have to. We can sit right here where it's dry."

She sank to a seated position on the top step. I sat down beside her.

"When your family was murdered," she said, turning to me, "did you ever consider killing yourself? Did it ever get to that?"

I thought for a time before answering. I needed to be honest. With her. With myself. "No," I said emphatically. "I've done a lot of things that were self-destructive. I isolated myself. I ignored my relatives, my wife's family, our friends. I removed myself. I knew what I was doing. For years I felt like I lived trapped at the bottom of a well and day by day, year by year, I was slowly drowning. Sometimes I still feel that way. But, no, despite everything, as bad as it got, I never considered suicide. So really, it is a thing I cannot comment on from any point of knowledge."

"Neither can I," she said. "Right after Danny tried to kill himself, I thought, I'll show him. I'll show him how it's really done. I planned just how I'd do it, the whole sad, dramatic thing, the bathtub, the blood, the note. I spent a lot of time in my head obsessing over the note. But really I was never close to doing it. Not even a little. I didn't want to. Which kind of pissed me off in a way. But I knew I could never cause that much pain. I've seen the results."

I exhaled, letting go of some fear.

"You know," she said. "Sometimes I felt guilty for not being so depressed by my brother's botched attempt that I couldn't go on. But it just wasn't true. As much as I want my brother back, I wanted to live. Is that selfish?"

"Selfish?" I asked, feeling relief wash over me. "Wanting to live? Not at all. What he did was selfish."

"That's not fair," she snapped. "You didn't know him."

"You're right," I admitted, sorry I'd said it.

"But I know what you mean," she said. "I don't like to admit it, but sometimes I think that too, and then I feel guilty for thinking it."

"I don't mean to imply that you should hold it against him. Obviously, he felt desperate."

"What do I do now?" she asked. "My family is broken. I'm supposed to graduate in May. And then what? More school? Spend my life working? Doing what? What's my life supposed to look like? Two kids and a job and wake up every day wondering if one of them is going to try and off himself? They tell me I'm supposed to leave home and go off into the world and start a life. I don't know how to do that."

I leaned back, sitting up straight. I turned my head and looked out the glass toward the street and stared at the empty space where the property review notice sign had once stood. I watched the rain. When I turned back to look at Monika, fresh tears dribbled off her jaw and onto her coat. "I'm not the one to offer advice," I said.

"Thanks for nothing," she said flatly. "I should have known better." Her expression did not change.

"One would have thought so," I agreed.

Anger interrupted her defeated appearance. "I should have expected this from you. I don't know why I came here. You're like…like the definition of selfish."

"Precisely right," I said, turning away from her defiant glare and focusing on the wooden step between my feet. "I am entirely selfish. I am ill-equipped to offer advice. Look at my life. What advice could I possible offer?"

"You're here, aren't you?"

Her question stopped me as if she brandished a weapon. I wanted to retreat down the stairs. Her question clung to the air. When I replied, I could not muster more than a whisper, like I'd been cooped up so long my voice struggled to recall its proper function. "Look at my life and do the opposite," I rasped.

She was silent for a time and then abruptly she rose and said, "Seriously? That's the best you could do?" Then she threw open the door and sprinted away, engineer boots exploding the puddles that had formed in the earthen path.

The door banged against the wall and back again, then stood partly ajar. I rose and closed the door on the rain.

25

The memorial service was scheduled for the following Tuesday evening. I found the notice in the local paper on a special library trip for that purpose. I assumed that Monika's parents had chosen an evening service so that Danny's friends could attend without interfering with school or after-school extracurricular activities. There would be no grave-side service, no casket. In place of a casket, an urn stood on a small marble pedestal at the front of the church, and next to it, dominating an easel, was a large unframed portrait of Danny painted in bright acrylics. The portrait, a canvas well over three feet square, commanded the attention of the service and focused the attendees on Danny in a way that had little to do with the generic, pedestrian words the minister spoke.

Monika had crafted a largely realistic portrayal of her brother, although she had employed nearly neon colors that sprang off the canvas and edged against one another—an electric blue face against fluorescent green hair. In the painting Danny was smiling, more of a smirk to be accurate, as if he refused to share a private joke. I could not get beyond the youthfulness of the face, an adolescent but a breath beyond childhood. His face appeared, like his sister's, nearly androgynous. His hair was an unruly nest of curls. Monika had highlighted her choice of neon green locks with jet black, and on close inspection after the service I saw that the highlights formed musical notes and cursive words, and near his neck, a thicket of flowers. A necklace encircled his throat, a hemp strand featuring homemade beadwork that carried the words:

"Fade far away, dissolve, and quite forget…"

My Dartmouth education served me after all and I recognized Keats's language. I finished the line in my head:

"What thou among the leaves hast never known,
The weariness, the fever, and the fret Here."

I offered my simple condolences to Monika's parents without introducing myself. They appeared dazed, their gazes quickly veering off to the doorways and windows as if scanning a horizon for anticipated movement. I knew that they would forever feel as if they were trapped underwater listening to the muffled sounds of the living world. For now, they protected the other mourners with quiet thanks and grim smiles, stoic nods and stiff hugs—a couple isolated in grief and trying to preserve dignity.

The rest of the mourners tended toward the young, who tried on their newly experienced emotion of anguish in the same way they did anything—loudly, with energy and conviction. They far outnumbered the adults in attendance.

While her parents remained stationary in a receiving line alongside grandparents and an uncle, Monika worked the room. She'd transformed into the perfect hostess, and as she departed each little clumped gathering of mourners, she seemed to leave them having experienced a moment of healing grace, tears transformed from abject grief to enlightened sadness, like diners sated after a fulfilling meal. She moved from group to group, making some erupt with laughter, drawing others toward an inward-turning silence, eliciting smiles and more hugs from all. I watched as she touched her forehead to those of two girls a year or two younger than her, and they reacted as if a spiritual healing had occurred. The two girls fell into an embrace when Monika departed. She held elbows in handshakes with adult men like a practiced politician. Upon leaving one group of teens, a small device connected to an iPod suddenly appeared and Brian Wilson's voice erupted. The incongruity of "In Blue Hawaii" filled that corner of the chapel with layered harmonies. The song segued to a Bare Naked Ladies tune and Steven Page's voice lamented about lying in bed. One of the teens broke into a dance and another sang along.

I stayed largely on the periphery of the room but willed myself to stop and politely converse briefly with several groups, and I made a particular point of engaging anyone standing alone. The effort caused me considerable discomfort. Small-talk had never been something I'd label as a strength in my skill set. Seven years of isolation hadn't exactly helped those abilities. Add to that the rather stark fact that I'd never met the deceased and I'd never felt more awkward—discounting a certain horrific karaoke moment—but watching Monika work the room assuaging her own grief in consideration of others, I was inspired. For explanation of my presence, I settled on "friend of the family" and I tried to ask a lot of questions.

At one point I found myself trapped in a conversation without exit, or rather, as the recipient of an endless monologue from a woman near my own age who was apparently obsessed with llamas, or more precisely, with a llama she referred to as Marcy. Over the course of ten minutes I'd learned more than I cared to know about llama eating habits, digestive issues, and reproductive needs. She'd just started in on the superiority of llama wool fibers when Monika rescued me.

"Why in fuck's sake are you here?" she demanded as soon as she'd pulled me away.

"Who on earth was that?" I asked, deflecting, quick to fall into old habits.

"She's the crazy neighbor."

"I thought I was the crazy neighbor."

"She's our up-close-and-personal version of crazy. She lives across the street from us. We try to avoid her. I used to babysit her cat when I was little."

"Why isn't the city trying to evict her? Apparently she's harboring livestock for Christ's sake. Running a virtual llama farm."

"I asked you what you're doing here," Monika nearly shouted.

"Doesn't the city know about the llama? Her name is Marcy."

"No, the llama is dead. Has been since before she became our neighbor. Stop changing the subject. Get over the llama. It's Tuesday."

"What?"

"Oh my God, you're so frickin' predictable. You're supposed to be at your city hearing right now."

"I am?" I thought for a moment before realizing she was right. "I forgot all about it."

"Don't you care? Don't you give a damn? Can't you see anything anyone has tried to do for you?" The hostess routine was gone for good, replaced by her impression of a Catholic mom.

"Seriously, I forgot all about it."

"You so full of shit," she seethed. "What are you doing here?"

"I came to support you."

"That meeting was really important."

"*This* is really important, Monika."

"You're delusional. I don't know why I should be surprised."

"Honestly, I completely forgot." Smiling, I repeated, "I forgot," for I really had forgotten. This fact brought me strange, backward pleasure, like a toothache that makes a martyr out of its victim. I marveled at my ability to forget a thing I'd spent weeks obsessing over. "Even if I'd remembered," I said, "it would be more important to be here."

"Learning about llamas."

"Exactly," I said, falling into what I thought was our schtick. "Where else am I going to get information like that?"

"They could decide something tonight that could change your life."

"As if they'd listen to me if I were there. They'll do what they do. Let it go, Monika. It's okay."

"Maybe if you hurry, you could still make an appearance," Monika said.

"Let it go, Monika."

"You've blown it."

"Nah, it will work out. Besides, I didn't have any real ammunition. I'd be better off getting a llama. Or a whole herd of them. Are they herds? Or packs? Litters?"

She refused to bite. She looked really angry, so I prattled

along at warp speed. I'd carry both sides of the banter if I had to. "You know," I said. "I've been thinking about taking up knitting. It would be cool to learn how to dye wool too, you know. Crushing plants and berries and all that. There may be a whole enterprise I've overlooked here. Put the rooftop to good use. What's the carrying capacity per acre for llamas?"

"Stop," she said.

"The big money is probably with alpacas," I said. "Or cashmere sheep."

"Stop it."

"I came here for you," I said.

"You keep telling yourself that," she said. She turned abruptly and stomped away. I started to follow and she joined a cluster of couples her parent's age and immediately transformed again, as if there were a changing room filled with costumes I'd not spied.

I ducked through a group of Danny's friends who all wore matching skater shoes and who had pinned black carnations to their clothes. They appeared to be arguing over the plot details of a recent movie. I stepped out a side door and into a hallway. There were tall windows in the hall, and while it was dark outside, I could see by the movement of the tree branches that the wind had come up and I knew there would be a winterish bite to the air. I walked into the biting wind and did not look back.

26

Days passed and I had no contact from the city. Eventually, with the help of a librarian and some time passed on a library computer, I discovered that the city maintained an online archive of meeting minutes. I learned that a dozen neighbors had testified about what an "eyesore" my home was and the leading comment was that it "appeared out of character with the surrounding properties." I remain uncertain how a structure that is essentially invisible to these neighbors is considered an eyesore. The city review board, bureaucratic to a fault, focused entirely on policy, code, and paper trails. I had violated no architectural standards, one official had remarked. But he had added that the city could not afford to be seen as condoning the existence of properties "out of character with immediate environs." Much of the talk by officials centered on what they viewed as "substandard application of nationally derived construction codes" by the county at the time of my home's construction. The board tabled discussion pending more review of findings.

If there had been any neighborly concern about recent acts of vandalism as reported in the main daily local paper, I heard nothing about it. Apparently, as a sane person might surmise, the neighbors saw no connection between the two topics. Perhaps they'd never noticed, or at least they had not noticed certain gnome-exchanging mayhem, or perhaps they simply catalogued such incidents as further evidence that the very foundations of the culture were eroding and the city would one day be rampant with meth heads and vagrants.

The city had stolen a page from my Bartleby playbook. Past observations of American public policy behavior left me assuming, no matter decisions reached or not reached, my fate would be handed over to the jurisdiction of lawyers. I knew enough to recognize that the deals reached in the backrooms and party offices were always more authentic of true motivations, and more lasting, than anything discussed in a public forum.

Monika stayed away.

I found myself either dreaming more regularly than normal or better adept at remembering my dreams. I'd begun having dreams about my daughter. In them she was usually a giggling toddler finding joyous humor in the simplest things—playing in a pile of laundry, jumping on the bed, harassing the dog by pulling on its lips. Whereas I usually fear dreams, I came to love my middle of the night visitations.

Somewhere along the way my little home had become so quiet that I thought I heard things, thin voices, music that was not present. Each morning after a couple of hours of work, I found myself craving a cup of coffee and more and more, I wanted the clatter of dishes and the hiss of steamers and the hum of overlapping conversations as background, and so I ventured out on the excuse of seeking fresh air before the weather prohibited such excursions. Out of character, I found myself working on the book while seated at the coffee shop, as if the voices nearby helped me locate the voices that had evaded me in the words I wrote.

I'd also returned to the work of constructing Philadelphia, only now as I worked, I heard its sounds: growl of garbage truck compactors, squawk of bus brakes, roar of sirens, hollow thud of delivery trucks on the move rattling over sewer grates, shouted voices and laughter spilling from bar doorways. With the voices and sounds arrived the people, and I could not move my pen fast enough to keep pace. More and more as I drew Philadelphia buildings rising from their bedrock footings, the sounds rendered became those of another city, one with a different accent. While I continued to work only in pen and ink, the work occupying the table began to appear entirely different than that suspended above it on the walls, as if it contained color, as if it were a living city rather than the skeletal remains of a past apocalypse.

Indeed, little, perhaps nothing in my life beyond what lived on paper had changed. I suffered no interruptions. I listened for sounds from the above ground world. Eventually I employed the disc player and the turntable with greater frequency, digging further into the collection, the sounds from the past fueling the work.

A week after Danny's memorial service, abruptly and entirely out of character, I set about baking the only true casserole I'd ever had the stomach for, a cheesy, spicy Mexican dish that Susan had hated and that I'd been making since college.

I'd saved the memorial program from the funeral, which had included Monika's address for those wishing to accompany the family home after the service. I employed my trusty hemp bag from the Coffee Sisters and walked with my casserole gift until I reached the entrance gates of Cedar Ridge Farms, large stone affairs that incorporated no cedar.

I checked the address I'd tucked into my jacket pocket. I had no idea where I was going. As I passed street signs, a pattern of names emerged—absurdly the names of songs that included fruit in their titles, streets like Strawberry Fields Lane and Blueberry Hill Road, Lemon Tree Way and Grapevine Street—yet there was no identifiable order, no simple alphabetizing or pattern I could discern. I entertained myself by imagining the sort of developer who chose, as a lasting contribution to a city, such an odd and seemingly arbitrary heritage. What music, fruit, and cedar trees had in common was lost on me entirely. I'd begun to give up hope when at last I reached Coconut Telegraph Road. I shrugged and turned with Jimmy Buffet's voice infiltrating my head as I scanned addresses.

The addresses proved quite necessary as most of the homes offered small variations on a common theme played out in three earthy colors. They were attractive houses, precise and cared for, large homes on a street that looked like it belonged in a catalog. No wonder some turned to yard art, I thought. How else would they avoid turning into the neighbor's driveway at night? Pity the drunk arriving in the dark.

In the end, perhaps the address was unnecessary after all, for no other house hosted a brown Civic in its driveway nosed against a garage stall door.

Monika's mother answered the door. I recognized her from the funeral of course, though it appeared she had aged in the week that had passed. She had the look of a famine victim, all bones and sharp joints and sunken eyes. Yet she smiled brightly and greeted me warmly when she opened the door. I had wanted to hand off the casserole and be on my way, but she insisted I come in. I was sure she did not remember me—why would she—yet the warmth felt genuine, as if she'd been wanting guests. Despite the pointed angularity of her features, she was an attractive woman and she shared a small portion of Monika's nervous, fidgety energy. I did not know the woman, yet as I took the long fragile-looking hand she extended, a hand that offered that soft, effeminate fingertip touch in a horizontal handshake, instantly I wanted to sit her down in the kitchen and spoon feed her some of the casserole. I wanted to take over her kitchen and cook all day for her, wanted to learn her favorite recipes, her motherly comforts, and cook each and every one until she found the dish she craved. Instead I held the bag forward as a kind of offering and said, "I baked a casserole. It's a Mexican sort of thing. You can freeze it for some other time."

"Oh, that's so thoughtful of you. We'll enjoy it so much. Won't you join me for some coffee?"

"I shouldn't."

"You must stay for one cup. I insist."

She led me to the kitchen. I didn't want to be there despite my reaction to her grief a moment before. I remembered the awkward visitations I'd endured, all the casseroles stacked into the freezer I never ate. And still, despite the awkwardness and the frequent silences and the forced conversations, so often I'd wanted the presence of another human then, even if sometimes I only wanted them for distraction.

The kitchen was immaculate. Stainless steel appliances. A granite island stretched ten feet. The room smelled of candles and flowers, a place comforting and nurturing where one expected laughter, not a host to grief. I sat at the island and, searching for conversation, complimented the room's color scheme. We then moved on to kitchen appliances.

Julia appeared businesslike as she ground beans and prepared the coffee in a device that looked like it belonged on the space station. I feared we were quickly reaching the end of my appliance knowledge base when I was saved by Monika's sudden appearance. Her voice preceded her physical arrival by many seconds in the form of a shouted question: "Mom, are you okay? I hear voices."

When she crossed the threshold, she jumped back as we made eye contact. "What are you doing here?" she asked.

"He brought a casserole," Julia answered for me.

"A casserole," Monika said, her voice full with surprise. "Will wonders never cease, Mr. Badger."

"Oh, that's right," Julia cooed. "Mr. Badger. I'm so sorry. I'd forgotten your name and I was too embarrassed to ask."

"The apology is mine," I said without correcting her. "I should have re-introduced myself. There is no reason you would remember."

Monika giggled.

"What is it, dear?" Julia asked.

"I can't believe you cooked something," she said, ignoring her mother.

"I do cook, you know. Actually, I like cooking a great deal."

"A regular domestic god no doubt," Monika said.

"Monika, don't be rude," her mother said.

"Never fear," I said, sounding suddenly like a 1960s super hero. "This is how Monika and I converse. I don't take any offense."

Julia looked confused.

"Don't worry, Mom. What he means is that I give him shit and he dishes it right back."

"Oh." The confused look didn't change.

"I say things like, 'I didn't know you ran a meals-on-wheels operation there, Mr. Badger.' And then he says, 'It's more of a meals-on-foot gig.' It's how we avoid the difficult stuff."

Julia looked more confused than before. I was busy thinking that Monika had it right. That was exactly what I would say. Then I recovered. "She greatly undervalues my cooking ability," I said.

"Well, I think it is very thoughtful of you," Julia said.

"Mr. Badger's a thoughtful guy, a regular etiquette expert."

Julia looked at me as if embarrassed. For me, for herself, I wasn't sure. I tried to cover. "Teenagers," I said. "Sometimes they just can't help but find themselves amusing."

"Lord knows it's a humor I don't always get," Julia said. "Now, you're with the school, right?"

"That's right," I lied. I wasn't sure why. An easier explanation, I suppose. Monika looked at me like she was about to mount a protest.

"So you're surrounded by them all the time."

"All the time. Swimming around in their addled brains. You can't imagine the things you get provoked into doing."

"I can only guess. Raising them. It's a trial. No one will ever tell you my Daniel was an angel. And Monika here, if only I could get her to apply herself to her full ability. It's exasperating really."

Monika appeared to be either preparing to spring for the attack or fixing to leap out of the kitchen entirely. I wanted to intercept any reply she might be forming. And then it came to me, an idea wholly formed in an instant. I opened my mouth without so much as contemplating the thought that had occurred to me. "That's why I'm here," I said, "beyond the casserole, of course. I, rather we, the school that is, would like to establish a scholarship in Danny's name. Through an alum at Dartmouth. It would be for bright, promising kids but ones who sometimes approach things in—how should we say—unconventional ways. Kids who are gifted but don't always immediately fit the traditional profile."

Julia began to cry. I immediately felt bad. But then she interrupted her crying long enough to say, "Oh, you don't know how much that would mean. To have something good come out of this nightmare."

"Mr. Badger," Monika interrupted. A look of confusion creased by concern appeared. "Dartmouth's great, Ivy League." She whistled out loud then. "But it's very expensive. There's no way the school could help with that kind of tuition. It's a thoughtful gift, but I think they're getting ahead of themselves."

"They've identified an anonymous donor," I said. "It would be a full ride for four years and then it would renew to a new student. A legacy for the community."

Julia's tears made her eyes glisten and there was a spot of brightness within them, despite their red-rimmed hollowness. "Oh, my," she said. "I'm flabbergasted."

"Moreover," I said. "The school would like to see Monika be its first recipient. She's an ideal candidate—exceptionally smart, talented, capable, yet a highly original and independent thinker. She's the sort of student who needs to be surrounded by others who are gifted, and she needs to be exposed to a demanding faculty. We'd just need to see evidence in the consistency of her grades next semester that the scholarship would prove a sound investment."

Julia sat down heavily on the stool next to me.

"This would all be dependent on your approval of course," I said. "Not just to issue the scholarship in Danny's name, but to put Monika forward as a nominee. Needless to say Monika would have to agree that this is of interest to her. I realize Dartmouth is far away."

Monika seemed to open her mouth in protest but no sound came out. The new sensation threw her into one of her fidgety fits.

"We would hope," I added, "that someone with her elevated

talent would continue to pursue her art alongside her other academic interests or as her focus if she so chose."

"Her art," her mother said absently as if her mind had drifted away. I wondered if she were imagining the distance to New Hampshire and worried such remove could claim a second child. As soon as I had suggested my alma mater, a place where I knew people within the administration, I worried about my presumption.

"Her art demonstrates remarkable ability and maturity," I said. "Just the sort of dexterous, eclectic achievement teamed with high intellectual ability elite private schools seek out."

"Yes, I know she is talented," Julia said dreamily.

"Mom, you haven't taken the time to see anything I've painted since I was in the fifth grade," Monika said angrily. "Don't pretend differently just because there's a stranger in the room."

"Untrue," her mother said, completely unfazed.

I squirmed. I should have stayed home. Going above ground, suddenly inserting myself in another's life, reinforced the reality that actions had consequences. Interference altered the course of lives.

"What are you saying, Mom? You've never seen what I produce. It would probably scare you if you did. You have no idea who I am."

"I'm afraid my timing has been poor," I said. "I'm sorry." I got up to leave. They both ignored me, and I gathered my coat from where I'd placed it on the back of the stool.

"You're wrong," Julia said.

"Wrong? You've checked out, Mom. You checked out a long time ago. Don't try and pretend you're proud of my work when you've never seen it."

I'd reached the kitchen doorway and momentarily hesitated, debating if I should offer one more apology, when Julia seemed suddenly aware of my presence. "Sit down and finish your coffee," she said in a voice that commanded no alternative. I complied. Then, turning to her daughter she said, "I have seen your work."

"When, Mom? You've never been to one exhibition. You and Dad haven't even been to a parent/teacher conference in over a year. You haven't even set foot in the school."

"At that coffee shop. The mural you painted behind our backs."

"I did nothing behind your back. You weren't paying attention."

"No, you lied to us. But you're right. I wasn't paying enough attention."

"How'd you even know about it?"

"One Saturday I followed you."

"You followed me?"

"I wanted to see where you were going."

"You could have just asked."

"I should have, but I didn't. I saw you go into that shop. I was sure it would be filled with riff-raff, but I was glad you weren't going to some boy's house or going to buy drugs or something."

"Mom," Monika protested in an elongated whine.

"I couldn't find a parking place," Julia said. "I had this notion when I saw you go in the shop that I would go in too and we should have a cup of coffee together and talk. I haven't been very good about talking," she said. "I finally found a space nearly a block past the shop and when I got out of the car, I saw the mural. I knew it was yours before I ever saw you climb the ladder. I just knew. It was like I could look at that wall and hear your voice."

Julia turned to me then. "Have you seen it?"

I nodded.

"But why didn't you come to me, Mama? Why didn't you say anything? All this time…"

Julia looked at me from within her underground world and then she turned and focused once again on her daughter. "Because of your painting," she said. "Your painting was so beautiful, so beautiful and so sad, so…so full of you that I knew then the biggest part of you had already gone away from me. Into a place I would never reach."

"Mom, I haven't gone anywhere."

"Yes, you have. But I've come to see that it's all right. I saw even then that you would be just fine, that you knew yourself and could express yourself and you were ready to move beyond us. Not in the way your brother had given up, but in a way that showed me you understood the nature of sadness and could contain it. You have a rare gift. You can express desperation and turn it into beauty."

"Why didn't you tell me, Mom?"

I could see Julia thinking. She was reaching for something deep within.

"It's hard to explain," she said at last. "I saw something in you that gave me comfort without you knowing it. But maybe, if I'm honest with myself, I've hidden this for the wrong reason. Maybe I'm jealous. I don't know. You found your exit. Am I making any sense at all? Do you understand? I'm envious that you've found an outlet for your sadness. I'm happy for it too."

I had no right to be there, no right to witness this intimate declaration by a stranger. I wanted invisibility, the wish of a child.

"Do you see, Mr. Badger?" Julia said, turning to me and heightening my embarrassment. "I want nothing more than such an opportunity for my daughter. I want her to extricate herself from this place. She needs to be removed from her past."

Her comment couldn't have registered a more direct hit to my heart if she had tried. "I'm happy to provide an opportunity," I said. "I have every confidence that Monika can accomplish great things. But at risk of disagreeing with you, the opportunity to enter the larger world should not come at the sacrifice of her past. If there is anything I have learned from Monika, it is that one cannot try and hide from memory."

"*You* learned," she said mockingly, this frail woman turning suddenly mean, the muscles in her neck and on her arms growing taut. "What kind of school are you running? I thought you were the teacher."

"I have never been the teacher," I assured her. I rose from the stool once again. I looked directly into Monika's eyes. "The offer is real."

"You're smoking crack," Monika said flatly.

"Monika!" her mother admonished.

"He's full of it, Mom. I don't know what kind of delusional game he's playing. He's not with the school."

"Who are you then?" Julia physically moved between myself and Monika. "What have you done to my daughter? Why are you here?"

"He hasn't done anything to me, Mom. He's just troubled."

I'd come above ground and I'd been caught. I had ventured out of place. "I...I don't know why I came," I stammered. "I just wanted to offer my condolences."

"You need to leave," Julia said.

I stood, wanting to depart. But something had seized me. I can't explain it. I couldn't quite let go. "I'm not with the school," I admitted. "But the scholarship...that's real. That's something I can do. I want to do."

"We don't need a stranger's charity," Julia nearly shouted. She had shifted in an instant the way I'd seen her daughter do before. "We have means," she said, suddenly defiant. "We can take care of our own family."

I felt something near an out-of-body experience as I heard myself, calmly and as if this sudden notion had been the long cause of a professional life's work, explain the details of a scholarship I had never conceived of five minutes before. "If Monika chooses to accept the offer and you approve it, it's hers. If not, I promise that someone else who meets Dartmouth's admission standards will benefit. If she accepts and does not need the full tuition, the balance will be reserved in an endowed fund and be available for the next recipient. I would love to see Monika seize this opportunity, but regardless, if you would be willing to allow me to do so, the scholarship would serve as a memorial to your son. I would wish it to be something that honors your family. But the benefits would certainly not stop at your doorstep, which is only fitting, for your daughter has helped me see the importance of a more encompassing vision and more extensive sensitivity to others."

Julia appeared ready to protest but I cut her off. "Thank you for the coffee. Once again, I am very sorry for your loss." We may have both suffered loss that forever bonded us together within the experience of lifelong mourning, yet that bond, by its very nature, still contained no ability to meet the other's loss with articulation beyond the most elemental expressions of sympathy. And to her, I would likely remain nothing more than a madman intruding upon her family at a time of its greatest vulnerability.

I marched out of the kitchen, intent on seeing myself out and allowing them some privacy. Yet somehow, as if the house contained secret passages, Monika nearly beat me to the front door. She stopped me on the doorstep. "What are you doing?" she demanded.

"I'm just trying to help."

"You can't just insert yourself into people's lives and think you can change them."

"You did."

"I didn't try to fuck with your life."

"The hell you didn't," I said, surprised at the anger I felt. I stopped and gathered myself. I was the adult and it was about time I acted like one. "But that's not what this is about."

"Then what is it about?"

"Nothing more than I said."

"What is it you want?"

"I don't want anything, Monika. I really don't. I'm serious about setting this up as an endowment. I do want to help you. But it's more than that. It's not just about you and me. It's about believing there are other possibilities. I want others," I said, stumbling for words, "for other people, people like you, to have the opportunity to make the world different from what it is."

"I don't understand," she protested. "Why?"

"I owe you."

"For what?"

"For making me climb out of my hole. You've shown me kindness for no reason," I said. "I'm not so removed that I haven't learned from that."

"You really are serious," she said.

I nodded.

A mischievous look appeared in place of her stern expression. "You're full of surprises, Mr. Badger," she said.

"I surprised myself."

"I was talking about the casserole," she said and shut the front door on me in typical Monika fashion, which made me smile. I walked home, down streets named for songs about fruit and among the upright world of trees and houses nearly indistinguishable in their color palette. Songs arrived in my head unbidden, joining the ordinary noises of the world around me—the laughter of children playing, the crush of fallen leaves underfoot, the honk of Canadian geese overhead—with a kind of harmony.

27

I was momentarily confused when I heard the sound of my doorbell. It was only the second time I had heard its chime. A week had passed since my trip to offer condolences to Monika's family and the self-inflicted instigation of my newfound role as a philanthropist. But I had remained as serious in my desire to commit to funding an academic scholarship as I'd been dumbfounded by my spontaneous ability to manufacture a development officer's pitch in Monika's kitchen. The week had been a busy one, first with a flurry of exchanges with Dartmouth, followed by multiple conversations with an accountant and a lawyer, neither of whom I'd had contact with since leaving Boston years ago. All such exchange was made considerably more difficult given that I had no phone and no computer. Lamenting about the quagmire I had created while I was visiting with Gabby at the Coffee Sisters, she'd immediately offered me use of the coffeehouse as a communications center for my new venture, and I'd passed a good part of the week there. She'd joined right in and helped me. There was an odd sort of energy to the work, like I was being carried along by invisible forces. I had ventured out and been caught, and yet here I was returning to the world that had found me out so easily. All week, whenever I left my house I wore a hooded sweatshirt against the cold and against the prying eyes of neighbors.

As accustomed as I was becoming to a world filled with ringing phones and whirring espresso machines, the sound of the doorbell remained jarring. I climbed the steps to find a rail-thin man in a business suit at my door. My mind flashed to city attorneys and my pulse quickened. Of course the destruction of my home would arrive in the guise of a lawyer rather than the clanking of a bulldozer. This one bore thinning hair and designer glasses.

"I don't know who you think you are fooling," the man said by way of introduction, "but no pervert is going to get away with preying upon my daughter." A fleck of spittle clung to the corner of the man's mouth and his eyes appeared huge within the frames of his glasses. I stammered, trying to find words to mount a protest.

"You stay the hell away from Monika," he spat. "And you stay away from my wife and my home. I won't hesitate to involve the police."

He turned away and then turned rapidly back. His suit seemed to sag, as if he'd shrunk suddenly. "You're…you're a grown man," he stuttered, the words barely above a whisper now. "For Christ's sake, she just a teenager," he said.

I wanted to explain that Monika and I were friends, but I looked at the man, who seemed wedged somewhere between a desire to hit me and a need to cry, and I remembered that I was a father of a daughter who would remain forever a teenager and I knew if I were in his shoes I would imagine only the nightmare scenario, would never listen to a pathetic excuse of a man who had hidden himself away below the earth like a night-stalking predator.

How to explain that we were men united in grief, that he had entered the unwanted brotherhood of fathers who had lost children? In his shoes I would do most anything to prevent harm coming to my living child. The man turned, and I watched him cross my field to his car idling at the curb without saying a word, thinking all the while that the shot that gets you is never the one you see coming.

28

Days later, I was caught in deep rumination when I heard the doorbell again. I'd begun to think its installation had been the worst sort of tactical error. I had not left home in nearly a week, showering only twice and failing to change cloths with regularity. I thought perhaps I was coming down with the flu. There had been a day when I had never left bed.

The doorbell was a summons to face the world that existed whether I wished it to or not. It was, I thought, mostly a world of my own making.

Climbing the stairs, I saw that it was raining. A slouched pair of striped leg warmers I hadn't seen the likes of since the '80s, layered over skin-tight dark pants, stood in color contrast against the rain outside the door's glass. I reached the top of the stairs and opened the door.

"You said I should always think about what you would do and then do the exact opposite," Monika said as if we were in the middle of a conversation.

"Good morning to you too."

"Aren't you going to invite me in out of the rain?"

"I don't think that's a good idea," I said.

"Why not?"

"Because your dad came to see me last week."

"Oh," she said. "What did he say?"

"He accused me of being a pervert."

"You're not, are you?"

I didn't dignify her remark with a response.

"That was wrong of him to say such a terrible thing."

"I can't blame him," I said. "I mean, put yourself in his place."

"He has no right," she said. "He never even talked to me,

never asked who you are. Never trusted that I'm capable of exercising judgement. It's just like him to assume the worst of people."

"You're his daughter," I said. "He's only trying to protect you."

"I'm an adult," she said. "He has no right to control my decisions."

"You're seventeen-years old, Monika. It *is* his job to protect you."

"And you missed my birthday. I'm eighteen. I can vote. If I smoked, I could legally purchase tobacco. If I was a guy, I'd be required to register for the selective service. I could join the Marines tomorrow. In the eyes of the government—well, except for their historically archaic belief that I don't have the right to drink—I am considered an adult. Emancipated. So, I think I've passed the age where my parents can choose my friends." Rain dripped off the end of her nose and from her hair.

"I'm sorry I missed your birthday," I said.

"It kind of got swallowed up by the funeral."

The matter-of-fact nature of her statement made me ache for her. "Accept my belated best wishes."

"It's freezing out here," she said. "Can't you let me in?"

"I think it's only right that I honor your parent's wishes."

"And let me freeze to death? I won't come past the top step. I promise."

Reluctantly, I stepped aside. I could feel the steel of handcuffs on my wrists already.

She stepped inside and immediately sat down on the top step. I sat next to her. Without looking at me, she said, "Do the opposite. That's what you said. So, I decided I would ring your doorbell. Because I can't see you arriving unannounced at my house ever again."

"That would seem certain," I agreed.

"And, this whole scholarship thing. I'm not going to take it."

"How do you know that's the opposite of what I would do?" I questioned.

"After your rousing speech on the value of education."

"Okay," I said, "no scholarship."

"You're giving up that easily?"

"Yes."

"But you were serious?"

"I remain serious. I'll stick to my word. I've already been in contact with Dartmouth. I've spent much of the week working out the details. You can't be the only troubled genius in our school system who is deserving."

"How? I mean, where'd you get the money?"

"You mean the particulars of my lovely stairwell don't give you confidence I have the funds? I did just fine in my day, and frankly, my father did even better. But the scholarship money, well, there were substantial life insurance payments and a victim's compensation fund that have just been sitting in an account."

"Oh."

"I'd like to think that some good might come of that money."

"Still, no guilt trips? No fight. Who knew you'd give up on me so easily?"

"I'm not giving up on you at all. You've helped me see that you deserve the right to find your own way."

"Is that what you did? You found your own way?"

I remained silent for a while, thinking, remembering. "After my family was killed, I pitied myself. I ran from people. If you learn anything from me, you really should do the opposite of anything I have done." I paused. She frowned. "That's all I had done," I said. "I ran away. I left people behind in the process. I've learned by watching you that we all need people. We need to invest in others."

"That's all great," she said. "What's the good of money if it isn't spread around? But it takes more than money."

"I know," I said. I looked at our feet. A small puddle had formed underneath Monika's shoes.

"This is what I should have said the last time we sat here," I said, looking up into her face. "We only get one life. You know that better than most. Take your energy and your bright, eccentric mind and your vivid talent and share yourself with others. You need to live a life your brother would have been proud of." I patted her on the knee, a gesture I'd done with Renee countless times. "Stay true to your spirit, Monika, and not only will you be fine, you'll always know exactly what to do."

She sat silently for a while, staring directly at me as if daring me to break eye contact. She remained perfectly still, no nervous rhythmic tapping of a foot, no sporadic gestures or twitches or flinching. It seemed I should say something. At last she blinked and said, "My, my, that was quite the speech. And not a hint of sarcasm. That might be a first. You've been down there taking counsel from the gophers or something?"

I ignored her. "I meant what I said."

"I know you did," she said quietly.

"I need you to understand that I plan to be there for you, Monika. I haven't been anybody's friend for a very long time. I might not be very good at it."

"Okay," she said.

"But your dad has every right to worry. From here on out, we should meet in public," I said, adding, "like adults" in the attempt to cut off her argument before she made it. "We can meet for coffee. That's something people do, right?"

"Okay." She sighed. "I accuse my parents of trying to control my life, but honestly, I've not been good at all about talking to them for ages. I just figured they had enough on their minds." She moved the toe of her right foot as if drawing a circle in the puddle on the step. "We'll be coffee buddies. Like those old men who meet up the same time every week wondering which one of them will die and not make it. They probably have a pool going."

"You'll have an unfair advantage," I said.

"Yeah, but I'm reckless." She smiled and then looked away. "I'll talk to my dad. The irony is, of course, that I go to school surrounded by sex-crazed, testosterone-driven, addle-minded teenage boys. Statistically speaking, the risks of unwanted sexual approaches are much higher every day I set foot in that school."

I stood. I looked out through the closed door and saw that rain continued. "I'm going to make you some tea for the road. And get you a towel. I'll bring them up to you." I knew having her sit on the stairs was the silliest sort of compromise, for rumors, if started, didn't need substance for people to believe them and to take actions because of that belief. Labels have their consequences.

"Will you turn on some music at least?"

"Pick your poison," I said. She looked like a little girl waiting on the curb for a weekend with her grandparents. "Personally, I'm in the mood for blues," I added.

"My dad used to play old blues and lots of jazz. I get the feeling he may have been a cool guy in his pre-dad days. I haven't heard him listen to music at all in years. In fact, I can't remember the last time either of my parents had music on in the house."

"That's sad," I said. "Your mom? What did she listen to?"

"Show tunes and this awful pop crap. Every song she ever played seemed like it was written by a fourteen-year-old who hadn't been invited to the prom."

"It probably was."

"The show tunes were funny though. She'd sing along."

"How about your brother? What did he listen to?"

"Pop as a kid, like all the other freckle-faced, metal-mouthed freaks. But once the pimples set in and he sprouted his first chin hair, he got original. Like really early Pink Floyd and Emerson, Lake & Palmer. Huge Jim Morrison fan. There was this one album he played constantly last year. By the guy who left the Beach Boys, the one that was nearly lost forever."

"Brian Wilson. You have to be talking about *SMiLE*. That's quite a piece of musical history for an adolescent."

"My brother was obsessed."

"Some people had been waiting to hear that album for more than thirty years."

"And I thought you lived in a hole."

"There are some things I keep up with. There's some strange stuff on that album. Your brother must have been an interesting kid."

"He was. Most people wrote him off. Thought he was weird. But he could be the sweetest guy you'd ever met. He was always taking people by surprise. You'd never guess what he was like just to see him. By the end, he dressed totally Goth, makeup, black fingernails, dark clothes, the whole bit. It totally freaked my dad out. Danny had the long wallet chain and the big rings and this crazy haircut that was like in-your-face, don't-mess-with-me spiky thing and needless to say, people steered away from him. Still, he'd go out of his way to talk to strangers or find the people who were feeling like they didn't fit. He always won them over. Like there'd be this blue-haired grandma wanting to hide in the bananas when he approached and ten minutes later, he'd be carrying her groceries to the car."

"He sounds like he could be your brother."

"Everybody loved Danny," she said. "But he never actually let anybody in. Inside his own head, he was totally alone."

"He doesn't sound like the kind of kid who would trash someone's garden."

"Sometimes he'd do things just to fit in. He looked like he loved being the outsider, but mostly I think he was just lonely."

"So, he turned to vandalism."

"He wasn't like that," she said. "Don't you get lonely?"

"Are you still secretly worried that I'll start harboring gnomes?"

"Stop, I'm being serious."

"It's hard to explain," I said. "I guess people can adjust to about anything eventually. What choice do you have but to accept what your life has become?"

"That's one of the saddest things I've ever heard."

"The truth is, I don't think a lot about being alone anymore, or rather, I didn't for a long time."

"And now?"

"I guess sometimes you reach moments in your life when you have to make choices. Are you going to focus on the negative, try and protect yourself from harm and never experience anything as a result, or are you going to accept change and try and find the positive?"

She smiled at me. "See you really have grown wise down here in your rabbit hole."

"I thought it was a gopher hole."

"Nah, remember the rabbit hole led to Wonderland."

"Hmm. Wonderland always seemed kind of a strange place to me. Are you sure Lewis Carroll didn't drop acid?"

"And this place isn't weird?" she asked.

"Good point. I'll go put your water on to boil."

"No offense," she said. "I know playing the blues is supposed to make you feel better and all, but could we put on something happy instead?"

"Sure, whatever you want. After all, it's *playing* the blues that's supposed to make you feel better, and we both know how that would go. What do you want to hear?"

"I don't know. Something from your heyday, only happy. Something mindless. I don't want to think any more."

"I don't know," I said. "It's been a long time since these speakers played anything newer than about 1962."

"Recall that you're the one who gave the stirring lecture on accepting change," she said.

I went downstairs and bent over a crate of albums I hadn't perused in ages. A line of dust straddled the top edge of each jacket. "Ah, ha," I said, retrieving *The Completion Backward Principle* by The Tubes, thinking it ought to be right up Monika's alley. I positioned the needle arm so that it would drop onto the fifth track and "Attack of the Fifty-Foot Woman" filled the speakers. I would never have thought that B-movie nuclear meltdown inspired rock proved appropriate accompaniment for mourning, but then the world is a strange place.

In my ears Fee Waybill's voice, singing of an insatiable radiated blind date, sounded from a past so distant it nearly evaded recognition, his voice a cry from an entire body of music I'd long abandoned, but bring me back he did. I knew the next line before he sang it. I could name every song any DJ might partner with it, could name the songs and their composers and the musicians who performed them and could recall the news headlines from the months those songs were first transmitted from car stereos and living room speakers and concert arenas, just as I could see once again my beautiful Susan, eighteen and radiant in 1981, expectant, curious, open, open even to a shy, bookish, long-haired nerd who blasted the sarcasm of The Tubes out of dorm room windows.

29

I remain something of a reclusive man, though more and more I venture farther out into the world, moving, as it were, in expanding concentric circles. Mostly, I remain a man accustomed to contemplation and slow, deliberate decision making, my usual plodding, methodical nature.

Writing and drawing fit the slower pace I prefer to employ. I've long ago given up on the book. I have instead begun editing a series by other writers intent on telling the stories of the old musicians, and nearly always they are stories of courageous people who defied poverty and bigotry and tragic circumstances to pursue passion. Editing such stories inspires me. Once again I write lots of liner notes, some introductory materials to accompany compact disc releases, and the occasional essay mostly focused on the relationship between the economics of the music industry and its impact on creative output.

I stopped drawing cities, with one notable exception. Instead, I've returned to visiting them. I remain a stranger on their sidewalks, one who walks unnaturally close to the harsh angles where sidewalks meet walls, and my visitations are brief. While present I enter their noise and see the people I pass. I try to look within faces and see individual lives, for that is the difficult thing to do in cities where people are so numerous.

Lately I've taken to drawing trees, strange, detailed expressions of trees that imagine their capillaries and fibers.

The world is filled with ironies, of course. For instance, it turns out my little home was never entirely a home at all. Two months after the public meeting, I received another letter from the city, this one explaining that the completed review uncovered original documents—these from the days when my little parcel hosted a movable office for the gravel mining company—that showed my property had always been legally zoned "mixed use" for commercial and residential development. While such status remained the result of a simple error to modify certain documents upon incorporation of the property within the city—a not so atypical oversight somewhere along the cogs of bureaucracy—it so happens that the former gravel pit owner maintained significant land holdings throughout the city, including property that shared a thin boundary with mine just at the edge of the land donated to the city as open space, property that then connected to a large parcel he owned on the other side of the protected space. And there, within plain sight of my french doors, the landowner had plans for commercial retail development of considerable scale. More box stores and parking lots. Apparently, the city liked the tax revenue his development would produce more than they cared to listen to the protests of my neighbors—about my underground dwelling or about the proposed retail development within their sightlines. The landowner had no desire to establish the precedent of not honoring zoning determinations that provided him the right to build, no matter the age of those zoning ordinances. Of course, he conveniently also had a brother who served on the planning and zoning board for the city.

On the same day I received the letter explaining this surprising status of my property, there appeared in the local paper an article chronicling the exponential rise in a bizarre form of petty vandalism wherein lawn statuary frequently disappeared from homeowners' yards only to be replaced with statues belonging to someone else. The article explained that at first the incidents seemed restricted largely to newer neighborhoods west of the city center and were thought to be the work of an individual or a small group of "misguided pranksters," to quote a city official. But recently the strange crimes had spread throughout the city, so numerous and so frequent that it seemed it had become a new fad, with multiple groups participating and trying to one up another or that a "significant, coordinated" series of attacks had been carefully plotted by a kind of "home-grown terrorist" cell. In the most brazen act to date, on the very first night after the official lighting of the city hall Christmas displays, all of the figures from the nativity scene had been replaced with yard art—a cutout of a farmer's wife bent over in the garden took the place of Mary; Joseph had transformed into a silhouette cowboy; pink flamingos replaced the wise men; concrete sheep stood in for shepherds; and a gnome took center stage, the object of all the statuary's attention.

During one of our weekly coffee meetings, Monika took obvious delight in showing me the article, which included a large color photograph of the revised nativity.

"It does have a wonderful flair for dramatic comedy," I said, laughing appreciatively. "How on earth did you do it?"

"I didn't. I had nothing to do with it."

"Monika."

"Pinky swear. Cross my heart. I'd like to take credit but, honestly, this was way beyond me. I applaud whoever did it. It's brilliant, don't you think?"

"You are pinky swearing?"

"I am."

"Because this," she said, "is the work of genius. Obviously, you've allocated your scholarship dollars to the wrong candidate."

"In the spirit of irony, you might appreciate this as well." I showed her the letter from the city with something parallel to the glee with which she'd shared the article.

Of course, the irony fully registered, though even Monika appeared shocked at the proposal I presented. It should come as no surprise that it was to her I turned to solicit a logo for the commercial scheme I'd hatched while mulling the letter and mulling my life. As someone who had never previously met my neighbors, after the public hearing, I became the object of lots of taunts, letters to the editor, and a fair amount of disturbing mail. I vacillated between desiring a return to invisibility and longing to commit some violent neighborhood vandalism, nearly asking Monika for a loan of her brother's baseball bat.

But mostly I worried about the accusations raised by Monika's father and whether or not the fears he had held were shared by others, for if so, I knew the power of such rumors would seal my fate faster than any city action.

On the one hand, my days felt numbered. More importantly, Monika really had taught me, no matter how much fear the world seemed to hold, that I must reenter it. I seized opportunity and settled on a different tack. I must admit that I took no small pleasure in causing irritation to my neighbors by employing the zoning permit. I started by erecting a sign for this new venture: "Underground Studios." My former door now bears this name and a second copy of Monika's logo, one that features a gnome in mining attire complete with a headlamp and spinning a vinyl record on an extended middle finger along with the message, "Welcome to the Underground."

The transformation of living quarters to recording studio was no great engineering triumph in this nearly soundproof little box I used to call home. Aside from a great deal of electrical work, some ceiling modifications for improved acoustics and the erection of some seriously insulated partition walls, remodeling was minimal. The bedroom, it turns out, was nearly ideal for a second life as a mixing booth, and the bathroom is practically genius given the drinking habits of some musicians during extended recording sessions.

As soon as the sign went in, the neighbors mounted one last battle. They had intercepted inspection reports for my property and had seized on concerns about an additional point of emergency egress from what was officially termed "the basement." Residential dwelling or commercial space, the requirement held. Perhaps it was because of my newfound ally on the planning and zoning board, but I remained dumbfounded when the city approved of my proposal for achieving this second point of egress, and where once stood a raised garden bed, there now is a rather homely looking cement structure that looks like an exhaust vent. It turns out that my former home was perhaps a submarine all along, sporting as it does now an escape hatch in the form of an elevator shaft—city requirements for building code and American with Disabilities Act enforcement all met in one utilitarian bit of construction.

To witness the transformation from home to recording studio proved more satisfying than I could have imagined. Liberating, one might say. Given the pleasant oddities and eccentricities of people within the music industries, reconnecting with individuals I once knew offered a workable transition into re-entering society. I located an old acquaintance, a sound engineer looking to make a change in his life in a direction opposite my own. He wanted remove from the status quo, both in music and in the locations where most music is industrialized. He accepted rental of the studio space hungrily. I reminded him to remember the name of the studio as he sought new talent and passed along a note with a location for where he might have opportunity to hear a particularly talented, if gruff fellow given to taking the stage under an overpass.

Aside from the visible and purposeful taunts of the sign, the ugly access point to the elevator, and the presence of a handful of cars in a dirt lot, there is no audible impact for my former neighbors to complain about. The sound of recorded performances no more escapes this little bomb shelter than any noise I made during my years there. The weekly recycling truck has more to haul away, but that's about the size of it. The neighbors continued to complain, of course, loudly and regularly. But I doubt that their complaints can be heard over the earth-moving equipment now leveling the expanse on the other side of the open space.

Of course, such a transformation held a diversion for me too: homelessness. I have not become a regular at weekend karaoke nights in the netherworlds below bridges. I've simply left one dwelling space for another. I can see now that perhaps my place below ground was never a home, rather something of a hideout, for I did very little living there.

Monika turned down the scholarship as she had told me she would. For a solid month I assumed she would eventually change her mind. Why I thought such a thing demonstrates poor perception on my part, for when, in my short knowledge of her, had Monika ever proven anything but stubborn? I spent undue time being angry with her without giving that anger voice, and then moved to what can only be labeled "disappointment" and eventually, ever so slowly like the antiquated being she accused me regularly of portraying, I came to realize that the lesson she had truly taught me was to accept others as they are, not as I might wish them to be.

In truth, she would have been a poor fit for Dartmouth. She did agree to humor me and complete the application process, there and elsewhere. I view our friendship as having reached a point of mutual respect when she asked me to read her college entrance essays. They are stunning documents: essays that eloquently, if eccentrically, outline why, as individuals and as a culture, we must educate ourselves with a vision of promoting change in the future. I think her philosophical stance may well be a crock of shit, but I take heart that if proven fallible, it is a thesis that offers no harm.

She was accepted at several of this country's finer institutions, to their credit I must say, and she chose to defer entrance at Northwestern, claiming she needed a "gap year," an artificial term to cover insecurity if I ever heard one, on the pretense she needed a year to scrutinize her life. She has tested the waters—of life, I suppose, but of remove from family and exploration of underemployment too—and moved to Chicago. One must appreciate consistency in character. At present, she works in a "bead shop" though I have no idea what that is and she makes regular trips home to check on her parents. She reports inroads in her campaign to convert her mother to vegetarianism and told me recently she arrived unannounced to find her father with the stereo turned to full volume.

She has been very good about writing me, and even though the flourishes of her handwriting threaten to make me nauseous, I take delight in checking my new mailbox. One of her current extracurricular projects is volunteering at an urban community garden on the grounds of a struggling elementary school. She dutifully sent me pictures last week of the garden as it entered its first spring. It is an urban pocket garden surrounded by decaying buildings and looming tall walls, buildings, I might add, that now look something like garden scenes themselves, sporting elaborate murals as they do. I wrote her back, warning of microclimates and the heat the buildings will generate and suggesting efforts they must take to create shade barriers and misting systems for some of the more sensitive plants.

Meanwhile, I kept to my word. The scholarship went to a gangly, acne-ridden boy who played the trombone in the marching band and who appears to be something of an engineering genius, although there was the significant black mark on his record involving destruction of school property. He assured me that he'd shifted his focus to the robotics of advanced remote investigative planetary rovers and away from the rockets that might get them to their targets, citing the dangers of high-octane fuels. Dartmouth could not, however, balk at his GPA or his test scores, nor at the endowment account I opened in Danny's name. Officials at Dartmouth report that my new mad scientist is excelling in classes and has suddenly developed an affection for intermural lacrosse, maintaining his newfound athletic ability is rooted in an understanding of physics and mechanical intervention in ball movement.

As if intent on fulfilling a prophecy issued by a seventeen-year-old with striped hair, I have begun to draw Boston. My methodology is different now, for not only do I work on it at my leisure rather than in adherence with a kind of forced schedule, I now draw plein-air rather than from memory. I retain an uneasy relationship with this city of my birth, and I've discovered that skylines are best drawn from a touch of remove. The vantage point from which I now paint reminds me that cityscape and landscape alike have foreground, and in this instance, much of the foreground is comprised of two- and three-story brick buildings dating from the late years of an earlier century, and I now take considerable pleasure in honoring

the significant details of eroded brick and near ceaseless architectural modification these structures demand. Foreground affords another detail I have come to relish as well—the presence
of trees.

And given that I am the one creating this particular vision of
my hometown and may well be the only one to ever view the finished project, I have taken liberties as its creator. Chief among
those liberties, much to the chagrin of city officials should they
have reason to view my interpretation, I've taken to renaming
the occasional landmark. I've slipped names into plate-glass
windows, onto the edifices of office towers, into signs within
public parks. I've added seven names and they are these: Mary
Alice Wybonski and Allison Sue Kathroll, Maria Helen Linch-
ner, Diana Francis Treemont, Nancy Regina Parkinson, Susan
Elizabeth Dunbar, and Renee Alexandria Dunbar.

I'd forgotten the relative anonymity one has in the city, and as
I move now among people, I am cognizant that their presence
has little to do with whether or not I am of the mood to feel
lonely. Indeed, this decision to move back to the city of my
birth has taught me many things that have come as a surprise,
chief among them the realization that several good friends are
willing to forgive seven years of absenteeism and selfishness.
While most have likely forgotten me, I've learned to accept the
welcome of the ones who have offered it and not condemn the
ones who have not. The traits of acceptance and forgiveness
are apparently held by mothers and siblings as well, who in an
act of grace, have assured me that the love and acceptance of
family do not cease in the presence of distance or time passage
or heartache, neither heartache caused or heartache suffered.

I have missed a great deal of course. I have missed the passing of nieces and nephews from childhood to adulthood. I have
failed support of a sibling when faced with a crumbling marriage. I have lost a friend to cancer. In my seven-year absence my
mother seems to have arrived suddenly at old age. I have missed
uncountable moments, large and small, moments of joy and

of despair, of triumph and of failure, and still those who have re-welcomed me into their lives assure me I am wanted there. I am like a stray dog taken in and fed. There is little expected of me and an unspoken will to respect that my time astray has manufactured more than a few bad habits, multiple eccentricities, and a desire to nose about my own chosen terrain.

For the moment, I live in what one must label a conventional sort of residence, a small flat above a music store that meets my simple needs efficiently. Indeed, it is situated at the heart of the foreground neighborhood I regularly draw and so I now have the unexpected complexity of living within the scene that I study.

I still frequently find this aboveground world shocking. Too often I encounter events that cause me fear and confusion. At times the sheer numbers—the numbers of people, numbers of cars, numbers of buildings—threaten to overwhelm me. There is ample evidence of intolerance. Acts of selfishness and ignorance and greed are transacted so regularly and so mindlessly they can overwhelm. I am conscious of such behavior, of course, for it would be an altogether different brand of underground fantasy to miss this too frequent nature of the world. But I have also witnessed small acts of kindness among strangers that give me hope. Simple acts: an offer to carry a bag, open a door, voice a kind hello, give up a seat. These are the ordinary acts one should expect in a civilized world but does not always see. Witnessing simple, tender moments puts me in a mood to be forgiving—of others and of myself. In such moods, sometimes simply gazing out the window of my flat or in moments in the park where I often go to draw, I allow myself to remember other, brighter times passed within this city. And then I find the will to converse with someone who has stopped to look over my shoulder at the city rising off the easel there.

I have learned that one can only find hope if one participates within hope. Why, just the other day as I was walking back from the bus stop after having had lunch with my niece, I witnessed a young woman, who upon encountering a homeless man sleep-

ing on a bench under a sheath of newspapers, removed her coat
and draped it over him. I was so moved at watching her provide
this gift that I called out to her and offered her my own coat.

"Why would I take your coat?" she asked.

"For the same reason you gave him yours," I said.

"But then you'll be cold," she said.

"As you are now."

"I'm close to home," she said.

"I'm two blocks," I said. "How far are you?"

"Five."

"Then it's simple math," I said and handed her my coat,
which she accepted with a shy smile. We parted without another
word, unlikely to ever see one another again. It is the sort of
gesture I can manage, one that allows anonymity.

When I arrived at my little apartment, I re-entered the drawing I'd been working on most recently—a portrait of a tree—
with such enthusiasm you might call it giddiness. I spend considerable time daydreaming, designing in my head, as it were,
another sort of residence I might build one day, one promoting
views of the surroundings, one that affords the relative isolation that accompanies elevation from the street, a residence
that takes full advantage of winter light and summer shade, a
home that offers built-in cooling systems through the natural
exchange of carbon dioxide for oxygen.

It is a design that begins with the principle that one must
ascend to enter the place one lives, a design informed by a
childhood spent reading escapism and contemplating fantasy.
We all live different kinds of fantasies. I certainly have. Perhaps
for now, I have exchanged a Ralph Ellison underground for a
Robinson Caruso tree house, have bartered Melville's "Bartleby" for his fantastical island tales. Frequently I have come to ask
myself a question of late: which is the more harmful fantasy, to
choose belief that I can hide from a world I seldom understand
or to choose belief in a world that might never exist? I know
few things for sure, though here is one: if I should ever act
upon my daydreams and build a fantasy home elevated among

the leaves and branches, I must choose a tree with roots that dig deep within the earth, roots that probe for sustenance among those dark spaces we can only imagine and we so frequently fear. Sometimes the things that give us life come out of the darkness.

ACKNOWLEDGMENTS

Although I can recall with absolute clarity the moment this novel came into being, it took me more years than I care to count to complete Man, Underground. Those years included countless revisions and the assistance of numerous astute readers and confidants. Enough years that the likelihood I have forgotten someone among the many who have helped me find and shape the book is strong, and if that is the case, I hope that my frailty of memory will not be mistaken for a failure of appreciation.

I offer a special thank you to my late parents, Albert W. Leichliter and N. Jean Leichliter, who despite not having the opportunity to attend college, were insistent that their two sons would have the means and support to do so. Both lived through the Great Depression, and both were raised in tiny Kansas farm towns, yet neither ever challenged my absurd notion that I wished to become a writer. My father, who dropped out of high school to care for his mother and then to serve in World War II, seldom read beyond financial and computer magazines—two disciplines he had taught himself—yet he read every manuscript I ever shared with him. He once declared *Man, Underground* his favorite. My mother, in the spirit of that special brand of loving, proud mothers, dutifully saved everything I had written from childhood forward, including a surplus of stories about a group of small plastic animals that occupied a penthouse apartment.

My parents' faith in me has only been surpassed by that of my wife, Patti. Far more than enduring what must seem endless and largely nonsensical ruminations from me about the book I am writing at any given time, she is a dutiful and honest reader and helps ground the work from the fanciful flights to which I am prone. She has stood by my work when reasonable people would have counseled that I give up. Extraordinarily gifted in her profession and passionate about it, in truth she has worked more and worked harder in order that I might have conversations with people who exist only in my mind.

Sydney Choi remains my first reader, always quick to find time in an impossibly busy life to read still-inky manuscripts with a mix of care, tremendous instinct, and a willingness to challenge me and the emerging ideas. My thanks to Jen Leichliter for her insights on the role of music in the narrator's life. The novel was distilled and clarified with the assistance of readings at critical stages of development by Susan Yandell, Lucy Flood, and Kat Kerr. Tim Sandlin not only offered insightful commentary on the relationship between these characters with a timely reading of the manuscript, his support of my work and invitation to be a member of the Jackson Hole Writers Conference resident faculty has enlightened and informed my writing and sustained my sense of belonging in a vital writing community.

I wish to thank Monika, who, more than any character I have ever written into life, arrived in my mind fully formed. She is representative of any number of people I have encountered inside and outside classrooms: brilliant, passionate, idealistic individuals who view the universe through a lens of their own grinding, and who, as a result, are too often seen by conventional wisdom as misfits or nonconformists. Monika's original brilliance, her fierce independence, and her deep morality has been informed by countless women I admire and respect, traits embodied by my wife, my three daughters, colleagues over the years, and numerous close friends. As for those daughters and their wonderful partners, I am confident that they will raise their children within a balance of guidance and freedom to become precisely who they wish to become, to think independently, to act with compassion, and to find the universe ceaselessly fascinating. Might those children and all those of their generation find hope and solutions to the numerous problems I and my generation have passed along as an unfair birthright.

Monika is, in part, an amalgam of many students I had the honor to teach over a twenty-one year career in college and high school classrooms, so thanks go to those bright and wonderful creatures who showed the desire to ask difficult questions, challenged themselves to find the answers that require the tenacity and creativity of exploratory miners, and found wonder and bounty in the universe of words and sentences in an age when too many ignore books and accept those who traffic in "alternative facts," a phrase we have tragically grown to accept as ordinary and forgivable.

Because I had the good fortune to spend a substantial portion of my professional life as a writing teacher, I had no shortage of mentors, including in the early stages of my adult writing life, John Edgar Wideman, Robert Roripaugh, and Don Murray. Far earlier in my education were numerous teachers who gave the whole of themselves to their students, but two must be highlighted—Ann O'Neal Garcia and Pauline Kouris—creative, original and conscientious educators far ahead of their time. Among colleagues who supported a young faculty member and who, using their gifts as writers and grace as teachers, guided him are: Rita Kiefer, John Brandt, Ed Kearns, Paul Rea, Lisa Zimmerman, and Joonuk Huh. And then there were the extraordinary teachers who let an old man join their midst and taught him daily: David Caldwell, Drew Overholser, Shoshana Kobrin, and Ethan Lobdell. And one special posthumous thank you to an astoundingly gifted poet, Bob King, who upon hearing me read a comedic short, said, "You should do more of that," which I took as permission.

In a publishing marketplace where fewer and fewer publishers are willing to take risks and where too often manuscripts are rejected in the belief that readers do not have appetites for literary fiction, Regal House Publishing is unique, steadfast in its dedication to producing books of literary significance, and genuine in providing writers a home and readers books that enlighten as they entertain. I do hope this book can be included in that latter description. *Man, Underground* would simply not exist if Regal House Publishing's founder, Jaynie Royal, did not champion it, and I could not ask for a more gracious, charming, or precise editor. Jaynie, and managing editor Pam Van Dyk, have built a very special press, and I am honored to have my work included in their catalog.

Books have invoked my passions, informed my vision, and altered my thinking since the time I was first able to read. I recall being tasked with reading the ending to *Where the Red Fern Grows* aloud to the class when our first-grade teacher, Ms. Lewis, was too overcome with emotion to carry on, and that memory stands as a reminder for the power of story. I have no delusions that this novel will change the world or linger in a reader's memory for fifty years, but I do hope that some readers will leave it with renewed commitment to help shrink the divide that currently shapes American public discourse, culture, and politics. Fear of those we believe to be different from ourselves is testing the tensile point of the great American democratic experiment, and while I will be considered naïve by most, I do hope that this novel offers a reminder that we are more alike than different and that all our lives would be bettered by more acts of kindness, those given and those received.